Sister

Sister

A. MANETTE ANSAY

William Morrow and Company, Inc.   New York

FIC
ANS

Chapter Two first appeared in *Story* as "Sister."
Chapter Three first appeared in *The North American Review* as "Spy."
Chapter Four first appeared in *The Indiana Review* as "Nothing You'll Ever Need to Know."
Chapter Five first appeared in *The Northwest Review* as "Distance."

Library of Congress Cataloging-in-Publication Data

Ansay, A. Manette.
    Sister / by A. Manette Ansay.
        p.   cm.
    ISBN 0-688-14449-7
    I. Title.
    PS3551.N645S57   1996
    813'.54—dc20   95-52672
                                                               CIP

Printed in the United States of America

First Edition

  2   3   4   5   6   7   8   9   10

BOOK DESIGN BY M. KRISTEN BEARSE

for my father, Dick Ansay,
and my brother, Mike,
with love

Acknowledgments

The first half of this book was written during my time as the George Bennett Fellow at Phillips Exeter Academy, and I'd like to thank the English Department in general, and Peter Greer in particular, for many kindnesses. I'd also like to thank the National Endowment for the Arts, the Corporation of Yaddo, the Virginia Center for the Creative Arts, and the University Research Council at Vanderbilt University for their generous support.

My thanks, again, to the critics: Sylvia J. Ansay, Kim Dionis, Stewart O'Nan, and to my agent, Deborah Schneider. Thanks to Claire Wachtel and the people at William Morrow for believing in this book. And special thanks to Jake Smith for technical support.

Chapter Ten is dedicated to Janet Schrunk Ericksen and David Ericksen, with gratitude for warmth and light during a long dark year.

Finally, I thank Kelly Allen and Leah Stewart for their fresh, fast eyes. I owe you.

Contents

Sister (1995) 1

Distance (1975–1980) 27

Poison Creek (1995) 105

Back by Dark (1984–1987) 141

Grace (1995–1996) 191

Memory is, I believe, the human soul.
—JAMES McCONKEY

Sister

(1995)

One

*I*f you've never been inside a Catholic church, I'll show you what it's like to go there, believing, into the cool dark air with only the light from the sacristy to guide you. Imagine the half-filled pews stretched out in rows as quiet, as impossibly even, as the rows of corn and soy in the fields behind the houses that trail from the church in four directions, the way light beams radiate from a child's sketch of the sun. Pretend you've just come from one of these houses, as I have, as my grandmother has, as all the people around us have, and at first the measured stillness of the church seems torturous, unbroken, unbearable. But as your eyes widen to accept the dusk, you'll notice a handkerchief twisted from palm to palm, a jiggling foot in an open-toed shoe. And, too, there are smells: rose perfume wafting from beneath a loosened collar, whiffs of manure from rubber-soled boots, dust that (I read this as a child, wanted it to be true) is mostly organic, made up of epidermal cells and bits of human hair. There is dust layering the top of the holy water font, where we dip the tips of our third fingers before making the sign of the cross. There is dust smudging the colors of the stained-glass windows, dust on the legs of the table where we select this month's missalette, dust on the intricate statues with their deep, worried eyes. Everywhere there is evidence of the body's desire for its own beginnings, the soul's helium float back to God.

I want you to be here with us. I want you to feel what I feel, a teenage girl towering over her grandmother at the back of this small Wisconsin church. There is the altar boy in his cumbersome smock, peeking out from the doors off the sacristy, excused from English or Math or Civics to serve the daily noon Mass. There are the men on their lunch breaks, the smattering of older retired men, and so many women!—young mothers with their sleeping babies, older mothers in groups of three and four, and the dozens of widows, women like my grandmother, who are the raw heart of this church. When they speak, you hear the older languages floating around their tongues. They wear their hair in tight, curly nests; thin gold bands still dent their fourth fingers. They carry what they need in big black purses, secured with fist-like clasps, these women who remember times without bread when they had to feed themselves and their families on their own ingenuity and the Word.

The men of my grandfather's generation were like visitors, cherished as guests who could not be relied on to stay for very long. They went off to war and disappeared, they were crushed under heavy farm machinery, they shot each other by accident and on purpose, they fell off horses and rooftops and silos, drowned in rivers, succumbed to snakebite, emphysema, whiskey. After my grandfather died of tetanus in 1947, my grandmother raised their four daughters and maintained the farm; when land taxes threatened to rise, it was she who sent the oldest two, Mary and Elise, to work in the cannery. Men died young; you mourned, you kept their graves tenderly, and—somehow—you went on. But when fire broke out, snuffing the lives of those daughters and fifteen other girls into ash, the shock left Oneisha and all the surrounding towns senseless with grief. These girls were the seed of the community, some of them already married and putting down roots like their mothers. A tragedy like this must have happened for a reason, and for some, that reason was all too clear. A girl's place was in the home, not working for cash in an ungodly world where company owners locked fire doors, paranoid about theft. My grandmother was thirty-eight years old. For the rest of her life she would blame herself for my young aunts' deaths. She sold the farm and moved her remaining daughters to town, where she kept them close to her, forever close. By the time I was born, in 1965, she was in her fifties, sharp and strong. God-like.

We pause at the back of the church, lingering the way polite guests do before walking toward the area where we always sit, the heels of my grandmother's short boots meeting the floor with absolute certainty. I stay close behind her, feeling every inch of my height, my feet kicking after one another like loosely tossed stones. A place to sit. For some there are choices. One might choose to go all the way to the front, to sit half hidden from the lectern by the bulky old confessionals; one might stay by the new, modern confessionals at the back. There are favorite seats beside the pillars that support the fat, curved belly of the ceiling, with its painting of angels ministering to Mary as she walks in the cherry orchard; there are seats beneath the mounted statues, where a child might sit to admire the delicate toes of the apostles. But we sit in the middle of the church, away from the pillars, the statues, potential distractions, away from the drafts that pulse from beneath the warped frames of the windows, whisper from the long, dark line where the walls meet the floor. My grandmother rubs the knuckles of my hand with her thumb, her peculiar gesture of affection, and I glow with her touch, with the knowing looks of the women around us who observe me at Mass, day after day, and whisper the word *vocation*. Sometimes I am asked to sing while the other parishioners kneel at the altar, five at a time, to receive Communion. My musical talent, like all good things, is God's gift, and such a gift is both a blessing and a burden. You wonder if you are worthy. You wonder what God might expect in return.

I want you to be here with us. I want you to feel what we feel. This is the tray that holds the hymnal, attached to the back of the next pew. This is the old-fashioned hat clip beside it. That is the altar with its hand-sewn linens, which are laundered by the Ladies of the Altar. Here are the flowers these same women bring with them from their gardens or sunrooms to decorate the church. These are the woven wicker baskets that will be circulated twice during the course of the Mass by old Otto Leibenstein: once to help the missionaries, once to maintain the parish. And somewhere in the sacristy, trapped in a ring of gold, is the Body of Christ, the miracle that results again and again from the Mass. The Processional is about to begin, and you know exactly what to do, feel the weight of two thousand years behind each simple ritual. You cannot imagine a time when this feeling of absolute purpose will leave you. You cannot imagine losing your faith. You cannot imagine the loneliness.

When my brother disappeared in 1984, I began to see myself in the third person, as if my life were a story being told to someone else. Though I listened with no particular interest, on occasion I did wonder what this third-person self might say or feel or do. *She goes upstairs to her room, the same room they shared as children. She rearranges the glass figurines on her bookshelf, imagining her brother's face.* A man can take care of himself, my father liked to say, and though Sam wasn't yet a man, he was wiry and tall, made taller by the steel-toed boots he wore, his cropped spiked hair, his dangerous eyes. He had disappeared several times before, reappearing hung over, dirty, his face drawn thin as if to shut out what he'd seen. This time, he'd left the house on the afternoon of August fifth. He didn't come home that night; he didn't come home the next.

A peculiar heat wave drifted in from the west, capped by a low bank of clouds that isolated eastern Wisconsin from its usual cool lake breeze. After three days, my mother went to the Horton police, adding a fresh report to Sam's plump file: driving under the influence, vandalism, trespassing, disturbing the peace, disorderly conduct, truancy. "He'll be home when he's hungry, Therese," they told her. "He's probably shacked up with friends." No one was eager to look very hard for a kid who had virtually dropped out of school, disappearing each night into the cars of strangers, accelerating south, always south, toward Milwaukee. But three days became four days, then five, and then a week. Clearly, something was wrong.

My father took a personal leave from the car lot, distributing Sam's picture throughout Sheboygan, Green Bay, Madison, Milwaukee. My mother ran a small advertising company, and every morning she printed up new flyers for him to post on bulletin boards and telephone poles and in the windows of bars, new press releases to be sent to newspapers farther and farther away. Since she'd first reported Sam missing, there had been a series of break-ins: Dr. Neidermier's big lakefront house on August tenth, Becker's Foodmart and the drive-in theater west of town on the eleventh. Next came rumors of an *incident* involving an older woman in Oneisha, Geena Baumbach, a friend of my grandmother's. These rumors grew, threading their way through polite conversations, twisting between quiet suppers and afternoon cups of coffee. There were people who moved away from us when we sat down in our usual pew for Mass. There were men who would no longer shake my father's hand. Suddenly the police were eager to find my brother too. Perhaps, they told my mother, he was involved somehow—as a victim, or a witness. None of them dared suggest to her face that Sam had become a suspect.

All through the third week of August, strangers drove up the long gravel driveway to our house, parking on the shady grass beside the barn: police officers, detectives, reporters, all of them sweating dark necklaces around their crisp shirt collars. My mother split her time between her tiny Sheboygan office and our sweltering living room, where she served raspberry Kool-Aid and gingersnap cookies. She brought out Sam's baby pictures, his old drawings, the statewide art prize he'd won in fifth grade for a watercolor painting called *Tulips*. She didn't mention that, afterward, my father called Sam an "ah-teest," that he'd spoken with a lisp, saying "ah-teests" were fairies, and maybe Sam was a fairy too. Instead, she discussed my plans to leave for college the following week; she talked about Sam's upcoming senior year and how she hoped he'd be back to start on time. I knew she was trying to present an image she felt would make her client—in this case, all of us—appear most appealing. She'd gone through Sam's room, collecting rolling papers, loose joints, a plastic bag containing a piece of mirror and traces of white dust, and she put all these things in a bigger plastic bag and buried them in the field. "There's no sense in having his life ruined by this," she said, and she reminded me that I didn't have to talk with the detectives if I didn't want to. By the time the sheriff arrived with a warrant, Sam's room was as clean as my own, lightly scented with lavender air freshener.

"You know Sam wouldn't do anything to hurt anybody," she told me, and the way that she said it was like a prayer, as if she believed I had the power to make her words the truth.

So I watched as my third-person self told the detectives that, like her mother, she hadn't seen Sam since the afternoon of August fifth. She said she'd never noticed signs that Sam was drinking or taking drugs, and that Sam and her father never fought, and that Sam had been missing school last spring to look for summer work—not an uncommon thing in Horton. She told them that there was no reason Sam might break into people's houses, or steal, or *assault* a woman in her own home, a woman my grandmother's age. She told them she had never seen a knife like the one Geena Baumbach described. Suddenly the walls spiraled swiftly inward. I woke up on the couch; a strange man in a Kool-Aid mustache was fanning me with a legal-size pad. The weight of the past few weeks hit me like a punch, and I sobbed as I came back into my body, feeling every painful inch of my pounding head and hollow chest, the tension knot between my shoulders, the sourness of my breath from telling lies.

That night, unable to sleep, I said the entire Rosary, remembering those long-ago trips I'd taken with my mother to Holy Hill Retreat. We'd meet my grandmother and Auntie Thil, her children, Monica and Harv, and we'd walk the Stations of the Cross, retracing Christ's crucifixion over a mile of wilderness. At each station, we'd kneel down on stone to say a new Our Father and Glory Be, asking forgiveness for our sins. My father and Uncle Olaf never came along; Holy Hill was for women and devout old men. Sam had gone when he was small, but as he got older my father teased him the way he did whenever Sam wanted to do something with my mother and me. Harv's persistence past age ten was unusual: a blessing, a sign. At twelve he announced he planned to be a priest, and after that he worked freely beside the women, building altars of flowers to the Virgin in May, arranging the family crèche at Christmastime, making the pilgrimage to Holy Hill that left our lips blue, our teeth chattering, our knees wet and chafing in the chill air.

My father scoffed at Harv, at men who were not what he called *a man's man*. He was awkward around priests the way he was around all bachelors, loners, men who did not quite fit in with the others; he spoke a bit too loud, laughed a bit too long. As Sam approached adolescence, my father became increasingly concerned over his quiet ways, his attachment to my mother and me. No son of his would be a sissy, a priest, a man who belonged to no one. No son of his would serve as a mirror, reflecting back the things that frightened my father most about himself. And by the time Sam entered junior high, he was learning to see the world through my father's rational eye. Painting pictures was silly because you couldn't make a living at something like that. There was no point in picking out a dream house or boat or a sports car from a magazine; where would you get the money? If God was everywhere, then how come you couldn't see Him? "If there is a God, let Him drink this glass of water," Sam said, and he placed it on the windowsill, where it stayed for days. Yet, eventually, it was gone.

"Evaporation," Sam said smugly.

"Maybe that's how God drinks." I was willing to believe, but Sam said that if God could do anything, He should be able to gulp eight ounces of fluid. He should be able to make everyone happy. He should float facedown in the sky, like a balloon in the Macy's Thanksgiving Day Parade.

It's hard to remember the earlier times, when Sam was not spinning in his own lonely orbit. Without imagination. A man's concrete eye. It's hard to remember that my family once believed we were special, that God Himself would cup His hands over our house to protect us from each other.

In the choir loft above the sacristy, Eva and Serina Oben—still known in their seventies as the Oben girls—take turns singing and playing on the organ, which was purchased last summer from the profits of raffles and summer festivals, and it's important to think about the quilts you helped to stitch or the pies you made or the pine cone wreaths that took all fall to glue and mount on coat hanger frames. My brother, like the other boys, was tacitly excused from tasks like these, but I helped the women with everything, and now the organ is as much my own as the bed I sleep in every night. Each note a familiar voice, holding me in place. Belonging, like my grandmother, to something larger than myself. I remember how carefully she taught me to pray to Mary, to Mary's mother, Ann, to my guardian angel, a little girl who looked just like me. I remember her household shrines, the framed photographs of Mary and Elise in their flower-strewn coffins, the Infant of Prague on top of the refrigerator, the four-foot-high statue of the Virgin behind the house. Altars to family, to women and children. Even Jesus looked female, with his moist lips and flowing hair, his gentle mother's eyes.

Eight years after my brother disappeared, I married a man who was raised without religious beliefs. Our wedding was a trip to the courthouse in the upstate New York town where we now live; my grandmother refused to acknowledge it. She returned my letters unopened. She hung up the phone at the sound of my voice. She died six months ago, believing that I, like Sam, had been lost for good.

"At least light a candle for her intentions," my mother said, when I told her I couldn't make it to the funeral. Work, money . . . I had good reasons, and my mother had heard them all before. Since leaving Wisconsin, I'd visited only once, and that had been ten years earlier. So on the afternoon of my grandmother's burial, I drove to one of the Catholic churches in our town, a town with two universities, six movie theaters, an arts center, bookstores, outdoor cafés; a town thirty times the size of Oneisha and Horton combined. I sat in my car, remembering my Sunday school classes at Saint Ignatius Church, where girls were forbidden to step on the red carpet that sprawled down the aisle. Girls were confined to the pews, while boys got to finger the glittering chalice on the altar. Girls had to curtsy to Father Van Dan, got called into the rectory, one at a time, to place their hands on his Bible and pledge to *keep their virtue*. Girls could never be priests, because they weren't made in God's image. Girls were made to stay home with their babies and raise them; even the latest Pope said that was true. The harder I tried to think about my grandmother, to remember how close we were when I was young, to do the one thing that would have made her happy, the angrier I became. I could not imagine leaving my car and walking up the stone flight of steps into the church. I put my head down on the steering wheel and cried, and then I drove away.

But in dreams I still take my place beside my grandmother, fold myself eagerly into our pew. The voice of the organ is full of anguish, the rich wood reflecting darts of light that burn larger, brighter, when I—no longer an individual but part of this congregation—rise and begin to sing. How the dust shines in the air! The priest floats into the sacristy, genuflects before the altar, prepares to transform bread and wine into the body and blood of Christ. Think of how it feels to behold a miracle. Imagine the power of such a belief, how you might cradle it for warmth, a treasured glowing coal that whispers, *I am loved*. When the priest raises the host above the altar and speaks the magical Latin, that dull bread glistens like a full moon. We burn our faces in its heavenly light.

And then I am bursting through the heavy front doors. It is winter. Ice shines on the chipped stone steps, icicles hang from the railing. I exhale the white dress of an angel, which dissipates into the air. Or perhaps it is a lovely summer day, the sky filled with the faces of high drifting clouds, and still there is nothing I recognize. This is the point when I always awaken, with Adam sleeping beside me, secure in a world I inhabit until my grandmother appears to me and I'm left to wonder, What is this place? This room, this house, this life accountable to no one but myself. My brother's disappearance, my grandmother's death. The feeling after loss finally hits. The deepness of it. The hurtling down.

Church bells ring in the distance, faint as a faucet dripping. First light mists the windows. I slip from beneath the covers, sit shivering on the edge of the bed. It's Sunday morning, early spring, 1995. Icicles drip from the eaves. The clock ticks on the wall. I cannot imagine what I will do next.

Two

$\mathcal{I}$'m trying on maternity dresses, hand-me-downs from Adam's sister, Pat, all of them childish, ugly. There's a full-length mirror on the closet door, and I twist and pose in front of it. The dresses billow like sheets on a wash line. Nine weeks into my first pregnancy, I cannot imagine how it will be to occupy that much space. "You'll know soon enough," my mother has assured me, but right now my stomach is its usual soft pouch. If it weren't for this lingering tiredness, I'd think the doctor's test was wrong.

"You want some toast?" Adam calls from the kitchen.

"Yeah. I'll be there in a minute." But I pull on another dress, turn sideways, stare critically as any teenage girl. Though I look the same as I always do, it *feels* as though I should look different.

Lately, I catch myself studying my body the way experts look at the body of a car, trying to determine where it's been, what it's done. I remember my brother once claiming my father's car had been dented by a hit-and-run driver. My father called the police, and they came after a long, impatient hour, two stout men who questioned Sam about the slivers of wood they found embedded in the paint. "Looks like a hit-and-run phone pole," the older one said, his lips pulled back into the wide grin of an unfamiliar dog. Sam was sixteen. His memory frequently suffered these gaps, visible as missing teeth. *Where were you last night? I don't know. What did you do? I forget.* It took him three weeks of community service to pay the six thousand citizens of Horton, Wisconsin, what it cost to fix that pole.

When I try to think of Sam, I see the blurred edges of a figure done in watercolor—I have to stand back before he eases into focus, and even then I can't see him clearly. Did he have wide-set eyes? Large, clumsy feet like my own? Were there freckles in the shape of the Big Dipper on his shoulder, or was that just something I told him once, giggling as he spun round and round, unable to turn his neck far enough to see? Sometimes I worry that the things I've invented outnumber the ones that are true. Then I recite the facts my mother gave to the police: the last time we saw him he was seventeen years old, he was five feet ten inches tall and weighed one hundred thirty pounds; he had blond hair and gray-green eyes, and yes, he did have older friends, men from Milwaukee we did not know, and yes, though he'd left the house on the afternoon of August 5, 1984, in his usual hurry, there was nothing peculiar about that day except that he never returned. Whatever happened next remains a mystery even now; there are suspicions, speculations, but no concrete clues. The possibilities wander through my dreams, catch me at odd moments like a skipped heartbeat. I have even tried to pray, crossing right thumb over left the way my grandmother taught me: *Tell me, please tell me where he is.*

It's hard to remember being seventeen, but these few things I do remember as I tug the last dress down over my head: the town of Horton, my father's lectures on citizenship, the stinging green odor of alfalfa fields stretching for mile after rippling mile, the brittle feathers of week-old pigeons—*pinfeathers*, my mother called them, and they did feel sharp against my hands when I'd climb into the belly of the silo to visit their nests. Adam is the sort of person who remembers everything, easily: what we had for lunch, the first time we made love, directions to a pond in Vermont where we swam three years ago. His mind is ordered as neatly as his dresser drawers. Pants to the right, shirts to the left. Socks rolled into balls, their lips pulled back to swallow their own bodies. Every so often, he'll straighten out my clothes, refolding crumpled cotton, stroking creases out of linen. *See, it's so easy to find things now*, he says, but within a day the crisp boundaries blur, long-limbed socks embracing shirts, panties twisted between them.

There are times when finding something only means risking another loss. Close to the mirror, I note the fine lines at the corners of my eyes, the deeper ones crossing my forehead, the slight downward curve reshaping my mouth. My body is slowly dissolving the landmarks of my childhood. Soon there will be others: stretchings and scarrings, a more complicated adult map. But I can still find the dent on my shin from where our neighbor's retarded son kicked me, feel the incredible warmth of the blood as he stood over me on the playground, crying too. I strip off the dress and there are my chicken-pox scars: three along my breastbone, one beside my navel. There is the downy hair on my stomach that made me afraid, for one awful summer, that something had gone wrong and I was turning into a boy. All these things I find and more; perhaps there are others, evidence I've overlooked.

My mother still gets responses from the ads she places in newspapers, at the backs of magazines. Three years ago a woman thought she saw Sam in Salt Lake City; last year a man insisted he waited on their table in New Orleans. By now he would be starting to age the way, at thirty, I am aging, his shoulders creeping forward a bit, his stomach comfortably soft. I wish I could look at my changing body to see the person I'm becoming, not the person I have lost. My earliest memory is of Sam, newly born, one red fist corking his mouth, but though I examine myself from every angle, I can't find one mark, one scar, the slightest clue I ever had a brother.

———

After breakfast, Adam and I sit on the back porch, drinking what we're pretending is coffee. In fact, it's a caffeine-free herbal substitute that tastes a little like dirt. He's already wearing his work clothes: an orange T-shirt, a baseball cap, jeans with a list of Things to Do poking out from the left hip pocket. I'm back in my nightshirt, and whenever I look up from the dun circle of liquid in my cup, the color of the world overwhelms me: tiger lilies along the porch, summer sky, emerald grass. There are butterflies, birds, our marmalade cat, Laverne. There are brown tree trunks and speckled stones and the neighbors' potted geraniums.

"How were the dresses?" Adam asks.

"Polka-dotted. Lots of little bows."

"That figures," he says, making a face. Pat is the queen of ticky-tacky things.

"At least there weren't any of those T-shirts that say 'Baby on Board.' "

He grins. "I'll have to get you one."

"Save your money."

"Or maybe one that says, 'Baby,' with an arrow pointing down."

"Ugh."

We are spending the day at home, officially to celebrate our third anniversary but in reality to finish all the projects I've started around the house. There's the partially stripped bureau in the garage. There are the seedlings I haven't transplanted even though it's June: peppers, melons, tomatoes, their tangled white roots peeping out from the bottoms of the peat pots, tasting air. "So what do you want to do first?" he says.

"I was thinking I'd tackle the garden," I say, and I cradle my cup in my hands.

"Then I'll finish the bureau." He stands up, whistling, and carries his cup inside. I can see his shape moving around the kitchen, and it looks like the shadow of another, larger body. It could be my father's shadow scraping the cast-iron pan, loading the dishwasher, wiping the table, except my father never did any of those things.

In Horton, there were names for boys who did dishes, who played indoors, boys who stayed close to their mothers. My father didn't understand when Sam wanted to play with me instead of making friends with boys in town. Sometimes he tried to play with Sam himself, but Sam cringed away from his blunt, tousling hands, his booming voice that always seemed too hearty, too cheerful. Nothing annoyed my father more than what he called *a sissy*. He began to keep a closer eye on us, listen in on our private talks. If Sam picked up one of my dolls, my father asked, did he want to be a mommy? If Sam crept into my bed in the night, frightened by some dream, my father jerked him up out of the blankets and told him he was a big boy, old enough to sleep by himself.

"You look beat," Adam says from the doorway. "Why don't you go back to bed for a while?"

"I'm OK," I say, although I feel as if I could put my head down on the table and sleep forever.

The seedlings are waiting for me in the back bay window. Beneath them, the wooden ledge has turned pale from the damp. I carry their trays outside to my little garden, two at a time, making trip after trip. Each year, I buy too many plants for the space that I have. My mother's garden sprawled for half an acre behind our house, well out of reach of the shadow cast by the derelict barn. The doors of the barn were kept boarded shut, but I found other ways inside, and as soon as Sam was old enough I hoisted him in through the broken windows at the back. The old metal poles of the stanchions rose up around us like trees. Cobwebs swam through the air. "Don't tell anyone," I warned Sam, and I led him through the cow barn to the silo and my secret: the white, glowing bones of mice and opossums and raccoons that had fallen the twenty-foot drop and died after lonely weeks pacing that concrete circle.

Summers, we spent entire days in the barn. We hunted for field mice nests, stroking the soft blind bodies that were no bigger than our own fingers. We caught the barn swallows that fluttered against the windows, and when we opened our hands to release them, they lay briefly still in our palms, shiny blue, and we felt their beating hearts. Sam was like those swallows when I sat on the edge of his bed at night, his pale throat exposed as he closed his eyes to listen to my stories. I made paper hats for him and tin can shoes. I taught him to make the sign of the cross, top to bottom, left to right.

He was beautiful—you could tell by the way strangers stopped to talk to him, bending their faces too close. "What a waste!" they said about his long, thick lashes, the deep coral color of his lips, his golden-pine complexion. I was the paler, chubby version; I looked adults squarely in the eye. "My brother is shy," I'd say in my coldest voice, and Sam would duck behind me and grip my hand, my father's old watch rattling on his wrist. The watch was one of my father's bizarre, infrequent gifts; it didn't work, but as Sam got older he began to wear it everywhere. It made him look even smaller than he was, sweet, the little boy pretending to be a man. I hated that watch. It was heavy, scratched, ugly; it glowed in the dark like a disembodied eye, and I didn't understand how Sam could like something I didn't. *I* was the one who decided what we liked. At first, I tried to swindle it away from him; when that failed I used force, until my mother intervened. "That doesn't belong to you," she said, not understanding that I wanted not to own it but to destroy it, this thing that distinguished my brother from myself.

I dig holes for the seedlings, add rotted leaves from the compost, sink the frail roots into the soil the way my mother taught me. It seems to me now that Sam began to change when we were first separated from each other—one day, we were simply brother and sister, and then, abruptly, we became boy and girl, *too old* to share a bedroom, *too old* to play together with my dolls or Sam's small Matchbox cars, *too old* to kiss each other good night, to touch. I did the dishes and vacuumed and dusted and worked in the garden with my mother; Sam mowed the lawn and helped my father change the oil in his car. I was given books to read; Sam was given things to build. I changed too, becoming self-conscious about my clothes, my hair, the too-flatness and too-fullness of my body. As a Catholic girl, I was to model myself on Mary, who was both a mother and a virgin. Mary, who Jesus allowed to suffer most because He loved her best.

The winter before my spring confirmation, I came downstairs wearing the confirmation dress my mother and I had made. It was white, of course, with frail puffed sleeves and two thick rows of lace at the hem. I was eleven, and I moved past Sam on tiptoe, pretending I was holy, a saint, an eager bride of Christ lifted by His breath so my feet wouldn't touch the ground. "That looks fat on you," Sam teased, and I whirled around and kicked him with my sharp white shoes. To punish me, my mother made me change clothes and then she put me to work lining the highest pantry shelves with fresh Con-Tact paper. The paper was orange and green, and it stuck to my hands. Sweat prickled under my arms as I wrestled it into place, carried armloads of pots and pans up and down the stepladder, all the while smelling my bitter, human smell. I wasn't holy, and it was Sam's fault, and I would make him pay.

It was a few days before his birthday, a particularly cold, gray January. We were still on vacation from school. The snow had drifted up to the windowsills, and the fields around the house stretched vast, empty, as if the soul of the world had been exposed. There was nothing to do except pick at each other, and later, as I sat reading in my mother's rocking chair, Sam began to pester me about his birthday present.

"I didn't get you a present," I said, even though I had. "I

mean, you're going to be ten now, and that will change everything."

"What do you mean?"

"You know, you'll be *ten*. Nine is much better."

"Why is nine better?"

"There's no sense in worrying about it," I said. "You're going to be ten, and there's nothing you can do about it."

For a moment, he searched my face for a sign, but I made
my expression like the snowy fields, smooth and white and without
a landmark. He frowned, his gray-green eyes deep as the eyes of
horses, full of want. "Will you love me as much when I'm ten?"
he asked, choking on that shameful word *love*, and when I told
him no, his face shattered. "I didn't mean it," I begged him, but
he ran down the stairs to his bedroom in the basement and locked
the door against me. Until the previous summer, we'd shared the
bedroom that now was mine, just across the hall from my parents'.
I knew how his body would be twisted on the bed, the pillow
tucked to his abdomen, his mouth hanging open and silent between sobs. I knew the flush that crept up his chest to his neck,
blossoming in his cheeks, the redness of his eyes. I'd been one and
a half when he was born, and my mother has told me how I
examined every inch of his tiny, perfect body. How I watched as
she bathed and fed and diapered him. How his first word was my
name.

I water the spindly seedlings, careful not to wet their leaves.
My mother's garden was something out of a picture book: tomatoes, sweet tapering carrots, melons that split at the whisper of
a knife, the rich dark soil spread around them like a fancy cloth.
She knew everything about vegetables and fruits, their special
needs, their swift diseases, and she passed these rituals to me, along
with her favorite casseroles, her belief in God, my grandmother's
quilt patterns, herbs for cramp tea. Sam got the keys to my father's
dirt bike, whispered jokes in the shed, blueprints and power tools
and fine-print instructions, the sharp, secret language of men.

Looking back at the way our lives have worked out, it would seem I was the luckier one, but at the time I resented being shut out, left out, left behind.

My mother did her best to comfort me, but she had grown up in a family of sisters, women who learned early to love women. She didn't understand how my flesh crawled when she hugged me or touched my hair, how the smell of her body disturbed me because it reminded me of my own. "You need to spend more time with other girls your age," she said, and by the time I turned sixteen, my friends and I took all the same classes, slept over at each other's houses, spent long hours on the phone. We may have talked about our classes, but mostly I remember talking about boys. We discussed ways to handle them as if they were poisonous snakes: on the surface they might be smooth glide, flickering tongue, but underneath they were hiss and venom and coil, never to be trusted. Each morning, I dressed for school as if I were dressing for a play. Everything from my blouse to my forbidden eye shadow (applied in the girls' bathroom, wiped away before I went home) was chosen for a deliberate effect. A successful combination of effects projected someone who did not at all resemble my real self, someone who could smile the proper smile, express an interest in appropriate things, and always be *a good girl*, bright but not brilliant, stable, cheerful, kind. *If you can't say something nice, my mother taught me, don't say anything at all.* I was a consummate actress, but at night my jaws ached with all the things I'd bitten back during the day. Even my prayers were censored, for fear of offending God's ear.

I don't want to raise my child the way Sam and I were raised, blue-for-boys and pink-for-girls, our assigned differences confirmed by the teachings of the Church. It never even occurred to me then that Sam might be lying awake himself, trembling with his own mute loneliness. In high school, he made friends with boys who dressed in black, who looked at the world with sullen, staring eyes. Of course, my father hated them. They weren't the wholesome boys he admired, that he wanted Sam to be. They smoked cigarettes and pin joints behind the shed, and if I came out into the yard, they whistled and called me terrible, filthy names. No one dared call Sam a sissy now. The last of his youthful prettiness was gone. Nights, my father paced the house, turning the TV on, turning it off. When Sam finally came home, long past curfew, their arguments rang through the darkness, brief bursts of shouts like gunfire. I'd lie awake listening to Sam's new deep voice, my father's throaty rage. In the morning I'd go downstairs to find the tipped chairs, the smashed plates, and, once, a crack in the plaster where my father had thrown Sam against the wall. "If you want to live in my house," my father said, "you better learn to live by my rules."

It was the same thing the Church said to us. I didn't yet know I could leave God's house, but Sam found ways out of my father's. He started hitchhiking to Milwaukee, where he met new, older friends. We heard their voices when we answered the phone, men's voices, curt like my father's, and sometimes Sam wouldn't get home until the following afternoon. "In my day, a young man knew how to work," my father began as Sam sprawled, hung over, on the couch. "Do you think I'd be where I am today if I had your attitude?" Sam just closed his eyes the way he did when he listened to his heavy-metal music, and I envied how he could make it seem as if he were no longer there. Yet I became more and more aware of his presence in the house, and I tried not to be there when I knew we'd be alone. He smelled of cigarettes and stale, dark air. He stole from my mother's purse. He stole from me too, creeping into my room during the day while I was at school, searching my closet and under my mattress, going through my dresser drawers until he found my baby-sitting money.

At lunchtime, I carry our anniversary cake out to the side yard, where Adam builds his outdoor sculptures. He's completed two since we bought this house: a six-foot sunburst made of mashed tin cans, and a life-size human figure made of more cans, copper wire, and pieces of the body of a Mustang. Why do you make them? neighbors ask, but he just tucks his hands into his pockets, smiles, shrugs. *Why not?* Summer nights, he comes home from whatever construction site he's been working on, locks his toolbox in the garage, and walks between his sculptures in the twilight, whistling. His new piece is my favorite—a grasshopper, two feet high and six feet long. When it's finished, the right wind will make it sing, a sound like breath blown across the open mouth of a bottle.

I spread an old blanket in the midst of the sculptures and we eat, alternating chunks of sweet cake with sips of sour lemonade. Laverne climbs into my lap, nails scraping my thighs, and settles into the nest my legs make for her. Today I am missing Wisconsin, the wide, flat spaces that stretch for miles. "But you wouldn't ever want to move back to the Midwest?" Adam says when I mention this. His voice shapes a question, but his eyes are pleading *no.*

I shake my head and pick up his hand, turn it over, spread his fingers. Jealous Laverne hops out of my lap, fixes me with a cat stare.

"I'm happy right where we are," Adam says.

"Me too," I say, and I scoot around to sit behind him, enclosing his legs in mine; I lift his shirt and press my face against his smooth, damp back. His skin is freckled from too much sun, and here's the nick of a mole removed last year. His left thumb, smashed by a hammer, still isn't able to bend around mine. I trace the firm scar on his stomach left by a childhood appendectomy. Evidence embedded in bone and flesh. Perhaps it's just a matter of knowing how to read what's written there.

One hot day in the middle of July, less than a month before Sam disappeared, I heard the soft *whup* of a BB gun and realized the shots weren't coming from the fields. *Whup. Whup.* I followed the sound to the backyard and saw Mom crouched in the shrubs at the corner of the house. One knee was bent, braced against the earth; she propped her elbow on the other. She looked like the statues I'd seen of Saint Bernadette as she bowed down to pray to Mary in the grotto.

"Mom?" I said softly, but she shook her head, and I caught a glimpse of her face. It was the face of someone grieving, a widow's face, the face of a mother whose child has died, and I recognized it even though I'd never seen it before. I squatted beside her and peered through the hedge. All around the garden, the bird feeders my father and Sam had once built for her stood like sentries: finch feeders, songbird feeders, hummingbird feeders. She had low bluebird houses and another, higher house for purple martins. She had two concrete birdbaths, and between them she kept an old china plate spread with oranges to attract summer orioles.

Sam was squatting barefooted in one of the birdbaths, firing on robins and finches, starlings and grackles. The birds kept coming, used to the noise my mother and I made in her garden, some of them so tame they would eat out of our hands. A song sparrow fluttered in the grass, merely stunned; Sam aimed at it, fired, fired again.

"Make him stop," I whispered, and then Sam looked up. He stared at us as we cowered in the bushes with our long hair trailing over our shoulders, our eyes wide. We looked like women. We looked like rabbits. We must have looked like prey. He raised the gun. Even now I have dreams in which I'm looking down the barrel, only the gun is one of my father's Colt .45s, and I wake up feeling the end of my life rushing toward me like a great gust of wind. But Sam didn't aim. He didn't fire. I do not carry beneath my skin a kernel of lead, smaller than a pea, which would almost be like a part of Sam carried with me forever.

Just after my grandmother's funeral, my mother phoned, her voice bright with news. "Oh, Abby, we may have really found him this time," she said. I listened to my mother's latest story—Sam fixing cars at an auto shop in Los Angeles—and I remembered how it was after Sam threw down the gun, after my mother had turned and walked away, when I stepped out of the bushes, stooped to touch each crumpled bird body, and he watched me for a while, hands in his pockets, no longer able to recognize a sister.

Distance

(1975–1980)

Three

$\mathcal{E}$ach year, my parents leased our fields to one of the larger local farms, and spring rumbled in with the roar of the cultivators circling the perimeters of our land. There were no other children living close by; our nearest neighbors, the Luchter- hands, ran a horse farm three quarters of a mile down the road. My brother and I grew up in the company of beets, which stained our hands and mouths a bloody red; during luckier years, there were sweet peas or snap beans, sugar-sweet to the tongue. Once, the renters sowed field corn, which attracted rats the size of gourds. But the summer I was ten and Sam was nine, they planted sixty acres in sunflowers, and by August our house was surrounded by a fiery corona that swallowed the usual deep summer greens in an elaborate golden yawn. When the damp wind blew off Lake Michigan, we could hear the petals rustling, sexual and fierce, and Sam and I paused during our games, whirling to look over our shoulders; it was a summer we never felt completely alone. We avoided the cellar, the smokehouse, the walk-in closet in our bed- room; at night, we leapt into our beds so that anything lurking beneath them wouldn't be able to grab our ankles and pull us down. Mornings, I'd wake up and look out the window, and there would be the bright, broad faces of the sunflowers, all facing east like so many wise kings. In his bed on the other side of the room, Sam was still sleeping, his head thrown so far back that his body formed a question mark. Even now, the memory of him frozen in that vulnerable arc fills me with an aching protectiveness, as if he were my child and not my brother.

That summer, Sam and I played only those games that involved wearing dark clothes and crouching behind shrubs and using words like *covert* and *operation* and *ambush*. A boy at school had an older brother who'd gone to work for the CIA; when we pressed him for details, he combed his hair with his fingers and said, "Classified," in a way that let the rest of us know there were things in the world we had not yet begun to imagine. I remember that I wasn't discouraged when I heard that girls could not be spies, any more than I was discouraged by all the other things that, as a girl, I wasn't supposed to do, because I had a vague idea that becoming an adult meant turning into a man. It was not a fully conscious thought, but it was present in the same way that God was present, a concept you trusted you would understand when the appropriate moment arrived.

Until first grade or so, I had been just as securely convinced that I could grow into any animal I wished, and after careful consideration I chose to become a cat. To encourage this metamorphosis, I made cat noises and licked my skin and ate cat chow from the house cats' bowl beneath the sink. I pinned a piece of twine to the seat of my pants, wriggling my butt to make it swing from side to side. Once, I managed to elude my mother and board the school bus that way, and the older boys nearly strangled me with my tail before the driver intervened. Still, I believed in my right to choose my destiny, and when one of the semiwild barn cats had kits, I recognized this as a moment of truth and knelt beside her to nurse. But she scratched me—three parallel lines across my forehead, which lingered for weeks like a signature.

The summer of the sunflowers, I decided that the years I

had spent practicing for cathood had had a purpose after all: They'd given me all the skills I needed to be an effective spy. I could scale high walls and jump off cliffs and fight dirty, using my teeth and nails; I could contort my body to fit into small, dark places; I could move with the fluid stealth of a cat intent on a kill. Of course, Sam wanted to be a spy too. After morning chores, we filled our afternoons with secret missions, ambushes, and code words like *smokey bear* and *10-4 charlie*. We painted elaborate, colorful scenes of spies climbing up the walls of castles and parachuting out of airplanes, and these we hung above our beds for inspiration. But by August, we were forced to face our greatest limitation. There was nobody to spy on. My father was seldom home. My mother ruined the mood by saying things like: "If you want to know something about me, just ask. There's no need to follow me around." The Luchterhands down the road were not an option because of the stallions; we remembered, from a visit to the barns in spring, the sound of those gunshot hoofbeats and high, crazed whinnies, the chill of those rolling devil eyes. And so we loitered around the house and barn, waiting for a mission, trying not to notice the watched feeling that followed us everywhere we went, invisible as breath and just as urgent, brushing the tops of the fields like wind. My father had grown up on this farm; it had been a hard life, one he rarely discussed. But he'd told us about the German POWs that my grandfather, himself a German immigrant, had hired as cheap summer labor. On hot, still nights, we thought we could hear them: their choked, guttural voices, the music of their chains, the hungry scrape of their bent tin spoons as they ate beneath the quarter moon.

My mother believed in intuition, God, and the power of prayer. The future came to her in quiet dreams and chilly flashes, a gift she'd had ever since her oldest sisters were killed in the cannery fire. One week after the funerals, she told her youngest sister, our auntie Thil, "You come away from that stove," and seconds later, the stovepipe exploded. She sketched my father's face on a napkin the day before they met. When she carried me, she dreamed that I appeared to her, a perfect baby girl who asked to be named *Abigail Elise.* Where did I come from? I asked whenever she told the story, and then she'd describe the netherworld she'd seen, a universe of unassigned souls, churning in a sort of primordial soup, each shrilling, *Choose me! Choose me!*

Foolishness, my father said. But the time my mother begged him to stay home from work, he did. Later, we learned that the highway had been closed, due to an accident involving four cars. Two people were killed. How had my mother known? She just did. The artificial nature of spying puzzled her, though she tried her best to play along, to help us out and, in the process, convert our interest into something useful. She sent me to the garden to "ambush" slugs with saucers of beer; in the morning, she suggested that Sam "case the beans" for signs of Japanese beetles.

"That's not the same," we told her, but neither Sam nor I could explain why. We flung ourselves at the furniture and moped: two combat-trained, sophisticated, deadly bored spies. It was this boredom, rather than our former sneakiness, that began to wear at her nerves. One day late in August, she decided that we could take our bikes into town, three miles away. We were to pick up some dishwashing detergent at Becker's Foodmart, stop for ten minutes at the dime store—just to look—and then we were to head straight back home.

For years, we had begged to go all the way into Horton by ourselves. We dug our battered Schwinns out of the shed and coasted down the long gravel driveway toward the road, making elaborate hand signals in case my mother was watching from the kitchen window. It was a warm, humid day. The east wind off Lake Michigan, which usually cooled our afternoons, had been stalled by a low, gray bank of clouds at the horizon. Buttercups and Queen Anne's lace choked the ditches, and every now and then we passed a pale green patch of wild asparagus, delicate as mist. At first, we raced each other, because the flat length of road was a novelty, but after a mile or so we settled into a steady rhythm, side by side, and we felt how small we were, surrounded by fields of corn and alfalfa and, occasionally, cows. They were Holsteins mostly, and because of the heat, they clumped together beneath what shade they could find, usually small stands of trees that the first German settlers had left behind. Sometimes there was an old foundation beneath those trees, a boarded-up well, a scrap of rotting fence—all that was left of an original homestead. The cows watched us pass, releasing powerful streams of urine that splattered their legs and bellies, their silent mouths working, working.

Horton was the sort of town that happened all at once. It began with an old grain mill, the only warning before an eruption of close-set houses that led toward the downtown. If you looked between those houses to the west, you could see the fields that stretched behind them; if you looked between the houses to the east, you could see more fields, and a glimmer of aquamarine that was Lake Michigan. We propped our bikes against a telephone pole and went into Becker's Foodmart. As usual, it was crowded with cans of food that no one ate unless it was a holiday: cranberry relish, Boston brown bread, mandarin oranges. The Dessert of the Day was always arranged on a long, low table by the grocery baskets. This time, it was a strawberry shortcake, cut into crumbling cubes. My mother never let us try these samples, though she sometimes took a plastic cup of the complimentary coffee for herself. *Who knows how long that's been sitting there?* she'd whisper, sweeping us past and into the sour meat smell. Now we popped the largest pieces into our mouths, but they were dry, too sweet, disappointing.

Mr. Becker prided himself on greeting everyone who came into his store. All children looked alike to him, so he simplified the matter by calling boys Bobby and girls Susie. Today he was stocking soup; we tried to slip past him to the household aisle, but there were jingle bells attached to the electric doors, and he'd heard them when we came in.

"Susie! There's my girl," he bellowed, dropping the carton of soup cans and charging up the aisle. "What can I get for you now?"

"We know where everything is," I said, in the voice I saved for adults like Mr. Becker. But Mr. Becker dropped one cold, heavy hand on each of our shoulders.

"What have you got to say for yourself!" he shouted at Sam. Sam looked at the floor and did not speak; I fixed my gaze on a pyramid of Fancy Artichoke Hearts. We both knew that when attacked by a bull or a bear, your best option was to play dead. "Cat got your tongue?" Mr. Becker asked, and then, mercifully, he released us and chuckled his way back to the soup. Sam and I headed for the dishwashing liquid, embarrassed for both ourselves and Mr. Becker. Rounding the next aisle, staring grimly ahead, we saw a tall, thin girl slipping a package of Hostess Ding Dongs into her purse.

She was about fourteen. She wore silver sandals and a gold ankle chain and frayed jean shorts that crept so high you knew she wasn't wearing any underwear. Her shirt was a man's white T-shirt with the sleeves and the collar ripped off. A gold star, the kind the teachers stuck on our papers when we spelled everything right, was glued to her cheek. She looked over at us, a slow, too casual glance, and we got very busy comparing the prices of Ivory and Palmolive. Without saying anything about it to each other, we knew we had gone undercover, real spies with a very real mission: follow the thief. I imagined our names in the Saint Ignatius Parish Bulletin, perhaps with a picture of us shaking Father Van Dan's hand. I imagined Mr. Becker rewarding us with cash, prizes, maybe even a trip somewhere.

"What should we do?" Sam whispered. The girl was heading

toward the automatic doors; they sizzled open and she disappeared, like an angel, into a pool of light.

"Go pay and then meet me outside," I said, pushing the money into his hand, and I walked quickly up the aisle and plunged into the sudden bright heat of the street outside. The girl was standing at the edge of the curb as if she were waiting for me. Her purse bulged at her side. "Hi," I chirped, trying to be cool. "Hey," she said noncommittally. I thought that perhaps I'd seen her before, one of several girls who liked to sit smoking on the half-wall in front of the bank. She braced herself against the telephone pole where we had left our bikes and lifted first one foot and then the other to unbuckle her silver sandals. Each had a braided noose, meant to ensnare her big toe, and I thought I'd never seen shoes that looked so terribly cruel. They reminded me of the traps my uncle Olaf kept hanging in his basement, with bits of fur still clinging to the metal. There were red marks on her toes, and she rubbed at them the way an animal licks a hurt. I wanted to touch them; I wanted to ask her name. I wanted to be beautiful in the way she was beautiful, wearing silver trap shoes and a look that shivered inside me. This was the sort of girl my mother referred to as a *wild girl,* and suddenly I loved the sound of those words. They made me remember my cat days, moving by instinct and intuition only, prowling through the darkness with twenty-twenty vision, striking with a neat, clean blow. Her eyes did, in fact, look like the eyes of a cat: They were narrow and green, outlined in green eyeliner, made wider and brighter by green eye shadow. For the first time, I imagined my own eyes painted: fierce, mysterious, untamed.

By the time Sam came out with the dishwashing liquid in a paper sack, the wild girl was walking up Main Street in the same direction we'd come from, those cruel shoes swinging from her hand. "Let her walk ahead," I told him. "If we tail her too close, she'll get suspicious."

We got our bikes and crossed to the opposite side of the street, riding so slowly that we kept toppling into each other. Once, still walking, she stared back at us evenly, but then she tossed her hair and continued on, her bare feet slapping the sidewalk. We had almost reached the mill when she made a military left and marched up the steps of a rectangular brick house. It was an ordinary, everyday sort of house, with a birdbath and a statue of the Virgin in the front. It did not look like the house of either a thief or a wild girl. The screen door slapped behind her; the shades were already pulled shut. The house looked forlorn, the way houses look when no one lives inside them.

We rode around the block, buying the time we needed to come up with a plan. We rode around the block again. Finally, we left our bikes and the bottle of detergent behind the hedge across the street and scurried along the side of the house until we found an open window. Because Sam was lighter, I lifted him up for the first look, hoping there wasn't a dog. His tennis shoes dug into my wrist, smelling of manure and grass.

"I don't see anything," he said.

"Let's try you lifting me," I said, and we switched places so that I could look for whatever Sam had missed that would tell us what we should do next. As I gripped the shutters I could hear him below me, exhaling in little grunts, and I knew he wouldn't be able to hold me there much longer. I pressed my face against the screen and saw a shadow moving rapidly toward the window, and then I was staring into the wild girl's face. Up close, she looked much younger, and she had sweet, crooked teeth. She was eating a Ding Dong, licking the white filling from her index finger. My mother wouldn't let us eat Ding Dongs, which she said had a shelf life of eighteen years.

"Do you see anything?" Sam called up at me.

I couldn't breathe.

"Are you trying to see me naked or something?" she said in that low, noncommittal voice.

"No."

"What?" Sam said.

"Then what do you want?" she said.

I wanted to look just like her, to become her, to lick eighteen-year-old frosting from my finger and survive, but this was not the sort of thing she meant. I knew all about extortion; still, money seemed too much to ask. "A soda," I said weakly. It was the only other thing that came to mind. My mother didn't let us drink them, not because of their shelf life but because the sugar would rot our teeth. The girl lifted the last bit of frosting into her mouth. I imagined how it would nestle there inside her, a puff of white growing smaller and smaller.

"Come around front," she said. I pushed away from the house and tumbled to the ground, pulling Sam down too. His eyes were the feverish eyes of a hunter. "Are we going to arrest her?"

When I shook my head, he gave me a look of absolute disbelief. I could see I was a failure in his eyes, but I was tired of the game, vaguely embarrassed, and I wanted to go home. We weren't spies anymore—just a little boy and a not so little girl who was too old to play games of make-believe. Self-consciously, I licked my hand and smoothed my hair back from my face. "She's giving us a soda not to tell," I said, trying to make it sound like a victory. "Besides, she ate all the evidence."

When we got to the front of the house, she was already waiting on the porch, holding a can of Jolly Good Cream Soda. She had put on earrings and fresh, orange lipstick. She didn't look at me—she looked at Sam. "What's your name?" she asked him, and though I was used to people noticing Sam first, I ached with jealousy.

"Boris," I said.

"No it's not," Sam said.

The girl laughed. "You got a girlfriend yet?"

"He's got five," I said, meanly. "One of them's even married."

The girl looked at me for the first time. It was a look of approval. "Boys are all the same," she said, and then she pressed the soda into my hand as if it were a secret between just us two. It was the first time I had seen Sam as a boy instead of my brother, and his face became part of the broken blur of faces that swam to the girls' side of the gym once a year for square dancing, boy faces with grinning teeth and strange-smelling breath and hands that dug in with short, blunt nails. The wild girl's fingernails were long peach opals, glistening as if they were wet. She saw me staring at them. "It's my mother's color," she said. "You want me to do yours?"

She turned and went back inside without waiting for me to answer. The soda was sweating in my hand. I gave it to Sam without looking at him, dried my palm on the back of my shorts. "How come girls color their nails?" he asked reasonably.

"They just *do*," I snapped—it had never occurred to me to wonder why—and then the girl came out with the nail polish and led me to the porch swing. She put my right hand on my own bare thigh. I felt my own flesh, warm and slightly damp, and I was conscious of the dark silky hairs that grew there.

"I want to go home," Sam said.

"Spread your fingers like this," the girl told me, and then she painted swift peach strokes across my pasty nails, brushing the edges of my chewed cuticles. It stung, but I didn't say anything. I was hoping she would do the other hand too. "You've got nice hands," she said. "Not too big, like mine."

She seemed to be waiting for something, and I struggled to figure out what it was. I hadn't yet learned to speak an adolescent girl's language of false denials and subtle cues. I looked at her hands, which were perfect, and then I understood. "Your hands *aren't* too big," I said, and I glanced meaningfully at Sam. His lower lip stuck out in the peculiar way that meant he wanted to cry.

"You have *stupid* hands," he said.

I started to laugh—I couldn't help it—and suddenly Sam laughed too. The girl's face grew longer, thinner, and she pushed my hand away. "I'm going into the house now," she said, "and if you don't get out of here I'm calling the police to report you for trespassing."

"I'm calling the police!" we mimicked in high, shrill voices, scuttling down the steps, racing for our bikes. The clouds that had banked the horizon all day were finally moving inland, bringing the cool east wind along with them. We rode home one-handed, no-handed, holding hands, passing the soda between us, choking as the unfamiliar carbonation fizzled in our noses. The fields around us bucked like ocean waves. *I'm calling the police!* we shrieked again and again, our words swallowed into the clouds. Lightning winked inside them, delicate, darting tongues, but we were not afraid. For the moment, we'd forgotten we were late, that my mother would be worried. We'd forgotten that my father would be home from work by now. We'd forgotten the peach polish that glistened on my hand.

My father was fifteen years older than my mother, away at the car lot most of the time, and before that night he'd never seemed as real to me as she did. He was the shape on the couch after supper, the distant whine of the drill coming from the shed, the crunch of gravel in the driveway that meant he was leaving for the car lot, or else coming home. The absentminded voice that told me to *be a good girl.* The sharper voice that said to *simmer down.* On holidays, he lit a fire in the fireplace, cursing the bursts of smoke, the newsprint on his hands. In summer, he mowed the lawn in grim, unswerving lines, and whenever I heard the cough of the mower, I rushed outside to rescue grasshoppers, butterflies, the occasional terrified toad. Sundays, he gave me and Sam each a dollar to put in the collection basket. Unlike my mother, he did not tell amusing stories about when he was our age, or make up silly knock-knock jokes, or join us in games of Sorry! He seemed to have a lot of rules; he worried about what he called *appearances*. My mother always took his side, saying he was no more strict with us than with himself.

He did not talk much about his family. It was my mother who told us he'd had a younger brother, our uncle Arnold, who had died in World War II. It was my mother who told us that their father, our grandfather, had liked to drink whiskey and gamble, and he'd liked these things so much that he'd died with barely this farm to his name. My father was known throughout Horton as the farm boy who'd made good, honored for valor during his own tour of duty before coming home to work his way up through the ranks at Fountain Ford. He was the absolute head of our household, the decision maker, the one we approached—my mother included—to request our allowance or a new pair of shoes. He was sort of like God; we knew he was supposed to love us, but it was an all-powerful, distant sort of love, a love that was not given to explanations. A love that wasn't quick to forgive mistakes. "This is my house," he'd say, and those words were enough to silence any disagreement.

At home, I told my mother Sam had gotten a cramp, that we'd had to walk our bikes and that's why we were late. She accepted the lie, as well as the detergent, and sent us straight into the kitchen for supper. My father had already helped himself to the mashed potatoes and roast, which were drowning in a muddy slick of pepper-and-flour gravy. "In the name of the Father, and of the Son, and of the Holy Ghost," he began. There was nothing he hated worse than cold food. I crossed myself and closed my eyes, folding my hands beside my plate. Outside, it had started to rain, and the rumbling in my stomach matched the distant thunder. Food smells rose around me like a thick, warm mist.

"Look at that," my father said.

It was a tone I'd never heard before.

"Ten years old and it's starting already," he said, and I opened my eyes. He was looking at my fingers. "Where were you this afternoon with those painted nails? Showing off for the boys?" Foolishly, I tucked my hand under the table. My father had never hurt me before, yet, strangely, it didn't surprise me when he rippled like a shadow over the space between us, grabbed my hand, jerked me up out of my chair. "This I'm going to nip in the bud," he said as I dangled there absurdly. What I felt in my shoulder was not pain but *color*, and that color ripened into a grand, glowing rose as my father hooked his free arm around my waist and carried me out of the house, slung over his arm like a garment bag, to the shed, where he dumped me onto the low stepladder. The rain on the roof was gentle, sweet. It reminded me of spending the night at my grandmother's house and falling asleep in the attic bedroom, closer to the stars and to God.

I have often wondered what my mother did while my father selected a rusty can from the row on the high wooden shelf, the way one might choose a good book, and fed oily turpentine into a strip of cloth from the rag box by the door. His expression wasn't angry anymore; he looked tired, distant, resigned, the way he did when he came home from a long day at the car lot. It took him several minutes to remove the last sliver of peach-colored paint, working the rag deep into the crevices around my nails before, in an odd, uncertain gesture, stuffing it into my mouth. Perhaps my mother simply ate her supper, pretending nothing was wrong so that nothing *would* be wrong, the way she believed if you thought you couldn't catch a cold, you wouldn't catch one. Perhaps she helped Sam fill his plate and told him, *Eat now; this is between your father and your sister.* My father interacted with us so infrequently—

small children, he believed, were best left to their mothers—that she might have felt this was, at base, something good.

"No makeup," he told me. "No nail polish, no high heels. None of that nonsense. Is that understood?" He went back to the house, and I waited, and still my mother did not come. I spit out the rag, licked my hot lips. After a while, I got down from the stepladder and crept into the house and up the stairs to the room I had shared with Sam since he was a baby. My shoulder had begun to throb. I held my arm against my side and listened to the familiar after-dinner sounds of the dishes being washed and stacked to dry. My head ached from the turpentine smell, which seemed to lift me in a glistening cloud until I could see myself far below: a dark-haired girl sitting on the edge of a neatly made bed; and, beside her, a stuffed pink rabbit, with its ears tied into a bow beneath its chin; and, across the room, another bed, hastily made, the rumpled sheets decorated with trains and octagonal signs that said STOP! The girl was rubbing her feet back and forth, back and forth, on the braided rug, and I watched her for a while, thinking it was an odd thing for her to do.

The rain had ended by the time Sam came in to get ready for bed, both hands full of the green beans he'd swiped for my supper. The air was cool and still. I kept my hurt arm against my side and ate the smashed bean pieces with my other hand. "You OK?" Sam said. I didn't know. When the beans were gone, Sam went downstairs and told my mother there was something wrong with my arm. She came in then, but she wouldn't look at me. "You better not be faking this," she said.

Dr. Neidermier met us at Saint Andrew's Clinic in Fall Creek. It turned out that the shoulder was sprained. A nurse gave me a sling for my arm and a shot that made me very sleepy. As we walked back out to the car, breathing in the clean after-rain smell, I leaned against my mother out of habit, but her whole body flinched away. Without touching me, she unlocked the car door. "Fasten your seat belt," she told me, and I did.

The movement of the car towed me into a warm, rich sleep, and I thought it was part of my dream when I heard my mother crying. She cried all the way home, as I tried to open my eyes to see if it really was her or just another liquid thought I couldn't hold on to long enough to understand. When we got home, she lifted me carefully and carried me into the house. My father was there. I twisted to hide my face, and I felt how tightly she was holding me. She stepped past him and started up the stairs. Then she stopped. I felt us both sink a little.

"Take her, Gordie. Please," she said, and I was in my father's arms, my sore shoulder trapped painfully against his broad chest, and he carried me up the stairs and tucked me into bed with the blanket folded down and my rabbit half under the covers just right, like this was something he'd been doing all my life. "Shh, sweetheart," he kept saying. On the other side of the room, Sam was lying in his bed, eyes open wide, as if I were the strange girl I'd seen earlier, and he didn't recognize her any more than I did.

That night, I lay awake for hours, listening to the rise and fall of my parents' voices coming from their bedroom across the hall. As soon as I closed my eyes I felt I was slipping through the floor of the earth, an endless whirling distance. So I kept my eyes open and listened for the sound of the POWs moving through the fields; I listened for the scratching of whatever lived under the bed; I listened, and I heard nothing at all. Mysterious things, it seemed, did not bother to hide themselves. That's what made them so frightening, for they drifted before your eyes in the brightest daylight, clothed in everyday, human forms. Suddenly I was suffocating. Beneath the sling, my arm was slick with sweat, and an odd smell came from my body. I sat up and pushed the window open as wide as it would go. Under the hushed moon, the sunflowers raised and lowered their heads in the slow night wind. After a while, I went over to Sam's side of the room. He was sleeping in his usual arc, his hands thrown out oddly in front of him. I nudged them together, so they folded into themselves like hands in prayer. I meant it to keep him safe somehow, but when he sighed and rolled onto his back, I realized I had arranged him into a corpse. Was he dead? I got in bed beside him and pressed my hand against his chest. His heart was beating, just like my own, and the sound of it absorbed the terrible silence. I rolled up against him, propped my sling on his shoulder, and slept.

At breakfast the next day, my father announced he had decided to turn the southwest corner of the basement into a bedroom, with wood-paneled walls and a lowered ceiling and a special sub-floor to resist the damp. This was going to be Sam's bedroom. I would remain in our old room upstairs, which my mother would help me redecorate. Sam stared into his cornflakes, and I looked down too, embarrassed, ashamed, as my mother explained I was growing up, perhaps faster than she and my father had realized, and it was time for me and Sam to sleep in rooms of our own. Nobody mentioned my bright white sling, and I wondered for an odd moment if it was part of a terrible dream, something that I had imagined. But the ache in my shoulder was real. When I'd finished eating, my father pulled me into his lap, and I perched on his knee for a polite moment, uneasy as a cat waiting to be put down, gathering strength for the leap.

After breakfast, in a controlled and careful voice, my mother explained how bad he felt about the night before. "It frightens him to think about his little girl growing up," she said. She was washing the breakfast dishes with extra vigor. I had been excused from table chores, and now I fumbled with the thought of having made my father afraid.

"But why?" I said. He had taken Sam to the lumberyard to pick up materials for the new room.

My mother sighed. "Because you'll be a young lady pretty soon, and you'll have boyfriends and dates, and then you'll start wanting a family of your own." She stopped, considering. "It makes him feel old, I guess. Maybe a little uncomfortable. People didn't talk about things like this when your father was a boy. It's scary for him, that's all."

I put my head down on the table. I didn't feel like a person who might make another person afraid, but then again, I didn't really feel like myself either.

"Not that it's an excuse," my mother said quickly. "Not that what he did wasn't overreacting. But he didn't mean it, sweetheart, do you understand? He asked me to make sure to tell you that."

I tried to nod without hurting my shoulder. My mother gave me two aspirins and a cup of tea with a tablespoon of whiskey. "Why don't you go back to bed," she said. "I'll be up in a bit to see how you're doing."

I finished my tea and went to bed, and I didn't wake up until late in the afternoon, when the sound of hammering poked me out of my sleep. Soon I heard the scream of the circular saw biting wood, and I realized my father had already started working in the basement.

"How did you sleep?" my mother said. She was standing in the doorway, and as I turned my head I saw that the bedroom was filled with flowers: gladioli, zinnias, hollyhocks, dahlias, lilies. Each bunch was clasped in a tin can or a jelly jar, and they perched in every crevice of my bookshelf and desk, even peeking from the drawers of my dresser. The cedar chest at the foot of my bed was covered with more bouquets, only these were held by my mother's good vases, the crystal she got when she married. I didn't need to go outside to know my mother's flower gardens all were bare, each blind stalk buried deep within the greenery of the leaves.

My father wouldn't let me help with Sam's new bedroom in the basement. "You'll hurt yourself," he said sternly if I picked up a board with my good arm. "That's too heavy for you." But he gave Sam bigger boards to carry, even though Sam was smaller than me, and if he complained, my father said, "Aw, that's light as a feather. Where's your muscle, son?" He seemed to be constantly guiding Sam's arm with his own broad hand, gripping the back of Sam's neck, moving Sam's body through a particular set of motions that would result in an even cut, a sharp angle, a flush edge. "Not like that, like *that*," he'd say, and he made Sam repeat each thing over and over until he had done it perfectly, twice. Often, my father lost his temper; Sam didn't have much of a knack for carpentry. He carried the hammer with two hands the way my mother insisted we carry her heirloom plates. He winced each time the head hit the nail. He plugged his ears when my father ran the circular saw. "Don't act like such a girl," my father told him. "That little bit of noise is nothing." And Sam unplugged his ears, set his teeth against the grinding sound.

One week before school started, my mother took me back to see Dr. Neidermier, who raised and lowered my arm and said I could stop wearing the sling as long as my shoulder felt OK. When we got back home, I ran upstairs to tell Sam and discovered his bed was missing, and his dresser too. His posters. His little blue floor rug. The room smelled different. It was as if he'd never lived there. I sneaked downstairs past the kitchen, where I was supposed to set the table for supper, and crept down the basement stairs, using my keenest spy stealth. The new bedroom walls were completely finished; the door to the bedroom was closed. I put my hand to the knob and eased my way inside, my feet padding over the rubbery brown indoor/outdoor carpet that now covered the floor. There was Sam's bed, his dresser, new shelves made of cinder blocks and wood, spray-painted brown. The closet, which had been merely a skeletal shape, was now a real closet, with a set of sliding doors. I opened them up, and there were Sam's clothes, hanging in a cluster. A dehumidifier hummed in one corner of the room. Everything smelled of harsh, fresh paint.

When I heard footsteps coming down the basement stairs, I

46

slipped into the closet and crouched beside the shoes, pulling the doors closed behind me. I could see perfectly through the slender crevice between them, and when Sam and my father came in, I felt a lurch of adrenaline. Without the cumbersome sling I was myself again, graceful and whole. I breathed the doors open, inch by inch, and I thought about all the time Sam and I had spent developing potions that would make us invisible, blending choke-cherry blossoms and pounded-up stones, beer stolen from the little refrigerator my father kept in his workshop, our own spit. Mixture after mixture we rubbed on our skin, and still we could see each other, squinting hopefully as we stood eye-to-eye, waiting for one of us to fade. Now it seemed I was finally invisible as I walked toward them, slowly, step by step. They were putting up new posters of airplanes and motorcycles, a HORTON WILDCATS pennant that had once been my father's. I was close enough to reach out and tap them on the shoulders and still neither one of them saw that I was there.

Four

The fall I started junior high, my mother, who had never worked outside our home before, took a part-time job at a weekly advertiser called the *Sell It Now!* Three times a week, she drove twenty-five miles to Cedarton in our "second car," a rusted Oldsmobile that conked out in a dramatic cloud of smoke if you let it idle too long. Years before, on the way home from the grocery store, Sam had spilled a gallon of milk across the back seat. Even now, and especially in wet weather, it gave off a moist, cheesy smell. But my mother didn't seem to mind. "It runs," she said, and if she ever envied my father's Ford, with its sleek blue sheen, its air-conditioned silence, I never heard her mention it.

One Saturday in September, just after she got the job, she invited me and Sam to come along and see where she worked. It hadn't been too long ago that my father had taken us to see his office at Fountain Ford, and I remembered the thick gray carpet, the water cooler with its magic hot and cold, the magnificent fish wandering the tank in the lobby, my father's name, GORDON SCHILLER, in gold block letters on his desk. The other men greeted him with shouts—*Hey there, Gordy! Gordo!*—and they shook

Sam's hand and told my father I was good-looking, and one of them bought us paper cups of hot chocolate from a machine. It made me proud to see my father that way, surrounded by people who admired him, the tie we'd given him for Father's Day dividing his chest in a fat splash of gold. His voice, which at home seemed too loud, too forceful, rang out like a bell in the vast showroom, drawing everybody to the sound. Outside the plate-glass windows, beautiful cars had been lined up in perfect shiny rows, and my father walked us up and down the aisles of the lot, one hand on the back of each of our necks, quizzing Sam on the names of various different models. "Maybe someday you'll come work for your old man—how would you like that?" he asked. I knew Sam wanted to be a famous artist or an actor or a daredevil stuntman, but he didn't tell my father that. I wanted to be a nurse or a veterinarian; still, I hoped my father would ask if I wanted to work for him too. Later, behind the closed door of his office, he showed us all the plaques he'd been awarded for his outstanding service to Ford. "My dad sure had nothing like this to show for himself," he said, and he gave Sam a poke on the shoulder. "Remember what I'm telling you. You've got to work to get ahead in this world. Nobody's going to hand you anything."

It was hard not to be disappointed when my mother unlocked the door to the windowless room she shared with four other people. When Sam said he was thirsty, she poured us each a plastic cup of water from the bathroom sink; I sipped it politely as she spoke about her work, bending seriously over a mock-up, planning the layout of the center page. But I felt vaguely uncomfortable, shy, as though I were listening to a familiar stranger, perhaps a friend of the family, someone I almost didn't know. Until that moment, it had seemed like the only things that happened to my mother were the things that happened to us. She felt my scraped knee and Sam's burned finger; she sweated our fevers, suffered our bad dreams. There was nothing that belonged to her alone except her past, and even that she shared easily, telling stories about her childhood until Sam and I remembered them as our own.

The night she first told us about the *Sell It Now!*, she had made a special dinner of lamb chops and boiled new potatoes, the first of the fall crop. She'd applied for the job in secret, she said, because she had wanted to surprise us. She hoped we would all be able to help out a little more around the house, because she would be pretty busy for a while. Sam and I nodded and said we would, but my father stopped eating, which was not a good sign.

"I can't believe you'd go behind my back on this," he said. My mother kept on eating like nothing was wrong, which was not a good sign either. Sam and I looked at our plates. "I thought we agreed there was no need for you to work."

"I just want something that gives me the same satisfaction your job gives you."

"What about us? Don't we give you any satisfaction?"

"Of *course*," my mother said. "But the kids are growing up and you're always at the lot and I don't just want to sit around, getting older. I want to meet people. I want to learn new things."

"The reason I'm at the lot so much is so that you can take it easy if you want. Don't I provide for us well enough? Don't we have a comfortable life?"

"It isn't that," my mother said. "There's more to life than being comfortable."

"Well, excuse me," my father said, "if my best isn't good enough for this family."

He stood up, grabbed his coat from its hook in the hall. The door slammed, and then we listened to the gravelly sound of his car moving down the driveway. "Don't worry," my mother told us. "He'll get used to the idea. Your father is a little old-fashioned, that's all."

But he didn't get used to it. His anger bubbled and simmered like a thick soup, filling the house with its smell, and every now and then it boiled over into a fresh argument. Sam and I sat close to the TV, the volume turned up as loud as we dared, and still we could hear them fighting in the kitchen as my mother got ready to leave for work.

"I'm asking you to resign, Therese," my father said. "For me."

"This isn't about you, for a change."

"Where's all this coming from? We never had a quarrel until you started this career woman crap."

"We never had a quarrel because I never asked for anything you didn't want. I'm asking for this. This one thing. Three nights a week, Gordon; it's not like I'm neglecting you."

"What about the kids?" my father said. "What about Abby? A girl that age needs her mother's supervision when the young bucks come sniffing around."

"*Gordon,*" my mother said.

"Young *bucks,*" Sam whispered, and he made kissing noises into his hand.

"Shut up," I said. That males of any species might show an interest in me—or I in them—was something I still considered ludicrous. Boys were ungirls, ill-mannered, unpredictable. In the hallways at school I hugged the rows of metal lockers to avoid their sharp shoulders, their swinging hands. In biology, when we had to choose microscope partners, I quickly picked another girl; at lunch, I sat on the "girls' side" of the cafeteria. Boys were citizens of another, stronger country. If you opened your mouth to speak in class, a boy would say it first. When you raised your hand, the teacher's gaze flew past it, straight into the waiting glove of a boy's eager palm.

Sometimes, falling asleep at night, I tried to remember if the differences I was noticing between boys and girls had always been there. Perhaps the shock of starting junior high had caused my perception of things to change, the way my father's binoculars changed after I dropped them, knocking loose the fragile prism inside. But tucked in the cedar chest up in the attic, I found the outfits my mother had made for Sam and me when we were very small. A green and red checked suit for Sam; a green and red checked dress for me. Twin yellow play pants, with flowers sewn over the pocket on mine and a sailboat sewn over the pocket on Sam's, so that people could tell who was the girl and who was the boy. It had always pleased me when people got it wrong. This happened frequently after the first of each month, when Auntie Thil came over to cut our hair in the style that she and my mother hopefully called a pixie. "Look at the little pixies," my mother would say afterward, and we'd struggle up into her lap, adoring and eager as puppies. I'd close my eyes, divided between the pleasure I felt at my mother's attention and the fear that, perhaps, Sam loved her more than me. I thought about this often, and at night, in the bedroom we still shared back then, I'd pose hypothetical questions for him, whispering across the dark space between our beds.

Me and Mom are attacked by mad dogs and you can only save one of us. Who do you pick?

Me and Mom are drowning and you're in a boat, but there's only room for one more person. Who will you save?

Pretending he was asleep didn't help—I demanded an answer. "You," he'd finally say, and only then could I sleep, bigger and brighter and stronger because there was someone who loved me best. With everyone else I felt my inadequacies, which I knew were abundant and terrible. I was nothing at all like the girls in the books we read in Sunday school, girls who were pretty and good, who dedicated their lives to worthy causes. I was too heavy and my voice was too loud and my hair wouldn't curl no matter what. I asked too many questions. My teachers said I had a tendency to "carry things too far."

"You can call me Mom," I told Sam one afternoon while we were playing dress-up. I was in third grade, Sam in second. We'd had to play dress-up in secret ever since the time my father came home from work and found Sam and me in Mom's high heels, wobbling between the window and the full-length mirror in their bedroom. Our hair was sprayed to stand on end; our lips were puckered red hearts. *"Hel-loh-oh!"* we trilled. One look, and we knew we had done something wrong.

"For heaven's sake, Gordon, they're *children*," my mother had said, but my father said it wasn't healthy for a boy of any age to put on lipstick and a dress. Still, I loved to outline Sam's lips in red, to highlight his deep-set eyes with lavender and blue, to clip earrings to the tops of his ears so the weight made them fold down like a little lamb's. I loved to dress him up in the clothes my mother had worn back when she and my father still went out dancing on Saturday nights. High on the closet shelf were the trophies they'd won, lined up like grinning gold teeth. Sometimes they'd sit at the supper table long after Sam and I had been excused, recalling those competitions, friends of my father's they'd double-dated with, plans they'd made before my father started working such long hours at Fountain, before Sam and I came along. Then you could see how it must have been when they'd first fallen in love, back when my mother was barely eighteen and my father was thirty-two, capable, confident, picking her up in his shiny new T-bird. There was something between them that changed the color of the light, brightening the dusk, and, perhaps, they'd clasp hands between the dirty dishes.

"Say Mom," I told Sam. He looked just like a doll, so sturdy and small in a pink speckled dress, and I wanted him all for myself.

"That's dumb," he said, but he changed his mind when I offered him a quarter. At supper that night, he said, "Thank you, Mom," when I passed him the scalloped potatoes. My father, intent on the TV, didn't notice, but my mother got the expression she wore just before she said something that might trigger an argument.

"Your sister's name is Abby," she told Sam.

"I know." He looked down, the potatoes plumping his

cheeks. My father snapped his fingers, meaning that we should be quiet so he could hear the evening news.

"*I* am your mom," my mother said to Sam, and I hated her then because I knew she was right, that long ago she'd made Sam up deep within her body, and for this reason he would always be a part of her in a way he would never be a part of me. I got up and ran through the house, slamming doors: the kitchen door, the hallway door, the heavy front door, which shook the warped porch floorboards and scattered the cats from the cool, dark earth beneath them. I climbed high into a pear tree and stared out over the fields toward Horton and its hazy light, the summer moon ripening in the distance. It seemed to me then that I had nothing of value, that I would never be anyone interesting or important.

After a while, the porch light snapped on and my mother came outside. She had told me once how she had felt when she first came to live in this house, my father's childhood home, and how she did things, deliberate little things, to make it her own: tying back the front curtains with a knot instead of a bow, interspersing yellow tulips among the red ones in the flower bed. Now I watched as she began flaking paint from the old porch railing with her thumbnail until the brown beneath it appeared, grew longer, proof beyond a doubt that she had been there.

My parents never lingered at the table anymore. The moment my mother sat down to relax, my father picked at her, pointing out things around the house that she needed to do. "You're not being sensible about this job thing, Therese," he said. "You're needed here. To go all that distance is hardly worth the little bit of money you make."

"You could help out now and then," my mother said.

"That's not cost-effective," my father said. "You want me to stay home and put on an apron so we can live on the seventy-five dollars and change you bring home each week?"

But I didn't mind helping out; it made me feel important, and my mother always thanked me and told me what a good job I had done. It was 1977, and a few of my friends' mothers worked too. It didn't seem like such a big deal to me. "And it isn't," my mother assured me. My grandmother disagreed. Even Auntie Thil couldn't understand why my mother wouldn't just admit the whole thing had been a mistake. "Olaf would never let me work," she said proudly. "I don't think he'd be able to find his way around the house if I weren't there."

We were at my grandmother's, still sluggish from a big noon dinner. My mother and my grandmother and Auntie Thil were playing cards at the kitchen table; underneath, Monica and I were setting up a line of dominoes, hoping they'd forget we were there and talk about something more interesting. Their legs hung down like prison bars, and we felt deliciously trapped, safe. "Gordon's a big boy," my mother said. "He had an apartment before we got married."

"He still drove home to eat at his mother's table every night," my grandmother said.

"She died in '57, Mom. We didn't marry until '62."

"She died in '58."

"I thought '57," Auntie Thil said.

"She died the spring we had those floods."

"It was '57," my mother said firmly. "And then he moved back to the farmhouse and spent five years cooking and cleaning for himself."

"From what you said when you first got married, it doesn't sound like he cleaned so much," Auntie Thil said, laughing.

"And he took his meals at Poppy's Kitchen in Horton," my grandmother said. "A man marries because he needs certain things. You can't go changing the rules, Therese. You promised to love, honor, and obey, and that doesn't just mean if you feel like it."

"When *I* get married," Monica whispered to me, "*I'm* sure not going to work."

55

"I am."

"Then you're weird."

To punish her, I let my knee nudge one of the dominoes, and they all went down. "Hey!" she said, forgetting to whisper. "That was my turn!"

"Girls?" my grandmother said. "Why don't you take those into the living room?"

Thursday was the advertising deadline at the *Sell It Now!* and on Wednesday nights my mother seldom made it home before midnight. After school, I'd hurry from the bus up the drive and into the house, where I'd find her careful dinner instructions taped to the refrigerator door. I preheated the oven and prepared casserole or pot roast or lamb, remembering to stab the potatoes so they wouldn't explode. When my father came home, I called Sam to supper, enjoying the grown-up feeling of serving the meal as if my father were my husband, Sam my little boy. My father grumbled about my mother's absence, but by then Sam and I were so used to it that it was easy to ignore. Afterward, I'd clean up while Sam did his homework in front of the TV and my father reread the *Milwaukee Sentinel.* Then I'd spread my homework on the kitchen table: English, French, Science, Math. Usually, I finished the first three in an hour so I could linger dreamily over basic geometry, resketching the various shapes until my father sent me upstairs to bed.

One night, as I was fitting the stubby pencil back into my compass, he came into the kitchen with his newspaper and sat down across from me in one of the orange vinyl chairs that matched my own. Air wheezed from the seat cushion, a ragged sigh. His regular place was at the head of the table, in the wooden chair with arms that his own father had made long ago. He glanced at the rows of figures I had written in my notebook. He reached out and touched the neat labels with his fingertip: *parallelogram, rhombus, triangle.*

"Para-what?" he said.

"Parallelogram. It's a figure with opposite sides that are parallel."

He tapped his finger on *rhombus*. "What's that?"

"An equilateral parallelogram."

I was proud to know something he didn't. But my father shook his head. "You'll never need that fancy stuff, you know," he said. "You should be learning about things that matter. Your mother should be teaching you the things you need to know."

He often said that his time in the service was where he'd gotten his real education. But I liked school; I especially liked geometry. I wanted to go to college someday. I went back to my compass and drew a circle with a one-inch radius. He opened the paper and slipped it between us, a textured wall of print.

"Here," he said, "just listen to this," and he read an article about a young woman in Milwaukee who'd been followed to her apartment by three men. When she unlocked her door, they forced their way inside, where they took turns raping her at knifepoint. She was unable to recall their faces. She was treated at a local hospital and released.

I pressed the sharp point of the compass into my thumb; when I took it away, there was a tiny red hole. I knew about rape from catechism; there it was called *violation*. But the women always died protecting their virginity, and then they were rewarded by God, glorified as saints, which made the possibility of rape seem as abstract, as unlikely, as a virgin birth. A window opened up in myself, and I saw what I could not know: the hallway that led to the woman's door, poorly lit and carpeted in orange, the apartment number screwed into the smooth, painted wood, the way she jingled the keys, thinking, *Hurry, hurry*. Then my mind winked shut. I smelled the sharp, after-dinner smell of the kitchen, and there was the circle I'd just drawn. I sketched a smile on its face. I wrote: *The diameter of a circle with a one-inch radius is two.*

"Has your mother told you about sex yet?" my father asked.

I nodded. Sex happened after marriage. At first it would hurt, but afterward it got better.

"When you live alone like that, you're at risk, you see," my father said in the utterly rational voice my math teacher used to explain right angles. "You have to learn to be careful," he told me. "You're not a little girl anymore." Sam came into the kitchen then and leaned against me, his body warm and faintly sour-smelling, twitchy from lying too long in front of the TV. "What's that?" he said, and he pointed to *circumference* in my notebook.

"The distance around a circle."

My father put his tongue to his teeth. "Nothing you'll ever need to know," he repeated. "It's the school of hard knocks that counts," he said.

"What's the school of hard knocks?" Sam said.

"Life," my father said. "What you've seen and where you've been."

"Oh," Sam said, and I was not surprised when he moved away from me. He no longer crept up the stairs at night and into my room, where we held flashlights under our chins, or played Scissors-Paper-Rock, or dipped our feet over the edge of the bed into piranha-infested air. He kept his sketchbooks hidden under his mattress, and he'd given me his watercolor paints and his calligraphy set, though sometimes he borrowed them back. My father said Sam was too old for all that, that it was time for Sam to grow up. He said it was time for me to grow up too, and yet it was clear that growing up meant one thing for Sam and, for me, something else. Boys were expected to live in the world; girls needed special protection. They had to be careful, and some girls, it seemed, never learned to be careful enough.

From then on, Wednesday nights as I worked my way through geometry, my father read to me about women who walked alone after dark, or talked to strange men, or went to bars with professional athletes, women who let themselves fall into the wrong place at the wrong time, women who suffered the consequences. Women who didn't have my father's respect for the world and the way it worked. Women who had learned the hard way, who hadn't been told, the way he was telling me now. " 'Entering through an open second-story window,' " my father read, " 'a juvenile, armed with a gun, sodomized a sixteen-year-old girl while her horrified sister watched.' " He shook his head. "What a world!"

I wrote out my math problems in clean, dark script. *A rectangle with four sides of equal length is a square.* The next day, I consulted the big red dictionary on display in the school library. *Sodomy: abnormal sexual acts: bestiality.* It made me think of the screams I heard from the horse farm down the road when the mares were bred by the stallions. I began to have trouble sleeping. During the day, I drifted through the halls at school, bumped by the flood of bodies that seemed drawn in one frenzied direction like magnetized bits of iron, and by association I became magnetic too. Each day, I got where I needed to go. I sat, I took notes, I swallowed my lunch in small, careful mouthfuls. Perhaps it was then that mathematics began to frighten me, the bent-necked evil sevens, the pregnant sixes, the snickering twos. I'd squint as I copied assignments from my textbook to the page, but it didn't help my growing sense of vertigo. The numbers loomed three-dimensional, rising and falling like sharp black lungs, and it was all I could do to guide my pen down between them, to coax a brief, flat line from the tip, to take my pen away before that line began to swell.

"What's wrong?" my mother asked frequently. "Honey, you seem kind of out of it."

"I'm just tired," I said. But I started to wonder if maybe my father had a point when he said my mother's job was hard on us all. It seemed to me that we'd been happier when she'd devoted her time to us alone, greeting Sam and me at the door after school, asking my father questions about his day at work instead of talking about her own. She'd already been promoted to assistant editor. Once, she and the associate editor, a woman named Cindy Pace, met for coffee to talk about ways they could improve the look and distribution of the *Sell It Now!* My mother came home flushed with excitement, to find my father waiting for her in the kitchen, home early from work as, lately, he so often seemed to be, asking where she had been and who she'd been with and what they had done.

"A cup of coffee with a friend," my mother said. "I'm thirty-seven years old, Gordon. I didn't think I needed to ask your permission!"

It was easiest to leave their angry voices behind and disappear into my room, where I'd lie on my bed and listen to the sound my heartbeat made inside my body, feel the pulse in my wrists, my throat. I found myself concentrating on only those things that were exactly in front of me. I peeled my cuticles until my fingers bloomed red; I twisted my hair around and around my second finger; I stared into my lap, or at the soft, smooth knees of my jeans, or at the toes of my sneakers, which I found strangely pleasing, narrow and pointed as the muzzles of dogs. Every day after school, I read the paper, skimming through the pages until I found the word *rape*. I read hungrily, shamefully, shivering with the same thing I felt when I saw people kissing on TV. Afterward, I felt sick with the cries of women beaten and molested and torn, the wailing of children who were never seen again, the swollen necks of strangled prostitutes, the spidery limbs of teenagers wearing skimpy clothing or too much makeup or polish on their nails.

One night, my father didn't read to me from the paper. Instead, he told me something he'd heard at work. A woman's car had broken down, and she'd last been seen with two men who'd pulled up beside her, offering assistance. Her body was found in a ravine months later. Raccoons had carried away the fine bones of her hands, a small portion of her skull. I imagined my mother's car breaking down on the dark rural highway from Cedarton, woods for miles around. As I chewed my pencil tip, I saw the truck pulling up behind her, baking my mother in a bright white beam like the probe from a UFO. She was under the hood, knowing it was a hopeless gesture because she wasn't even sure where the oil went—my father took care of all that business—so she squinted happily at the figures approaching her, blocking the light like coils of smoke. "Am I ever glad to see you!" she sang out, and here my mind shut like a terrible fist, holding in the poison, choking me inside it. That night, when she sat on the edge of my bed to listen to my prayers, the holy words lodged in my throat like bones. *The Lord helps those who help themselves:* This was something I'd been told for as long as I could remember, and every time I visited my grandmother's house I read it again, cross-stitched in gold and blue, hanging on the living room wall. My mother was not helping herself. Each time she left for work, she put herself at risk. God had little sympathy for fools, but I asked Him to make an exception in my mother's case, promising Him all sorts of things even though I knew it was a sin to bargain.

"You're so quiet lately, honey," my mother said, picking bits of nubby wool from my blanket.

"I'm worried about you," I said.

"About me?"

"What if your car breaks down?" I said. "What if you get stranded on the highway?"

"My goodness," my mother said. "I'll just walk to the nearest house and ask to use the phone."

"What if somebody attacks you?"

My mother looked at me. "Where would you get an idea like that?"

"It's in the newspapers," I said, and I closed my eyes so that I wouldn't cry. My mother kissed me and stroked my hair and told me that nothing was going to happen to her, but I knew that she was just being *naive*. That was another word I'd learned. My father had used it to describe me.

The next Wednesday night, I waited in the kitchen, defenseless, not even pretending to do my homework as the owl-shaped clock over the sink chirped the quarter hours. I stared at the owl and I followed the movement of its wings, and still my father did not come in. Finally, I went into the living room, where I found him polishing his business shoes, Sam beside him, half a dozen pairs fanned around them on sheets of newspaper. My father worked carefully, scrubbing polish into the crevices with a bristled brush before passing the shoe to Sam, who patted the excess polish away with an old diaper. The unpolished shoes waited, unlaced and open-mouthed; the room smelled strong and sweet.

"Finished already?" he said, without looking up.

"I guess."

He didn't say anything else. I waited for a minute or so, and then I went upstairs to bed. My father never read aloud to me after that, though sometimes he still brought the paper into the kitchen and sat across from me as I worked. "All that fancy stuff," he told me, shaking his head at my Introduction to French book. "Who do you know who talks French?" It was as if those other Wednesday nights had never happened. Perhaps he stopped because he felt he'd made his point. Or perhaps he simply grew bored with the routine. Maybe he noticed my increasing nervousness and realized he was frightening me far more than he'd ever intended. But I continued to read the paper on my own, furtively, secretly, shamed. Wednesday nights, I thought of my mother stranded on the highway, and the numbers in front of me collapsed into piles of short black sticks. Then I got up, casually, as if to get a glass of juice, or to scratch whichever cat happened to be slouched across the counter. But my father caught me glancing at the door, making sure it was locked. "You're safe with me," he'd say. "No need to be so jumpy." Sometimes he'd even get up and open the door, twisting his neck to peer at the stars, while I stared down at the knees of my jeans, imagining the wolf glide of a man's shadow slipping from the barn.

Halloween fell on a Wednesday, and my mother asked if I would mind staying home to wait for trick-or-treaters while she worked late at the *Sell It Now!* This year, for the first time, my father would be in charge of Halloween, driving Sam to Horton, watching closely while he approached each house, rang the bell, came back with a miniature chocolate bar or a fistful of sweet hard candy. There had been icy rumors about razor blades in apples, arsenic in Pixy Stix. Even Girl Scout cookies weren't safe; someone had discovered a pin. "You check everything before he eats it," my mother told my father. "Nothing unwrapped, nothing homemade. I'm *serious*, Gordon," she said, because my father had started to laugh.

"You worry too much," he said. "Sam's not afraid of that horse crap, are you, Sam?" and Sam looked between my mother and my father, anxiety creasing his forehead.

Other years, my mother would have driven us into Horton and dropped us off at the band shell, with strict orders to return by nine o'clock. We were never late. After curfew, the high school kids roamed the streets, the sweet tooth of childhood gnawing in their throats. They couldn't go trick-or-treating anymore; they were too old, too angry, stiff-legged in their freshly washed jeans. A few of the biggest boys dressed up as girls, while the girls painted their faces in the usual ways—white lipstick, green eyeliner, blush the color of beef. To us, they had become a part of the terror, no less essential than witches and demons. If they found a younger kid scurrying between the houses, the next day at school that child would be without candy, humble, eager for even a few stale pieces of chicken corn.

This year, I had planned to be an angel, my wings pinned

into a clever V to minimize wind resistance. But as my mother pointed out, a lot of kids my age would also be staying home, and I began to enjoy the idea of answering the door, looking over the costumes, deciding if they were worth one candy bar or two. So on Halloween night, I put on my everyday jeans and helped turn Sam into a vampire bat, stapling black streamers to the arms of his shirt for the air to ripple like wings. With his white plastic fangs and spiky bat ears, he looked the way I imagined a real-life vampire bat would. But just as he was ready to try his first flight off the couch, my father announced that costumes were for sissies. "You can be your old man, how's that?" he told Sam, scrunching his company hat over Sam's cardboard ears. It was a blue baseball cap, with a bent visor and *Fountain Ford* scrawled across its brim. "Dad!" I said, but Sam did not say anything, not even when my father plucked the streamers from his arms and took away his plastic jack-o'-lantern, the hollow kind all the other kids had, and gave him a brown grocery bag instead. "It'll hold more," my father explained. "This is a bag that means business."

Sam spit out his fangs. "Maybe I should carry a briefcase or something," he said, tilting the visor to hide his eyes. "So it looks more like a costume."

"Not necessary!" my father said. He was bristling with enthusiasm, clapping his hands together the way we'd seen him do at Fountain Ford when talking with the other salesmen about a hot deal. I could see how it was going to be, my father hustling Sam door to door, block to block, jeering him on when he stopped to catch his breath. Sam would have more candy than he'd ever had with me—my father would make sure of it. He winked as he guided Sam out the front door, his hand at the back of Sam's neck. I did not say good-bye; I was angry with my father, but even more so with Sam, because he did not fight back. The door slammed shut, forcing in a puff of air, rich with wood smoke and damp.

I finished the dishes and wandered around the house, waiting for trick-or-treaters. I looked out the windows. I opened the refrigerator door and closed it. I examined the row of family pictures hanging on the stairway wall. My parents' wedding portrait. My mother's high school graduation, a picture of my grandmother, Auntie Thil and Uncle Olaf. A snapshot my mother had taken of Sam and me when we were very small, sitting back-to-back in a gigantic pumpkin my father had bought from our neighbors. There were no pictures of my father's parents or his younger brother, Arnold, who had died in the war. No, he said, when we asked, he did not miss them. "How could I miss anybody when I have such a fine family right here?"

Sam's favorite cat, Rose, rubbed against my legs, but when I tried to pick her up she switched her tail and stalked away. To console myself, I began to eat the miniature Snickers bars from the candy bowl. The taste was flat and chalky, the way something on sale would taste. It didn't taste as good as trick-or-treat candy, which was sweeter because you sensed it wasn't really yours, something deliciously stolen. I imagined Sam in my father's baseball cap, holding out his ugly grocery bag, and I ate a few more Snickers, mixing the remaining ones with my fingers so it looked like there were more. My mother had said we probably wouldn't get many trick-or-treaters anyway. Our house was too far from Horton, set back from the highway. The trick-or-treaters we did get usually came just as we were ready for bed, kids from the neighboring farms huddled close for warmth in the open bed of somebody's pickup. The glowing end of a cigarette watched from the cab, a red devil's eye.

Tonight the first group of trick-or-treaters didn't arrive until well after dark. I had long given up sitting by the door and was watching a Charlie Brown special and nibbling Snickers bars when I heard footsteps on the porch. I ran into the kitchen and peeked carefully through the window: a group of clowns and one tiny, shivering fairy. When I opened the door they all just looked at me, shifting foot to foot.

"What do you say?" I said, because it didn't seem fair they should get something for nothing.

"Please," the fairy chirped. The older ones tittered a few "*trick-or-treats*" and held out their plastic jack-o'-lanterns. I wondered how I looked to them, too big to go trick-or-treating, perhaps, but not big enough to be mistaken for a grown-up. They had come in a rusted blue station wagon that was idling by the shed, and when they ran back and opened the doors I heard a woman's shrill voice telling them to hurry up and shut the goddamn doors, did they want to freeze her ass?

Suddenly it seemed that every five minutes I'd hear a knock at the door. There were witches and elves and Martians; there were ingenious salt and pepper shakers, a martini, an airplane, even a Tweety bird with real chicken feathers. I began to worry about running out of candy, and I wished that I hadn't eaten so much of it myself. I was jittery from the sugar, and every time I heard a new group at the door, the sound tickled my spine like a burst of electricity.

At precisely nine o'clock I gave the last Snickers bar to a rabbit; his sister scowled at me through her ballerina eyes when I handed her an apple, still cold from the crisper. "It's all I have," I pleaded. The rabbit giggled and scampered toward the waiting truck. The ballerina held her stare an extra moment before pivoting elaborately, then stomping down the steps, her long braid swinging. I shut the door, locked it, and turned off the porch light. I considered putting a sign on the door saying *Sorry, just ran out,* but Uncle Olaf did that every year so he wouldn't have to pay for candy, and last year he'd gotten his windows soaped. Maybe there would be no more trick-or-treaters. With that, I heard another car creeping up the drive. I ran around the house turning off lights, until everything was dark. The car hesitated in the courtyard, then turned and headed back toward the road. I was relieved. It was nine-fifteen; my father and Sam would be home soon. Maybe we could give away some of Sam's candy, the kinds he didn't like. I found a flashlight in the kitchen drawer and amused myself by letting the cats chase the floating white circle of light across the floor. The furniture loomed in the silence, the couch and the chairs rubbing shadows. The big fern rustled from the cold air seeping in beneath the front window.

By ten o'clock I had started to worry. My father and Sam should have been home by nine-thirty, and I wondered if they'd been in an accident. There hadn't been any trick-or-treaters for a while, but I still didn't want to turn on the lights. To pass the time I went upstairs and changed into my nightgown and slippers and robe, leaving the flashlight, still lit, on my bed. When I picked it up, it flickered uneasily. I turned it off to save the batteries. Outside, the wind had blown back the clouds to reveal a nearly perfect full moon, and after a moment I could see everything clearly. I was heading back toward the stairs, stepping through the dappled patterns made by the moonlight, when I heard another knock at the door.

It startled me because I hadn't heard a car. It was almost ten-thirty, and I figured whoever it was would give up quickly. But that didn't happen. Somebody began to knock. Then I heard the screen door open; the person pounded on the inner door. I crept down the stairs to the living room window, wondering if it was anyone we knew. But when I looked out into the courtyard, there was no car. I went into the dining room and cupped my hand to the glass, looking down the long driveway to the road, but I couldn't see a car down there either. Whoever it was had come by foot.

I didn't know whether or not to be afraid, and I wished desperately for my father and Sam to come home. After a while, the pounding stopped and the screen door closed, almost gently. I heard the porch steps creak, the low murmur of a man's voice, and then I saw a shape outside the living room window. I dropped to the floor, listening as it moved around the house, testing each of the windows, one by one. The cats listened too, their green eyes glowing. If someone got inside, they would disappear like shadows and wait patiently for whatever was happening to me to be finished, so they could return to their favorite chairs and lick their paws. I hated them then. I wanted to put my hands around their smooth, smug throats and squeeze. And I hated my mother and my father and even Sam, who had left me at risk, all alone.

Now someone was working on the back door, making quiet, careful sounds, worrying at the lock, jiggling it, cajoling it, until I heard the bolt slide back with a hollow crack. I got to my feet and backed into the kitchen, thinking I would get a knife from the drawer, but then I decided that the sound of the drawer opening would reveal that someone was home. Instead, I reached for the largest cast-iron pan hanging on the wall. Just as I was lifting it down, the kitchen light snapped on, and I spun too hard too fast, the heavy pan jerking my body toward a man. The pan sailed past him, hit the wall, dropped straight to the floor, and bounced in a cloud of plaster. "Jesus Christ," the man said, and he was my father, and he was laughing. Sam peeked out from behind him, his eyes huge and terrible beneath my father's *Fountain Ford* cap. "I locked the damn keys in the car," my father said. "We had to hitch back with some kids, and when you wouldn't answer the door . . ."

He was limp with his laughter, leaning against the wall beside the dent where the pan had landed. "How are we going to explain this to your mother?" he gasped. "She's going to think you've gone crazy."

"I am not crazy," I said, and I was dizzy with what I thought was pure embarrassment; I hadn't learned, yet, to recognize rage. "How was I supposed to know it was you?"

"Well, Christ, Abby, who else would it be?"

"A rapist," I yelled. "Or a *sodomist!*" My father stopped laughing. He stared at me, incredulous, as if I'd just done something obscene. *"Honey,"* he said awkwardly. My body was trembling beneath me, and with all my will I forced it to stay whole, to carry me step by step through the kitchen, past my father, past my brother, until I reached the stairway. There, shame broke over me in hot, sharp waves, and I took the stairs two at a time. In my room, I got into bed without taking off my robe, without turning on the light. After a while, Sam came in and sat at the foot of the bed with his bag of trick-or-treat candy, as if he wasn't sure whether to stay with me or go back downstairs to my father. I could hear his breathing, ragged and thick, as if he was crying too. "I thought you were going to kill me," I finally said, and then he crawled up the length of the bed and got under the covers beside me, the way he used to do. The candy bag rested, stone heavy, on my chest.

"Look," he said, but I didn't need to reach inside to understand it was more candy than either of us could possibly have imagined. I sat up and upended the bag across our legs. The contents slithered and spread, glittering in the moonlight like a blanket of jewels.

"Do you think some of them are poisoned?" Sam asked, and he sat up too.

I picked up a tiny carton of Junior mints and turned it over in my palm, but there was no way to tell. "We ought to turn on the light," I finally said, but neither of us did. Sam was the first to begin to eat; it was some sort of cookie, homemade, with lots of chocolate chips. He held it out to me, and I opened my mouth, bracing, bracing hard for the stab of the pin or the muffled whiff of poison, the edge of the razor biting bone.

Five

Though my mother had lived in Horton since before Sam and I were born, she still referred to Oneisha as *home*, drawing out the word so that it sounded like someone's name. Every Sunday after Mass, the three of us ate dinner at my grandmother's house, sometimes joined by Auntie Thil and our cousins, more rarely by my father and Uncle Olaf. The house was a pale pink two-story with a porch that wrapped around it like the snug waist of a girdle. The first floor listed slightly to the left, while the second floor listed slightly to the right, and when you compared them to the strict vertical lines of the porch railing, it made the house appear to be swaying to a gentle internal wind. In summer, squirrels nested in the gutters and rustled in the chimney; in winter, mice made scritching noises behind the walls. My grandmother's cats tracked the sound with their ears, while Sam and I watched, twisting our faces, still young enough to want our own ears to move with that same quick, swiveling grace.

My mother says that, even now, Oneisha hasn't changed. If you stand in front of Saint Ignatius Church, Highway KL and the Fox Ranch Road stretch in four directions like the arms of a cross, narrowing until they vanish at the point where they meet the horizon. Growing up, I believed these roads wrapped the world like flat, wide ribbon, and that if you followed any one of them, you would eventually find yourself approaching the wooden signs Uncle Olaf had carved to replace the green metal kind issued by the state of Wisconsin: ONEISHA, POP. 650. Home was a place you never escaped. Like an enchanted maze, the very steps you hoped might lead you away were, in fact, bringing you back to the same streets you walked with your friends, restless, your sneakers scuffing the pavement, all the while sensing things could change in an instant if only you knew what to look for.

But the year I started high school, I stopped looking and closed my eyes. I slept for hours on end, going to bed right after supper, sleeping through my alarm the next day, falling asleep in school. Friends stopped calling, puzzled by my lack of response to the things in their lives that mattered most—boys, curfews, parents, grades. Someone reported me to the school guidance counselor, who called me in for a few short "consultations." He was a heavyset man, who chain-smoked as he asked faltering questions about my home life; afterward, he sent my mother notes on pale blue paper, explaining his role in the school system, inviting her to make an appointment to discuss "life's rocky transition called adolescence." The principal sent notes too, only his were form letters printed on stark school stationery, two parallel columns with *Check Off Items That Apply* at the top. "Grades falling," my mother read aloud. "Attitude poor. Does not pay attention." When I began to lose weight, she took me to Dr. Neidermier, who took my pulse and palpated my abdomen before he said hello. I stared at the medical diagram on the wall, a man's head and torso, the skin and muscle peeled away to reveal his various organs. Just above his jellyfish brain, THE HUMAN ANATOMY was printed in bold black letters.

"There's nothing wrong with her," Dr. Neidermier said. I sat motionless on the edge of the examining table, clutching the worn green gown around me. My mother smoothed it over my knees, as if I were still a little girl and the gown was a fancy little girl's dress. I remembered her driving me to grade school birthday parties, the proud feeling of sitting alone beside her in the front seat like a grown-up. "Her weight's OK. Actually, she could lose another ten, fifteen pounds, no problem."

"But there must be something the matter," my mother said. I could see her shoulders rise as if she were pulling herself up by an internal string. After two years at the *Sell It Now!*, she and Cindy Pace had taken out a small-business loan and started their own advertising company. Cindy Pace had a college degree in English; she seemed nice enough to me, but she'd never been married, which, according to my father, meant she wasn't normal. He nick-named her "Windy Face," because she and my mother talked on the phone so much. At night, he listed all the reasons why A-1 Advertising was going to be a failure, but my mother tuned him out, reading books with titles like *Assert Yourself!* and *Yes, I Can!* As she spoke to Dr. Neidermier, she enunciated each word carefully, a technique, she had explained to me, that would make a person take you seriously. "You don't need a medical degree to understand this child isn't well," she said.

But Dr. Neidermier was smiling, the way he did at Sunday Mass when he turned around to give the Sign of Peace. "It's her age. You know," he said, "sweet sixteen and all that."

"She's barely fifteen. A freshman in high school."

"Fifteen, sixteen, eighteen, twenty. It's tough for a girl these days," he said. "Competing with the boys. College. Career." He winked at me, a gesture that always made me feel I'd missed something. "Join some clubs. Go out for pizza with the boys." I felt my eyes closing under the bright fluorescent lights. When I opened them, he was gone and my mother was standing in front of me, staring into my face.

"Wake up," she said. "Concentrate." Her eyes were hazel, with flecks of brilliant green, and I realized how seldom I looked past the thick curve of her glasses. Her nose, I knew, was a slender

replica of my own, and there was a small pink mole at the corner
of one nostril. "What are you thinking," my mother asked, "when
you look at me like that?"

"I don't know," I said, but I was wondering if I would be
able to recognize her if we met on the street in Chicago or New
York City or Paris or any of the millions of other places I had
never been. I wondered how I could be sure that it really was my
mother. This woman's hair, I noticed, was blondish at the temples;
didn't my mother have red hair? But who would want to trick me
like this, to pretend she was my mother when she wasn't? I began
to feel afraid. I closed my eyes again.

"We've got to do something," my mother said. "You're slipping away as we speak."

"Yes," I said. I was tired. I wanted to go home and crawl
into bed, where I'd been all afternoon, waking to the intermittent
whine of the saw coming from my father's workshop. He had a
rare day off from the car lot, and he was spending it making yet
another bird feeder with Sam. The backyard rattled with bird
feeders and birdhouses; they swung from the trees and from del-
icately curved stands, they stood at attention on thick posts, they
dangled from the clothesline, they stuck like barnacles to the sides
of the shed. "Do we really need another one, Gordon?" my
mother said, but my father said that Sam needed to practice what
he called *the fundamentals*. "Repetition leads to perfection," he told
my mother. "Anybody who can lie around drawing pictures of
birds should be able to build a house for them. Right, Sam?"

Sam glowered; he was thirteen, and glowering had become
his stock response to my parents, though he still got along all right
with me if nobody was watching. "Adolescence," my father called
it, shaking his head as if it were a sad diagnosis. I wondered if
adolescence was what I was suffering from too.

"We'll figure this out on our own," my mother muttered,
handing me my clothes. *"Doctors."* She spat the word. "What do
they know?" but I sensed she was more angry with herself for

letting Dr. Neidermier escape so easily. She had done everything the books said to do; what could she have missed? As we drove home, I pressed my forehead against the cold window, watching the town of Horton ripple past like a colorful river. On Main Street, the houses were painted pastel shades of green and blue and yellow; they were small and square, like candy houses, and I imagined I could taste them in the back of my throat, cloyingly sweet but with a bitter core. Outside town, the slender trees dividing the fields were already bare, the leaves blown down too soon, browned with frost. Crows rose from the corn stubble, and just up the road from our house, we passed a flock of wild turkeys near the drainage ditch where Sam and I used to build dams after the heavy spring rains. I remembered the feeling of the icy mud between my toes, the smell of it as we scooped it up and slapped it into a thick brown wall, the delicious panic as the water rose over our ankles, up to our knees.

My mother parked in front of the barn, and I started for the house, but she grabbed me by the sleeve and led me through the maze of bird feeders, car parts, abandoned household appliances, and rusty farm equipment until we reached the shed. Recently, my father had fixed it up as a place where he and Sam could spend time together. According to my father, my mother had done a poor job with Sam; she'd been too soft, too lax, overprotective. Now he was stepping in "to put some hair on Sam's chest," an expression that was painful considering how slow Sam was to mature. But Sam was changing in other ways. He kept to himself more and more. He lied about things, stupid little things, even when it was easier to tell the truth. He talked back to my mother, picking on her just like my father did, complaining about a meal she'd fixed, refusing to carry his plate to the dishwasher. "Make Abby do it," he'd say, when she asked him to strip the sheets off his bed or vacuum or wipe the table. And though my father insisted he obey, it was clear that he was really on Sam's side.

"That's why God made girls—right, Sam?" he'd say, winking at my mother so she'd have to take it as a joke.

A sign on the door said *Enter at Your Own Risk.* When my mother and I came in, my father leapt up from beside the metal cabinet where he kept his small tools. Sam was running a plane over a two-by-four again and again, as if he were making a giant spear. One corner of the shed was arranged like a small living room with carpeting, a refrigerator, and two overstuffed chairs. An American flag hung from one wall. Below it was a table made out of a door balanced on three sawhorses, and there were blueprints spread across it like the secret maps Sam and I once had made to find buried treasure, with X marks the spot. Beside the blueprints were two open cans of beer.

"I didn't hear you," my father said, and he walked toward my mother with careful steps, the way he did when he'd been drinking. "What's the matter—is she really sick?" A perfect dusty handprint clung to the thigh of his coveralls. "What did the doctor say?"

My mother went over to the table, picked up a can of beer, set it down. "You're not drinking this, are you, Sam?" she said.

Sam ignored her, shook his long hair across his eyes. Girl hair, my father called it. For weeks, he'd been trying to shame Sam into getting it cut.

"Sam?" my mother said. "I asked you a question."

My father looked annoyed. "Don't worry about it," he said.

"I can't believe you're giving a thirteen-year-old beer," my mother said.

"Don't come in here telling me what I can and cannot give my son," he said. "If it were up to you, Therese, he'd be wearing a goddamn skirt."

"Gordon—" my mother began, but my father had turned to me. "So what's wrong with you?" he said, interrupting my mother.

"Nothing," I said.

"The doctor doesn't know," my mother said.

"Is she . . . what's that thing girls get? Where they don't eat." For a moment, his voice was concerned; he met my mother's gaze.

"No. Thank God." They were silent for a moment, considering what to do with me.

"Well," my father said. He cuffed my shoulder playfully. "It doesn't sound too serious."

"Can I go now?" I said. The room seemed too warm, and it smelled faintly of turpentine, an odor that always made me queasy. My mother grabbed me by the sleeve again, as if she thought I might float away. "I'll come with you," she snapped, "seeing it doesn't look like your father's going to help."

"What do you want me to do?" my father said.

"For starters," my mother said, "I want you to stop giving alcohol to a minor." She swept the beer cans from the table with the back of her hand; they foamed on the carpeting before my father could retrieve them. Back in the house, in the cold mud room, she slipped my coat from my shoulders and spun me around to face her. "What do you want me to do for you? Tell me." She rubbed my shoulders hard, as if she were trying to warm me. "Because if you don't, I'll have to decide, and I might be deciding wrong. Maybe you need to see another doctor. Maybe you just need a change of pace. More exercise. Vitamins." She waited for me to agree or disagree. *"Please,"* she said, and I finally opened my mouth to speak. But the sleepiness lapped my chest, the back of my neck. "I just want to sleep," I told her, and she released me, exhaling a white flag of steam.

I woke up because something was wrong with my big toe. There was a snap, and then the smaller toes next to it stung. I sat up, picked the rubber band from between my toes. "Jerk," I told Sam, without malice. He still had the same giggle he'd had when he was six. *A late bloomer,* my father called him, pinching back his slender elbows until they touched, or pinning him helplessly in

76

the crook of his arm as Sam fought back silently, furiously, hope-lessly. Sometimes he'd grab Sam by his long hair, lift until he rose up on tiptoe. "You see, sport, why short hair is an advantage?" he'd say. The room was dim; it was late afternoon, and I felt peaceful and good, the way I always felt after I woke up.

"They're fighting about us," Sam said.

I rolled my eyes. "What else is new?" We listened for a moment; my mother's quick bursts of speech, my father's low rumble. The sounds seemed to settle in the corners of the room. My mother was quoting statistics that said people were more likely to become alcoholics if they started drinking young; my father said it was fine for a boy to have one beer with his dad, and that the kid they should be worrying about was me, and if my mother cared about me she wouldn't have started that goddamn business when it was perfectly clear I needed more attention. "You're turn-ing her into Mathilde," he told my mother, and I thought about Auntie Thil: her nervousness, her adolescent hospitalization, which was spoken about in whispers or not at all. Maybe my mother would send me to a hospital. I thought about how I'd look wearing a long white gown. The priest would come to visit me; my eyes would burn dark and fierce and holy, as my worldly body wasted away. One day, gold light would spin a ring around my head, sprout from the tips of my fingers. Then I would be whisked up to heaven. I imagined my father and Sam bending over my corpse, their faces torn with regret.

"What's beer taste like?" I asked.

Sam made a face. "Sour. Like somebody else's spit."

"How do you know what somebody else's spit tastes like?"

He raised an eyebrow lewdly. "I know all about girls."

"What are we like?" I asked, because I really wanted to know.

"Not *you*," he said, blushing, and I snapped him with the rubber band. He snapped me back, and I grabbed him; we were wrestling around on the bed when we heard footsteps on the stairs.

Instantly we let go of each other; Sam slouched to the other corner of my room, and I lay back on my pillow. When my father stepped into the room, he seemed to grow larger against the backdrop of my white wicker furniture; his breathing sucked up all the available air. My mother stood beside him. She was saying something. "Listen to me," my mother was saying. "Have you even heard one word I've said?"

"What if she doesn't want to go?" Sam said. His voice was too loud, shaking.

"Stay out of this," my father said.

"To the hospital?" I said.

All three of them looked at me. "To live at Grandma's, stupid!" Sam shouted. "And they can't make you go if you don't want." His voice cracked on the word *want*; perhaps it was changing after all. I looked at him, at my mother and father. They wanted a decision from me. They were waiting to hear what I had to say. I couldn't tell if the sound I was hearing was my own heart beating or the collective sound of theirs. So much noise! I thought of my grandmother's quiet rooms, the regular tick of her kitchen clock, the soft slap of cards on the kitchen table.

"I'll go," I said.

Sam kicked my white wicker rocking chair so hard it swung to and fro long after he'd stormed out.

My grandmother prepared the bedroom in the attic, the one that had been my mother's when she was growing up. Auntie Thil's old room was directly below; across the hall was a room filled with the things that had belonged to Mary and Elise. My grandmother slept in the first-floor bedroom, always on the left side of her marriage bed, which was worn lower than the right side, where my grandfather had slept. The departed were present in a quiet, constant way: in the funeral photographs lining the hallway between the kitchen and the living room; in the quilt, stitched by

Mary, spread across my grandmother's bed; in Elise's piano that my grandmother kept tuned. She'd collected recordings of all the pieces Elise had played; my favorite was "Für Elise," and I listened to it again and again. My grandmother told me that Elise had liked to pretend Beethoven had written it for her.

My mother drove me out to Oneisha the Sunday before Halloween, and it could have been any other Sunday, except that Sam wasn't with us. He'd announced that from now on he planned to attend Mass with my father, who went—or, at least, pretended to go—to Saint John's in Fall Creek, a larger, more modern parish, where Masses took only forty minutes. My father didn't like Saint Ignatius's hour-long services or my grandmother's custom of having us say the Rosary together in the afternoon. He'd come along every once in a while, if Uncle Olaf was going to be there too. Then, after my grandmother's big dinner, while the rest of us cleaned up, the men took the boys—Sam and my cousin Harv—into the living room to watch football on TV.

"But your grandmother's expecting you," my mother told Sam. "You should have said something earlier."

Sam stared pointedly at the TV.

"Leave him be," my father said in his end-of-discussion voice. "He's old enough to hang out with his old man if he wants." He leaned past my mother to kiss me good-bye, a loud smack that scratched my cheek.

" 'Bye," I called to Sam, but he didn't say anything.

"Don't worry about him, sweetheart," my father said. "You just rest up and feel better, OK?"

My mother drove at her usual swift pace, keeping toward the center line to avoid the soft, crumbling shoulder of Highway KL. Horton, at six thousand people, was one of the larger cities in the area, and now we were heading north toward the smaller townships: Ooston, Farbenplatz, Holly's Field, Oneisha. The sky was low and gray and bright, and the air tasted of the brittle snow that spattered against the windows. My mother's car had no heat,

and it was cold even with the blankets spread across our knees.
There were no other cars, and the fields were nearly empty. Occasionally there were horses, but they stood motionless, facing
north without expression. We passed the burned-out cannery site,
where Mary and Elise had died; I'd never once seen my mother
turn her head to look at it. When we crossed the railroad tracks
at the south edge of Oneisha, I jumped, startled back into myself
after all that smoothness. "Funny how it always gets you," my
mother said. "Those tracks. They're the last thing you'd expect."

When I didn't answer, she said, "Remember, I said I might
decide wrong. I don't know if this is the right thing to do."

"It's fine," I said.

"You should have someone with you all the time, till you're
feeling better again."

I nodded, but she wasn't seeing me.

"Maybe I should have cut back my hours, stayed home with
you for a while, but we've made such an investment, Cindy and
me—"

"Mom, it's OK," I said, and I meant it.

"I just can't be dependent on your father like I used to be."
She stopped, made a wry face. "I'm not the little girl he married.
There's more to my life now than him saying, Jump, and me
saying, How high?" The highway had dissolved into Main Street,
and she drove slowly now, edging past the row of nearly identical
houses until she reached the intersection. Jack-o'-lanterns leered
out of windows, perched on porch steps. Someone had erected a
corn-husk man; he pushed a real wheelbarrow filled with pumpkins and gourds. "Maybe you'll feel better just getting out of
Horton for a bit," she said. "You can spend time with your cousins—won't it be nice to have them next door? You and Monica
can run back and forth, make popcorn, sleep over."

We turned onto Fox Ranch Road, passing Saint Ignatius
and, beside it, the cemetery, with its low, sculpted graves. Each
winter, it disappeared beneath the snow until spring, when it

erupted with geraniums and tiny American flags. Across the street was the low brick rectory where Father Van Dan lived and, beside it, a cottage occupied by the two elderly nuns. On the other side was Geena Baumbach's cheery yellow house; she was the rectory housekeeper and her front yard was cluttered with rusted swing sets, a teeter-totter, a slide that tipped over whenever it stormed, and a few plank benches for young mothers to sit on while their children argued turns. In summer, the nuns were outside every day, working in their vegetable garden. Sometimes they'd cross behind the rectory to the swing set, where they'd arc toward the sky like blackbirds, weighted down by their strict religious garb.

My grandmother's house and Auntie Thil's tan brick ranch were next door to one another, divided by a single shared driveway. Jakey, my grandmother's old yellow dog, was lying in the middle of it; he barked once for show before ambling out of the way so we could pull in and park. "Where's your brother today?" my grandmother called from the door. "He isn't sick?"

"Oh, no," my mother said cheerfully, lightly, as if Sam hadn't been coming along for Mass and Sunday dinner in Oneisha ever since he was born. "He's going to Saint John's with Gordon."

"I see," my grandmother said, but it was clear she didn't.

"I think it's nice he and Gordon have some time together, don't you?" my mother said. She carried my suitcase inside, as my grandmother held the door. But then, instead of putting it down, she escaped up the long, narrow stairs toward the attic. The house looked oddly unfamiliar to me, though Sam and I had explored every odd-shaped closet, every corner from the attic to the musty cellar. I tried to understand that this was where I would live, the place I'd go to sleep every night, away from my parents and my brother.

"Things all right at home?" my grandmother asked me gently, kindly. I never could lie to my grandmother; I shook my head. *No.*

"Your mother has too many irons in the fire," my grand-mother said. "Starting that business . . . I don't know." It was 1980, and in Horton, Wisconsin, married women didn't do things like start their own businesses. "If it was a question of money, I could understand," she said. "But that isn't it, then, is it?"

My mother came back down the stairs. "What isn't a question of money?" she said.

"Your job," my grandmother said.

"Business is booming, thank you for asking," my mother said.

"Therese," my grandmother said. "Nobody's criticizing you. We're just concerned, that's all."

"We'll be late for Mass," I said quickly, and neither my mother nor my grandmother said anything more. My grand-mother stuck two stuffed Cornish hens into the oven, and we walked up the street to Saint Ignatius; by the time we returned, the house was thick with the smell of roasting hens. I chewed and chewed, but the food had no taste, and I slipped what I could to Jakey, who was begging beneath the table. Halfway through dinner I asked to be excused, and my mother walked with me up the stairs to my new room. It was cold and smelled of cedar; I shivered as I pulled off my jeans and stepped into my long underwear. She tucked the covers under my chin and listened to me say my prayers, her eyes bright with tears. "I wish I had something nice to leave with you," she said. "A ring or some-thing." She looked at her hands, which were bare except for her wedding ring. Her ears were not pierced. Her hair was cropped close, practical hair, which my father called *mannish*. "If you want to come home, just call and I'll come get you. I'll come get you right away—OK, honey?" She looked like someone familiar, someone I should know, and I was about to say her name, but I was already sleeping.

For weeks I slept, rarely leaving my room except to use the bathroom or eat. Those were the weeks I did not even remember my dreams. When I slept, it was as if the world I'd lived in blinked closed along with me. Years later, I would encounter the word *truncation* in a music composition class; it referred to lifting out a group of notes so neatly that when you played the piece through, it was as if they'd never been there. At last I had a word to describe those weeks of sleep. I ate breakfast; I ate supper. There was nothing in between—no fights between my father and mother, no slamming doors between my father and Sam, none of my father's remarks about my weight or my clothes or the dirty minds of boys. *Believe me, sweetheart,* he'd say, *I was a boy once. I know.* No Dolly Parton jokes, his heavy arm draped over my shoulders. No questions that made me uncomfortable: *Do you have a boyfriend yet? Been doing any smooching?* I never could tell how serious he was—after all, I was not allowed to date until I turned sixteen. No makeup or high heels or panty hose. No bikini swimming suits.

Sometimes I'd come downstairs for breakfast and my father would look at my face, at my body, as if he were seeing me for the first time. *My God, Therese, she's growing up!* he'd say, and he'd give a low wolf whistle. *Where did our little girl go?* I'm right here, Dad, I wanted to say, but I wasn't really sure anymore. A year before, at the beginning of eighth grade, my mother had taken me shopping for school clothes; she'd waited outside the JC Penny dressing room, insisting I come out to model the jeans and blouses and sweaters we'd chosen. In the three-way mirrors, my breasts looked huge—they were already much bigger than my mother's— and my stomach stuck out no matter how hard I tried to suck it in. "Stop doing that," my mother told me. "You have a perfectly lovely figure."

"I'm fat," I said. "Even Dad says so." I'd learned not to eat dessert in front of him, sneaking back to the kitchen for a scoop of ice cream or a cookie before I went to bed. If he caught me, he'd say, *A moment on the lips, forever on the hips.*

"He's being ridiculous."

"Maybe he's just being honest," I snapped.

"Abby," my mother said. We were alone in front of the mirrors. Everywhere I looked, a dozen Abigail Schillers seemed to be looking back at me. "You are a lovely young woman."

"Mom," I said. I couldn't bear the sound of that word, *woman.*

"Your whole life is ahead of you, and I think your father is a little jealous of that. Maybe curious about it too, because soon you'll be leaving us both behind. We'll never know you the way we did when you were a little girl."

She stood next to me in front of the mirror. *"I'm* jealous," she said. "I was never as pretty as you. Remember, the great artists didn't paint skinny beanpoles like me."

She convinced me to tuck the blouse into my jeans, ran back out into the racks to fetch a rust-colored vest. "Put this on," she said, and even I had to admit it was flattering. She made me buy two, in different colors. "It's so nice," she said, "to have my own money to spoil my kid if I want."

"I thought you said I was a *woman,"* I said, trying to maintain my sullen cool but smiling in spite of myself.

"You'll always be my kid," my mother said. "Woman or not."

The next day, I chose that outfit to wear to school, and when my mother complimented me at breakfast, I spun around like a model. But my father put down his toast. "My God," he said in a small, strange voice. "Therese, are those her real breasts?"

Sam giggled, and I blushed the color of my vest.

"Gordon," my mother said, furious, "she's fourteen, she's not a child anymore," and as they fought, I grabbed my backpack and slammed out of the house, ran down to the foot of the driveway to wait for the bus. At school, I carried my books in front of my chest; I sat slouched over in my chair. I hated the world and everybody in it. I wished I were invisible. I wished that I could simply disappear.

———

My mother had arranged for me to take a temporary leave from school. The agreement was that she would collect my assignments once a week and I would mail them back to my teachers, keeping up with my classes independently. I did this fairly regularly at first, then rarely, then finally not at all. Once, I did turn in a paper called "Volcanoes" for my sophomore science class. After a brief factual introduction cribbed from the *World Book Encyclopedia*, I wrote pages of vivid prose about a girl who had the magical powers of Jesus and lived inside Mount Vesuvius, untouched by the heat or the fumes. My midsemester report card showed a neat row of F's, which reminded me of merry little flags. I forgot how to write in cursive, a memory lapse that would prove permanent. My textbooks mildewed in my bedroom closet; mice nibbled the covers to lace.

My grandmother cared for me matter-of-factly, without pity but also without the slightest trace of impatience or scorn. Nights, when she listened to me say my prayers, she always asked me to name one thing—no matter how small—for which I was grateful. At first, my head filled with cotton, the *shushing* noise I heard whenever I was asked to think, to speak my mind, to do anything that called attention to myself. But gradually I could think of things to say. *The way Jakey sleeps at the foot of my bed. The recording of the "Moonlight" Sonata you played for me this morning. The mourning doves in the tree outside the window.* And after she'd gone: *You, Grandma. You.* Everything in my grandmother's house was predictable, calm, safe. Sometimes I'd wake up in the cold sweat of a nightmare, but as soon as I opened my eyes, the memory was blanched by the glow of the Jesus night-light she had plugged into the socket by the door. *Let My Light Guide You* glowed in gold across the front of Jesus' robe, and some nights I thought I could feel that Jesus was really there in the room, watching over me so I could go back to sleep. Warm at my feet, Jakey thumped his tail and sighed; I pulled the covers up to my chin. *Let My Light Guide You.* I was used to Mass on Sundays, prayers before meals and bedtime, but I'd never lived with God in the constant, quiet way my grandmother did. She didn't pray for me to get well; she prayed that God's will be done. "Offer everything up to God," she said, "and pray for those less fortunate than you." She gave me a German prayer book that had been Elise's when she was my age, and I'd lie in bed sounding out the strange words, translating as much as I could. This pleased her, and she wrote out the English so that I could compare the two. Soon I could quote them in both languages, and I memorized several of the Psalms from her German Bible as well.

When I first began to wake up again, to come back into myself, I took long baths, singing to myself while I waited for the old claw-footed tub to fill. The water pressure was poor at the top of my grandmother's house, and if she was doing the dishes downstairs, there was plenty of time to run through my repertoire of Christmas carols and hymns. I began to notice the deepness of my voice, the flicker of my pulse in my temples when I sang, the pattern the sunlight made as it splashed through the lace hanging modestly over the window, and because I had been able to notice nothing for so long, everything seemed precious to me, blessed. I liked to sing, which surprised me, because I'd never really taken conscious pleasure in doing so before. When I told my grandmother, she nodded mysteriously. She gave me a gold ring with a pink glass stone that had once belonged to Elise. To my surprise, it fit my finger perfectly. I did not take it off.

Every Wednesday afternoon, my grandmother and the other Ladies of the Altar met at the church to do the weekly cleaning. Just before Thanksgiving, I went with her for the first time. The women had decided to clean the Stations of the Cross, which hung from the walls fifteen feet above the pews. Their fear of heights made me fearless, tireless. I stood at the top of the ten-foot ladder, wiping the faces of the apostles with warm, soapy water, coaxing dust from the creases of their plaster gowns, from their weary shoulders and delicate toes, washing away the faint gritty layer of the past year of prayer. Afterward, we relaxed with coffee and cake in the windowless room in the basement where the cleaning supplies were kept. While we'd been busy upstairs, Auntie Thil had stayed back to prepare the food, and now she fixed my coffee, thick with sugar and cream. She was a big, soft woman, with fingertips swollen from constant nail-biting. Her face held the look of someone who was ready either to laugh or to burst into tears.

"Look at the roses," she said, gently touching my cheeks. And that night, preparing to take my bath, I saw in the mirror that my eyes were clear. The dark circles that had ringed them for months had faded, the nervous tuck of my lips smoothed away. I got into the water and soaped my breasts and stomach without feeling disgusted with my body. It was simply that, a body, and if it wasn't as attractive as my mother said, it certainly wasn't as ugly as I'd thought. I lay in the tub until the water chilled me blue, joy rushing over and over me. I sang myself the lullabies my mother use to sing me, my voice growing more and more confident until it echoed off the floor tiles, the tall windows, the smooth plaster ceiling.

The next day, I got up at six-thirty and made breakfast for my grandmother, shredding the bacon into the scrambled eggs the way she liked it. Over our second cups of coffee, she stared into my face as if she were searching for the heaviness that had been there. "Today I visit Mrs. Heidelow," she said, and understanding this was an invitation, I said I'd come along. Mrs. Heidelow was not expected to live until Christmas. A member of the Ladies of the Altar visited every morning, so her daughter could take time away to shop, to fill prescriptions, to light a candle at the church, to grieve.

My grandmother and I bundled up in our coats, and before we left the house, she handed me a colorful scarf that was identical to her own. I tied it firmly over my head the way she did, jammed my hands deep into my pockets, and together we began the icy walk to the other side of town. The sun was up now, tinting the snowy streets a pale, hopeful rose. My nostrils pinched together and stuck; I sniffed hard, smelling the cedar trees that stood beside each home. Light spilled from behind the drawn shades of tiny bedroom windows. We walked with our shoulders touching, stepping out into the street when the sidewalks disappeared, pressing close to the curb when a car drove by. Passing the crossroads, we reached the abandoned fox ranch that had given Fox Ranch Road its name. As children, Sam and I had wandered among the rusty cages, inhaling the peculiar smell that seeped from beneath them. It was easy to imagine that the ghosts of the murdered foxes still lived here, and I was glad when the ranch was behind us, the sun firmly above the horizon, and our stiff boots scuffing up the long driveway that led to Mrs. Heidelow's house.

Her daughter let us in, leading us through the house to Mrs. Heidelow's room, where she served us coffee before she left. We sat on folding chairs as Mrs. Heidelow drifted in and out of a medicated sleep. The tiny black-and-white TV buzzed on the dresser, the commercials too bright, too cheery. I watched Mrs. Heidelow's eyelids flutter; she was awake, but the effort of opening her eyes exhausted her. Still, when she spoke, it was to ask about me. Was I feeling any better? Was my grandmother taking good care of me?

"Yes," I said. "I'm feeling good again."

"How she sings!" my grandmother said. "Every night in the bathroom, it's just like Elise has come home to me."

I twisted Elise's ring. It was the first time I'd realized my grandmother could hear me, had been listening to me all along, but I was not embarrassed. And this was what made living here so different than living in Horton, where my father was always quick to laugh, to make you wish you hadn't sung, hadn't spoken.

"What do you sing?" Mrs. Heidelow asked, and, again, I understood the unspoken invitation. I sang "Stille Nacht," the first verse of "O Tannenbaum."

"Do you know the other verses?" my grandmother asked,

and then she and Mrs. Heidelow taught me, the old German words rolling easily from their tongues. Walking home, I knew my grandmother was proud of me by the way she clutched my arm, tightening her grip when we reached icy spots, allowing me to assist her. I began accompanying my grandmother on all her visits to the sick, the lonely, those who were specially chosen and loved by God. I waited the long rows of tables at the monthly church supper, while she and the other women cooked in the kitchen. Afterward, standing up beside the sweltering heat of the ovens, we ate crushed pies, a scorched roast, a pudding that hadn't quite set. Evenings, I learned to quilt, and soon I carried my own sewing basket when we met in groups of fifteen or twenty to make a "weekend quilt" for the missionaries to give to cold children far away. Wednesdays, I went with my grandmother to Devotions and, afterward, to the rectory, to visit Father Van Dan and the nuns, Sister Mary Andrew and Sister Mary Gabriel, who served us homemade pretzels, cookies, or chocolate cake decorated with perfect hickory nut meats they'd coaxed from the tough, pale shells. Father Van Dan, surrounded by women, was not uncomfortable the way a regular man like my father would have been, and the women spoke of the same things they spoke of when alone: farming and weather, religion and politics, children, sickness, money.

Thanksgiving came, and my mother asked me to spend the day in Horton—my father really wanted Thanksgiving at home, just the four of us, as a family—but I begged to stay in Oneisha and, at last, my mother relented. I was never far from my grandmother's side. Friday nights, Auntie Thil drove us, along with my cousins, to the Knights of Columbus hall in Ooston, and there we played bingo, mingling with the men, who wore their funny hats so proudly, smoking cigars that turned the air the color of dust, occasionally leaving their wives to slip outside for "a little something Joe forgot"—booze someone had in a brown paper bag. Uncle Olaf was already there, sitting with his pals at their usual table, and whenever he won something he'd carry it to Auntie Thil and present it with a flourish. The smaller prizes were made by hand: yarn-covered hangers, knitted booties, stained-glass Christmas decorations, a pound of divinity; but the prizes we crossed our fingers for were crisp twenty-dollar bills. We marked our cards with pieces of corn, gritting our teeth, holding our breath for that B-69 or I-19 that would launch us into the air, shrieking *Bingo!*

Saturdays, we'd take Jakey next door to visit Auntie Thil's Little Buster. The dogs chased each other around the pond in the backyard, while Auntie Thil and my grandmother played cards in the kitchen and discussed Uncle Olaf's drinking. My cousins and I went into the den, where Monica watched TV, and Harv and I talked about God. If God was both perfect and able to do anything, could He make a mistake? Why did He make suffering? Harv was a year older than me, and I saw my brother in his face, only here that sullen roundness had become stretched and angular, filled with purpose. Harv had a vocation; I was curious and envious and awed. He was still an altar boy, and because he *liked* to be, not because he *had* to be. He helped out with church bake sales, and he often went to Mass during the week. He was able to shrug away his father's teasing. He answered to another Father now.

"You guys are so weird," Monica said. "You sound like a couple of monks." She pointed her chin at me. "No wonder you cracked up."

"Don't mind her," Harv said. "She's jealous."

"You bet I'm jealous," Monica said. "I'd do anything to get out of school." She lay back on the couch, fanning her fingers in a practiced way to check the polish. I rolled my eyes at Harv; he struck a pose, rippling his fingers. "Dahling," he said, "do my nails have that pahrfect sheen?"

"Oh, dahling, yes, I believe they do."

We collapsed on each other, laughing.

"You guys are weird," Monica said again.

I didn't miss my mother as much as I'd thought I would, not even after she started going to Mass at Saint John's with my father and Sam. It was, she said, the only way to make certain they actually went, and though she still came out to Oneisha on Sunday afternoons, she didn't stay very long. When my grandmother pressed her, my mother admitted that she was afraid to leave Sam unsupervised. She'd caught him hitchhiking by the highway one Saturday, grounded him, and caught him at it again the next day.

"I thought he was spending time with Gordon," my grandmother said.

"They're not getting along so well," my mother said. We were playing cards at the kitchen table; she shuffled and reshuffled the deck. "What does Gordon expect? On the one hand, he encourages Sam to defy me. Then he turns around and complains when Sam doesn't respect *his* authority."

"What do *you* expect?" my grandmother said. "You defy your husband."

"Mom," my mother said. "It isn't the fifties anymore."

"Show me," my grandmother said, "where the Bible says God's law should change with the times."

I couldn't believe Sam had been hitchhiking. Getting into a car with a stranger didn't seem like something my shy brother would do. Yet Sam wasn't exactly shy anymore; *indifferent*, perhaps, was a better word. The few times I talked with him on the phone, he didn't have much to say beyond "yeah" and "no" and "I don't know." His voice was changing rapidly now, and I realized that soon it would be as deep as my father's. "Why won't you come visit on Sundays?" I asked.

"Don't know," he said. "Don't feel like it."

"We could set up the dominoes like we used to," I said, remembering the elaborate mazes we'd made in the living room only a year before, one of us keeping an eye on Jakey so he wouldn't knock them down with his tail. But Sam only made a scornful sound with his tongue. "That's for kids," he said. "You wanna talk to Dad?"

I always passed my father on to my grandmother as quickly as I could, and then he complained about how my mother was never home and Sam was running wild and there wasn't a clean shirt to be found in the house. "I showed him how to use the washing machine," my mother would say. "Mother, a man as worldly as Gordon claims to be should be able to push a few buttons." But my grandmother sided with my father; a woman's place was in the home. The deaths of her oldest daughters still weighed on her heart, and she worried that my mother was *tempting Providence*, upsetting the natural order of things by leaving my father to make his own bed and drive Sam to school when he missed his bus. And Sam missed the bus whenever he could, oversleeping, dawdling over breakfast. One morning in November, my father pinned him beneath the sheets, cut off his long hair by force, then bent him over the bathroom sink where he shaved off the rest. "Maybe you'll hear me calling you better without all that hair over your ears," he said. My mother told me the story privately; she asked me not to repeat it to my grandmother.

"I don't know what to do about them," she said. "Every time I turn around, they're at each other's throats."

One Sunday afternoon, she didn't come out to visit until late in the afternoon. My grandmother was napping, so we took a walk across the frozen fields at the edge of town, Jakey trotting happily ahead of us. When we got to the picnic table in the Yodermans' apple orchard, we sat on top of it, side by side, our feet propped on the benches. The ice weighted the trees, and it seemed they were bending down to listen as my mother spoke to me about all the wonderful choices my life would offer me, choices her own life had not presented. This year with my grandmother was a slight detour, but soon I'd be back in school, doing well again. When I graduated, I wouldn't have to get married right away. I could go away to school, find a career I loved. With her profits, she'd opened a special college fund for me and Sam. When I told her not to worry about me getting married or going to college, that I was praying for a vocation, she stopped, her breath leaving her mouth in small, irregular puffs. "The more you learn about yourself," she finally said, "the better you'll be able to serve God. Your grandmother says you're musical like Elise."

I nodded, slipping my mittened hands between my thighs and the cold surface of the picnic table so I could feel Elise's ring pinching my skin.

"Perhaps you could study music. Many of the greatest musicians praised God through their instruments." She put her arm around me. She'd been buying me books she had never read but had heard were books an educated person should read: *The Great Gatsby, My Antonia, An American Tragedy*. She used that phrase often now—"an educated person"—and whenever she said it, she'd gesture at me as if it were my name. But the books made me nervous; they were filled with un-Godly people, people who lived lives of sin. My grandmother told me not to read them. She gave me *The Catholic Digest*, a copy of *The Song of Bernadette* that had once belonged to Elise, pamphlets on dating, growing up, loving God, that were distributed through the Church. I liked them better than my mother's books. They showed only people who had a clear sense of purpose, the sort of person I wanted to be, bright with the secret of faith.

"I'd like you to start taking piano lessons," my mother said. "Maybe we could rent a piano for you when you come back home."

"OK," I said, although I wanted to tell her not to worry, I could just keep on living with my grandmother and playing Elise's piano. Usually, if I listened to a record once or twice, I was able to play parts of it back, and one day I managed to sound out all of "Für Elise." My grandmother listened in the kitchen doorway, and afterward she told me I could go through Elise's things and choose whatever I liked for myself. Now I drank from what was once her favorite mug, wore her nightgown to bed, decorated my nightstand with her piano figurines. I hadn't realized my own ear might have anything to do with my abilities, until Father Van Dan, visiting one day, said that I had "perfect pitch." The phrase reminded me of the way a dog's ears lifted whenever it heard something. Perfect pitch. I liked the sound of the words. I whispered them over and over to myself so there was no chance I would forget.

"I have perfect pitch," I told my mother.

"Really?" my mother said. "So does your brother—the guidance counselor told me."

"Maybe he can take piano lessons too."

"He doesn't want to," my mother said.

"Why not?"

My mother stood up on the bench, dusted off the seat of the jeans she'd started wearing. She climbed to the tabletop and stood there, scanning the flat, snowy countryside as if she thought something might be coming toward us—an unfriendly dog, a storm. The sun was already starting to set. "Your father will tease him," she said.

I shrugged as if it didn't matter. "That's just how Dad is. He makes fun. Like the nose-to-the-wall test." My father had found me reading the classifieds, imagining myself as a waitress or a teacher, a salesman or a clerk. The jobs were divided into sections, one for women and one for men. I'd been scanning the men's section because it looked more interesting, but when my father came in, I dragged my finger over to the women's so he wouldn't be able to tease me. "Looking for work?" he said. "Good God. A career woman just like your mother."

"I guess," I said, which was what I always said. It was neutral, unassuming, dull, which meant my father would lose interest and go away. But that day he sat down on the couch beside me.

"You got the right qualifications?"

I shrugged.

"Let's see," he said. "There's only one test a girl has to pass. Stand up," he said, and he led me over to the wall, his hand on the back of my neck. "Put your nose to the wall," he said, and when I did it, bending forward over my breasts, he laughed, shaking his head. "Nope," he said, "not quite. They'll have to hire someone else."

My mother came into the room and saw us standing there. I pressed my nose to the wall again; it was cool, unyielding, a good place to rest. I didn't understand. "Don't worry," my father said, still laughing. "Your mother wouldn't get the job either, that's for sure." My mother took me by the hand and led me from the room. "Don't listen to him," she said. It was Sam who finally explained the joke to me: If a woman's nose could touch the wall, her breasts were too small for the job.

"I'm so sorry about that," my mother said now, as if she had done something wrong. "That's why it's important for you to think about going to college, to have the skills to look out for yourself, even if you don't think you'll need them. I have no education, only three years' experience. This business is a huge risk, and it can't support two children. Your father and I both know that if it were just my income alone—" She stopped, then shrugged, and I briefly saw myself in that futile gesture. "It's not good to be too dependent on anyone," she said.

"Except God," I said.

"Well, yes," my mother said. "But God helps those who help themselves."

"If it's His will, God can help anybody."

"But don't you think it's His will that you go to college, make something of your life? Let your light shine instead of hiding it under a bushel basket?"

"I want to keep on living in Oneisha," I blurted. I hadn't meant to say it like that, and my mother gave me a hurt, surprised look.

"I know we're going through a tough time right now, but we're a family, Abby. We belong together."

"But I feel good here. I'm not sleepy anymore."

"You're still sleeping," my mother said, "only now you don't even know it. Abby, there's a whole world out there!" She waved her arms at the horizon, but all I saw were the Yodermans' cows standing shoulder-to-shoulder at the feeder like a black and white bracelet, Jakey's yellow tail poking up from the weeds, the small cross of houses that was Oneisha, Wisconsin. The world ended where the sullen winter sky met the stubble of fields not quite completely covered with snow. The world was the smell of frozen apple crushed beneath my heel, the wet black bark of the apple trees, my mother's voice saying, "I want you to come home. Maybe in another week or so."

For the next few nights I had terrible dreams, and in them I was running from a man who I knew was going to catch me and do unspeakable things. Sometimes the man was chasing Sam too, and then I had to make a decision, because he would be able to catch only one of us and, being older, I could run faster. Should I save myself? Should I fall behind, saving Sam's life with my own? Night after night I woke up on the floor, twisted in the blankets, with my shoulder or hip or head stinging from the fall, and always I was the one still alive, intact, safe, facing the open arms of Jesus. *Let My Light Guide You.*

When I told my grandmother about the dreams, she spoke to my mother, and after that there was no more talk of my going home in the near future. And soon the dreams were forgotten in the rush to prepare for Christmas. My grandmother and I spent entire days baking for the children living in the trailers south of Farbenplatz, the elderly in the nursing home in Holly's Field, the sick sentenced to Christmas in the hospital. I supervised the younger children on a hayride sponsored by the church. I helped make the queen-size hand-stitched bear paw quilt that would be raffled away on Christmas Day. I made ornaments for our Christmas tree—walnuts rolled in glitter, clothespin angels, paper snowflakes, tinfoil chains.

Father Van Dan arranged for me to sing the Ave Maria at Midnight Mass on Christmas Eve, and I rehearsed with Eva and Serina Oben, Eva conducting me with one long finger. Afterward, they gave me sight-reading lessons, loaned me armfuls of music I could study on my own. How easy it was to make music! I'd accidentally found a language I could use to express absolutely anything I wanted, even forbidden, sinful things like anger and desire. It was the first time I could remember feeling as though it was all right to speak my mind, and suddenly I was never at a loss for things to say. I practiced on Elise's piano two hours every day, and then I walked over to the church, where I experimented with the organ. Now that I knew the notes, I could sound out everything I heard. I could even transpose things into different keys without fumbling. My mother had heard about a Milwaukee Conservatory teacher who came to Horton twice a month. She got me on a waiting list for lessons, paying the reservation fee out of her own business earnings when my father insisted fancy lessons were unnecessary, that if I had to have lessons at all, a local teacher should be good enough.

"Are you nervous about Christmas Eve?" she asked. It would be the first time I'd performed for a real audience, including my father and Sam, who were also planning to come for the service. But that didn't bother me. I intended to sing for God and God alone. I'd been praying for a vocation, the absolute knowledge that my life was meant for Him. It was a feeling that, according to Harv, was unmistakable when it came. "I guess it's like the way you describe music," he told me, during another one of our conversations that left Monica rolling her eyes. "Understanding without words." I wanted to understand. I wanted to be chosen.

At eleven-thirty on Christmas Eve, my grandmother and I walked over to the church, and I was grateful for the stinging snow, the bitter wind chilling me awake. My parents and Sam were already there, and at first they looked like any other family, lined up in a pew, Sam's blond hair cropped so short I could see his scalp shining underneath. Then, as we got closer, I saw what my mother hadn't described, what I had not imagined: deep clotted nicks where my father's razor had bit in. There was a noise in my head like bees. Suddenly I was remembering all the times my father held Sam and me down, one at a time, rubbing his coarse whiskers into our necks as we screamed and begged him to stop. When he grabbed me first, Sam could have run, but he never did, pummelling my father's shoulders, trying to set me free. My father laughed and pummeled him back, too rough; did he think it was all just a game? Sometimes he would take us for drives, letting the car swerve over the median or off the shoulder, accelerating so our stomachs lurched and our heads snapped back against our seats. He would tell us he was going to drive into Lake Michigan, and he'd edge the car inches from the drop-off. Nobody sneeze, he'd say.

My grandmother called my name; I was blocking the middle of the aisle. I stepped quickly over my father's knees, kissed my mother, sat beside my brother.

"Hi," I whispered.

"Hey," he said. The worst of the cuts was behind his ear; he noticed me staring, sank lower into the collar of his coat.

Offer it up to God. When I rose to sing at Communion time, I stopped seeing Sam and my parents and grandmother. I didn't even think about the rest of the congregation. I walked to the altar, and as soon as Eva began to play, I opened my mouth and let my voice fill the church like a choir. As I sang, I prayed for God to accept the offering I made of myself, waiting for the feeling of absolute understanding that Harv had described. But I felt nothing except my own want, heard no voice other than my own—and then not even that. The song was finished. Eva swayed to stillness. In the long moment before the congregation burst into spontaneous applause, I knew I had been refused. Harv was assisting Father Van Dan; at the Communion rail, he slid the gold platter beneath my chin. I saw my reflection there, terribly distorted.

"The body of Christ," Father Van Dan said.

"Amen." I could barely say it. *I believe.*

After Mass, people nodded to me, pressed my arm; a few of them said shyly what a pretty voice I had, how much like Elise. My grandmother nodded proudly, accepting compliments on my behalf; my mother scooped me into a hug, and even Sam said, "That was pretty good." We'd been fasting since sundown, and when Harv emerged from the sacristy, we all walked back to my grandmother's house for pancakes and sausage and sweet fruit preserves, the same early breakfast we ate each year before everyone finally went home, stuffed and exhausted. My father put his arm around my shoulder, leaning too hard, the way he always did. "Congratulations," he said, and I offered him my hand to shake. But when he tried his usual trick of squeezing too hard, I bent his thumb back as if I were snapping a carrot.

"Don't do that," I shouted, "I hate it when you do that," and then I started to cry.

"Did you hurt her, Gordon?" my mother said.

"Who's the victim here?" my father said. "Christ, look what she did to my thumb," and he held it out, already swelling; I could see it under the dim light of the moon. But nobody was listening to him. Instead, my mother was rubbing my hand, my grandmother was patting my shoulder, Harv and Uncle Olaf were searching their pockets for Kleenex, and Monica was saying in her affected way, "Why does *every*thing have to *be* so *melodramatic?*" I cried all the way home and into the bright warm light of the kitchen, where the cats climbed into my lap and my grandmother fed me whiskey tea. I cried while my grandmother fixed an ice pack for my father's thumb, and later while Uncle Olaf secured it with tape from the first-aid kit, teasing him about the dangers of thumb wrestling with a daughter. It was clear to me now that I belonged in this world. There was nowhere else for me to go.

On New Year's Day, I told my grandmother I wanted to go back to school in January. She surprised me by giving me Elise's piano; Uncle Olaf had agreed to haul it in his truck. "For your lessons," she said. "It will fit nice in your mother's living room, and I'm sure Elise would want you to have it."

"Thank you," I said. I couldn't believe it. "Are you sure?"

My grandmother took my hand, rubbed her thumb across the top of my knuckles the way she did when she was pleased with me. "When God shuts a door, He opens a window," she said, "or, in your case, perhaps, another door." I'd told her about how much I'd wanted a vocation, how hard it was not to envy Harv. "Keep the piano and practice your lessons and remember Elise in your thoughts," she said. "If God wills it, you'll have the lifetime of music she always wanted."

Sam's fourteenth birthday was coming up on Saturday, the sixth of January, and we decided I would move back home then. My father hadn't spoken to me since Christmas Eve; I'd sprained his thumb badly, and for the next six weeks he would have to wear an embarrassing white splint. He told people he'd slammed his finger in the car door, but there was something about the way he said it that made them ask more questions. Eventually, some-one heard the story from someone who knew my uncle, and my father was teased without mercy. Sam told me about it the next time I called. "Serves him right," he said bitterly.

The night of the fifth was bingo night, and for the first time, I won twenty dollars. Auntie Thil won next, then, amazingly, my grandmother. People were laughing and rubbing our sleeves for luck, and we drove home happy and warm with our good fortune. As we walked into the house, the squat, old-fashioned phone was ringing, and I knew by the way my grandmother reached for the receiver that she also sensed something was wrong. It was my mother; Sam had been hurt in a car accident that involved two other underage drivers. She'd thought he was at a friend's house, doing homework, and when the police called, she was so certain they had the wrong number that she told them so and hung up. They called her back. She called us. The car, an old Pontiac, had spun out of control on Highway J, bounced through a ditch, and hit a tin shed. My father was already on his way to the hospital. Would we meet her there?

My grandmother phoned Auntie Thil, and within minutes we were on the road to Saint Nicholas Hospital, our twenty-dollar bills still crisp in our pockets, our coats giving off the festive smell of the KC hall. Auntie Thil dropped us off at Emergency, and for the first time I was scared. The receptionist knew my grandmother; she smiled kindly and gave us the number of my brother's room.

"Quit," my grandmother said when she noticed me sniffling. We stepped into the elevator, and she punched the floor button. "Abigail, use your head. If it was serious, they wouldn't have him in a room so quick."

There was my mother at the end of the hallway, talking with two police officers in their stiff uniforms. I knew the younger one. His daughter was my age. I went to her birthday parties when we were in grade school, and her father always helped us play Pin the Tail on the Teacher. Officer Holtz. He recognized me and smiled, but his uniform made me shy, and I did not smile back. The other officer had a pen and a pad. He seemed eager to finish and go.

"He has a broken collarbone, some stitches," my mother told us. "The other boys were sent home already."

"So you've never noticed any sign before this that he'd been consuming alcohol?" the impatient officer said. My mother looked at my grandmother, and her face darkened with shame. "No," she whispered. "I've already told you."

"We'll give a holler if we need any more information," Officer Holtz said quickly, and the two of them left in a jingle of keys.

"The other boys were older," my mother said, as if she were speaking to herself. "They gave him the beer. It was their car he was driving."

"Can we see him?" I asked, and my mother nodded. My grandmother took her by the arm.

"You go on ahead," she said. "Your mother and I need to have a private talk."

There were two beds in the room. The one closest to the door was empty. The second one was hidden behind a loose white curtain, but I knew it was Sam's because I recognized my father's shoes. I hoped that my father wasn't scolding Sam, but as I listened, I didn't hear either my father or Sam saying much of anything. What I heard were ragged gasps, like the sound of someone in pain, and for a moment I wondered if Sam was hurt worse than my mother had said. But when I peered around the curtain I saw that Sam was asleep, his face a white ghost mask except for his lashes and brows and the faint gold hairs that lined his upper lip. His shoulder was covered in plaster; he had stitches in one ear, black and spiky-looking, like a row of ants feeding there. My father was sitting beside the bed, one long arm thrown over Sam's chest, and the splint on his thumb seemed huge and glowing. His shoulders moved, and I heard that gasp again.

When he looked up, I recognized the man from my dreams, and as I stared at the shine of tears on his face, I understood why God had refused me. I had run with all my strength, as fast and far as my selfish legs would take me. The man had caught my brother instead. Now he'd never let go.

Poison Creek

(1995)

Six

I'm not ready for fall: the long, chilly evenings, the morning frost shining on the last of the peppers and tomatoes, the yellowing squash, the tattered pea vines still clutching their stakes. Despite its late planting, the garden has flourished; my cupboards look as full as my mother's ever did, and I'm proud of the rows of canned vegetables, the neat labels: pole beans, pickles, salsa. Yesterday I dug up the lavender potatoes Adam ordered on a whim from a catalog. I figured they'd be bitter, but they were light and sweet, and we ate a small mountain of them, boiled, with butter and salt. This is why we left Baltimore, where we shared an apartment for over five years, eager to exchange the city for small pleasures like these. "A good fall taste," Adam said, and I wondered how I could have dug onions and beets, caulked the north windows, walked beneath maples filled with leaves the color of fire, and all without realizing summer had tapered to a brief warmth somewhere in the afternoon, dried up, blown away. Too late, I'm wishing I'd savored it more, our last summer alone. Next fall, we'll have a nine-month-old child. I remind myself of this every day, trying to make the idea seem real.

How will we find time to plant another garden? How will

we keep up with the house, the yard, oil changes and dental appointments and regular exercise, the day-to-day maintenance that already demands so much room in our lives? It seems as if we are already as busy as we possibly can be, Adam with his carpentry work, me with my job at the Turkey Hill Nature Preserve, no parents close by to help out in a pinch. "There's Pat," Adam reminds me—another reason we moved to New York State. And already she's volunteered baby-sitting, but her house is a disaster, her little girls wild, and I'm not reassured when she tells me, "When you've got three, what's one more?" Of course, my mother would love to stay with us for a while after the baby is born, but she'd mine the house with green scapulars, prayer cards, and bottles of holy water, the way she did the time she came to visit just after Adam and I were married. It had been a long week for all of us. On Sunday, she went to Mass with a neighbor—I'd arranged that in advance. Afterward, over the brunch I'd made, my mother spoke of nothing but the graffitied state of my soul— one black mark for each missed Mass—while Adam ate in silence.

"What will you do when you have children?" she said. "Certainly you'll want them to have a moral upbringing."

"*I* am a moral person," Adam said, "and I never went to any church when I was a kid."

He picked up his plate and left the room, leaving my mother and me to glare at each other.

Now she wants to know if we're making plans for a baptism. "I've never been a godmother before," she hints. "Maybe Adam could get baptized at the same time. A two-for-one special."

I match her tone. "It's only a bargain if it's something you need."

I'm tired of my mother's hints. Today at Turkey Hill, watching lines of geese scarring the horizon, I have the urge to jump in my car and drive . . . where? Anywhere. Away. But it's autumn that's making me feel this way, the restless wind, the skittering leaves, and I realize it's the perfect time to open Uncle Olaf's wine. He called it Autumn Tonic, and though he's been dead for several years now, Auntie Thil still sends me a bottle each fall from what's left of his well-stocked cellar: dandelion or mulberry or plum. The names themselves are sweet to the tongue. Usually, Adam is amused by that sweetness—he prefers beer to sugary wine—but when this year's bottle arrived in the mail, he said, *You shouldn't be drinking; you should be taking care of yourself.* All summer, he's been busy with what he calls *the preparations*, finishing household projects, taking on extra carpentry work. He waxes the truck, vacuums out my car. He joined a shoppers club in Binghamton and comes home with boxes of bulk toilet paper, pasta, rice. When I tell him it feels like we're anticipating war, he reminds me of what I already know, what everyone with children has been telling us almost gleefully: Four months from now, there will be little time for anything other than the baby's needs.

For the next three days he'll be traveling across the state, scavenging for antiques he'll restore and sell at Pat's shop in Cobblestone. It's a lucrative sideline, something to do when construction work drops off for the winter. He left yesterday, one suitcase filled with clothes rolled into tidy logs, and when I come home from work, the dark windows remind me he's gone. At least there's the cat for company, but the moment I open the door, she weaves between my legs and runs to the edge of the lawn, where she rolls happily in the dead grasses. I think about getting back in the car, driving to Pat's house for supper with the girls. Pat wouldn't mind, especially if I picked up some ice cream for dessert. Right now I'd choose even my nieces' messy clamor over this silent house.

It's then that I remember Uncle Olaf's wine. I remember the low cedar barrels where he aged it, under the cellar stairs beside crates of yeasty pilsners, stouts, and ales, and his own potent invention, Raspberry Glog, which he stored in glass jelly jars. At Christmas, we kids got a taste on the tip of a teaspoon, perhaps the last sip that someone didn't want. But every now and then throughout the year, we'd sneak down the steps—me and Sam, Monica and Harv—to steal another swallow or two. The glog looked as harmless as Auntie Thil's canned fruits, plums and peaches and spiced brown pears, which occupied identical jars. I took a long, dizzying swallow, hiccupped the exquisite taste of raspberry, and experienced the light-headed chill of knowing I had done something I could not undo. The alcohol ferreted through my veins, tickled the hard-to-reach places in my mind. When I passed the jar along to Sam, it seemed as if it were taking an awfully long time for my hands to obey my wish: *Let go, Let go, Let go.*

The glog was eighty proof; I know that now, the way I know each sip of wine means death to a handful of brain cells. As I sit in the kitchen rocking chair with my glass, pushing the floor away with my toes, I imagine those cells—the baby's and mine—like frogs' eggs: clear, clumping jelly, thick with information. There is no way to know if it is information we might someday need. There is no way to know if it's information we are better off without. But this I do know: one glass of wine can't be any worse than these past few months of stifling caution—low-salt diets, doctor visits, vitamins that leave my mouth tasting strange, eight glasses of water every day, eight hours of sleep every night. Adam believes in these rules the way my mother believes in the Ten Commandments, as if they are a magic formula, an infallible recipe.

Beyond the French doors, I can see clouds of migrating birds rising and falling, dust devils blown by a hundred wings. Our house is the last on a dead-end street, perched on the edge of a ravine. We bought it when we got married, liking the back porch, which juts out like an impulse, and the side yard, with enough space for Adam's sculptures. Deer pick their way up from the ravine to strip bark from the apple trees we planted along the lot line, standing on their hind legs to nibble beyond the wire protectors. In Horton, the deer drifted in herds of fifty and sixty, like cattle. They came at dusk and grazed until darkness, finally invisible except for their eyes, which trapped light from passing cars and glowed like floating spheres. First frost always made them bold. Even the yearlings were anticipating winter, the long, gray days of bitter bark and tough, dead grasses, and they ate steadily, fiercely, as Sam and I watched from my bedroom window, wrapped in a quilt, our feet dangling off the edge of my bed to catch the heat that rose from the vent on the floor. I told him the deer were really souls of the dead. If we went outside, we'd instantly die too. During the day, they transformed into other animals—bears and fish and even dogs and cats—so you never should approach a strange animal, in case it wasn't what it appeared to be. My mother overheard our murmurings one evening and put an end to it by stomping outside, my father's jacket thrown over her nightgown, and startling the herd into white-tailed flight with an exasperated flick of her hands.

Where you got your ideas, she still likes to say, *Heaven only knows!* But looking back, I don't see them as any stranger than the things we were taught to believe. Once, when Sam and I were quarreling over some small thing, she told us that each time we raised our voices in anger, it was the same as holding a burning match against the flesh of Jesus, which made all the angels weep. I was filled with remorse, imagining the hot sizzle of Jesus' skin, the agony in His eyes, the wailing of thousands of white-winged creatures. But Sam ignored the kitchen match my mother had lit to emphasize her point. Undaunted, he looked around the room.

"I don't see any angels," he said, crossing his arms on his chest. "Prove it." My mother doesn't remember this. Her Sam was a boy who volunteered to lead Grace before meals. Her Sam sat up straight at Mass, hands folded just so, like in a First Communion picture. With age, she's becoming as religious as my grandmother ever was, and it's hard for me to remember there was a time when she urged me to rely on myself—not God alone—for answers. She recently joined a women's prayer group; they meet twice a month to pray. One woman has cancer of the liver, and when the group joins hands, they ask God to shrink the tumor. They pray for each other's children, for people in the community; they pray for news about Sam. They believe that if a person has faith the size of a mustard seed, anything is possible. "Why do you always look for negative things?" she asks me. "Or is that just what happens when a person stops going to church?"

Even now, she'll call with news, real or imagined, of Sam: a dream, an anonymous phone call, a hopeful letter from a missing persons organization, an insight from a psychic, saying, *Sam is thinking about us* or *Sam is ill* or *Sam is coming home soon*. Prove it, I want to say. There have been too many disappointments, too many trips across the country to discover yet another stranger, someone else's lost son. But since my grandmother's death, I'm eager to hear my mother's voice, as lonely for her company as she is for mine. When she talks about Sam, I keep the silence she believes means we agree.

Growing up, my house rang with many of these silences; the things you did not say because to say them would be wrong; the things you did not feel because they were sins. The things you wanted to do but couldn't because you were a girl, or a boy. The questions you could not ask because you might be acting *too big for your britches* or else *talking nonsense,* in which case my father would tell you to *simmer down. If you can't say something nice,* my mother told me again and again, *don't say anything at all.* And perhaps what I remember are things that should not be remembered, should not be spoken. *Simmer down. Simmer down.*

For my thirteenth birthday, my father gave me matches and a pack of Camels, wrapped up in pink tissue paper. I was in the backyard, where I'd been idly throwing rocks at a stump. It had been, until that moment, a normal kind of birthday. We'd had an early supper of meat loaf, my favorite, and a store-bought cake I'd picked out myself at the bakery downtown, a chocolate cake with green frosting and lavender sugar flowers and *Happy Birthday Abby* written in cursive across the top. My mother had given me a diary with a key and a glass horse tethered to two glass foals. Sam had saved his money to buy me a king-size box of Milk Duds and a key chain that was a flashlight too. Now my father was giving me a pack of cigarettes.

"Thank you," I said.

My father looked pleased. He played with the zipper on his *Fountain Ford* windbreaker. "Have one," he said politely, as if he were offering me a cookie, a stick of gum, some unexpected little treat.

I studied the Camels uneasily. My mother usually bought our gifts, and I figured my father just didn't know any better than to give me cigarettes. He'd given things to Sam that I'd considered strange; a Baggie of smashed butterfly wings from the grille of his car; his broken watch; chewed-up pens with the names of car dealerships trailing down their sides; a large inflatable spark plug from a gas-station window display. The Camels were just one more mistake, only this time the mistake was aimed at me. Or was it some kind of trick? *No makeup,* he had warned me. *No high heels, no nail polish.* He'd never said specifically that I wasn't allowed to smoke, but I knew it was something I wasn't supposed to do.

"I don't smoke," I told him.

His expression did not change. He took the cigarettes, put them in his pocket, and said, "C'mon, let's go for a walk."

The red and gold of the turning leaves glowed eerily in the twilight. I watched the faint crescent moon move with us, slipping from tree to tree as we walked down the driveway to the highway, and I tried to keep up with my father. He was a fast walker, a businesslike walker, head down, shoulders forward, hands jammed into the pockets of his windbreaker. Sam and I had once imitated his walk for amusement, stretching our legs like wading birds, tucking our chins to our chests. But lately, Sam tried to throw an extra inch into his own stride, my father's broken watch sliding up and down his arm the way the high school boys' class rings slid on the slender fingers of their girlfriends.

At the highway, my father turned right toward Oneisha, and I wondered if he was leading me there, if I would be expected to walk the ten miles behind him in silence. But when we came to the end of our land, he stepped off the road and followed the gully to the stand of hickory trees that belonged to the Luchterhands. There I paused, catching my breath. The hickory trees had a reputation: Older kids biked out from town to hold secret meetings here, to drink Southern Comfort from Dr Pepper cans, and to beat up younger kids like me. "C'mon," my father said when he realized I had stopped.

"Mom's going to wonder where we are," I said, but I picked my way toward him through the weeds. The wind moved in the branches of the hickories, and they clicked together, the sound my grandmother made with her tongue to mean *Shame*. My father took the cigarettes out of his pocket, and I knew then that he meant for me to smoke one. "Somebody's going to see," I begged, but the highway was a pale gray scar in the distance.

He opened the pack, selected a cigarette, put it between his lips. "I used to smoke," he said. "Did you know that?"

"Yes."

He lit the cigarette, drawing once, twice. His wispy hair lifted slightly in the wind. "Son of a bitches make me sick now," he said. He coughed, shaking his head. "I want you to have your first smoke with me, not with some kid at your school."

He held out the cigarette.

"Dad," I said.

"One cigarette," he said. "Then we can go home."

His face wore the look that meant, no matter what, he was going to get his way. I took the cigarette from him gingerly, stuck it into my mouth, and sucked. It tasted like dirt. I spat out a stream of smoke, watching it curl upward and upward until it blended into the sharp white tooth of the moon. The glowing end of the cigarette was oddly beautiful, like a ruby but deeper, etched with gray patterns of ash.

"Your mother would kill me if she knew about this," my father said.

I took another puff, inhaling this time. My stomach churned chocolate cake with green icing; I choked for a minute, tears streaming down my face. "Kids aren't supposed to smoke," I said.

"Tap the ash off the tip," he said, and he demonstrated with his finger. Sparks spun into the arms of the hickory trees. I tried smoking with my left hand, then smoking no-handed. I tried blowing smoke through my nose.

"I could teach you how to do a smoke ring," my father said after a while.

"That's OK."

"I guess you don't have to finish all of it," he said.

I handed it to him, relieved. He put it out under his heel and kicked loose ground over the butt. For a moment, I thought that if I stood on my toes the wind would lift me high into the trees, and their arms around me would be soft and warm, and the smell of them would be magic.

"You going to smoke when the kids at school give you a cigarette?" he asked.

I shook my head no. My mouth tasted awful.

"That's my good girl," he said. He turned away, and I followed him out of the field. We passed Mrs. Luchterhand, who was riding one of her black Morgans. Both her long braid and the horse's tail were clipped with reflectors, which glowed like eyes. "Wonderful evening for a walk," she said to my father, her voice high and airy, like my mother's.

When we got home, he led me inside through the back door so my mother wouldn't see. "Will Sam have to smoke a cigarette when *he* turns thirteen?" I said.

My father watched me kick off my sneakers by pushing my toes against the heels. "No," he said. "Take your shoes off with your hands."

"How come?"

"They'll last a long time if you take care of them."

"I mean how come about Sam?"

My father laughed and shook his head as though he were remembering something private. "Boys can take care of themselves. It's you I've got to worry about."

"Why?"

He smiled, reached into the pocket of his jacket, pulled out a small box wrapped in green paper. "Happy birthday," he said, and he watched me open it. It was a necklace with my birthstone. He'd picked it out himself. "For my teenage daughter," he said.

The clock by the bed glows 2:00 A.M. when I first start hearing music, or, more precisely, a muffled, driving beat. I close my eyes, half dreaming the long Saturday nights in Horton, the slow cars moving up and down the dirt road that followed the lakefront all the way out to Herringbone Beach, trawling for girls sitting in small groups in the grass. Music was the simplest bait— Led Zeppelin, the Stones, AC/DC. My friends and I floated toward that music and the heat contained in the sound of it, so much like a heartbeat, but faster, harder, freed from the limits of the body. *Hey, girls, wanna ride? Wanna ride?* and we came up out of the long trampled grass, brushing off our jeans, rubbing stiff knees. In the morning, I'd get up and go to early Mass, tamed by knee socks and a fresh cotton slip, penitent in my good church dress.

I led two lives when I was in high school, and each had its own sound track. Classical music was for church and home: my private voice, a gift from God. This was the music that accompanied the girl my parents knew, the girl my grandmother admired and my teachers praised. Mornings, I got up early and practiced on Elise's piano for an hour before school; after school, I used the grand piano in the school auditorium, taking the late bus home with the athletes and cheerleaders and pom-pom girls. They treated me kindly, if a bit uncomfortably; I was something of a bewilderment to them. But every now and then I'd show up at their parties, which made me acceptable, even marginally cool. Rock was for those forbidden nights—lurid, public, urgent—and this is the sound that unravels me from my sleep, peeling the layers away like onion skin, until finally I get up and step into my sweatpants. Pulling an old sweater of Adam's over my T-shirt, I go into the kitchen, open the French doors to the cold night. The moon is almost full, and the houses and trees are outlined in silver. I can hear lyrics, laughter, and I realize the noise is coming from the belly of the ravine. Sometimes I walk there in the morning before work, carefully following the faint deer paths until I reach the trickle of water at the bottom called Poison Creek. In spring, it swells into a river, seven or eight feet wide; Adam and I saw a dead raccoon once, swollen and stiff, its curious hands stretched skyward.

My next-door neighbor, an older woman whose name I do not know, steps out into her yard. She has a man's coat draped over her shoulders; she uses her hands to pin it chastely over the front of her robe. When she sees me, she walks over to our lot line and stops precisely at the edge, as if she's toeing a mark for a race. "You're new here," she calls, "so I'll tell you. They have parties down there every fall."

"Who?" I ask. She is wearing slippers shaped like rabbits, and they hop in place as she shifts from side to side in the frosty grass.

"Kids," she says, and she takes one hand from the front of her coat to shake her finger in the air. "High school kids. They wait till the weather gets cold and the police don't want to get out of their nice warm cars and chase them off."

"I'm Abby," I say, but she doesn't hear me.

"Goddamn kids. I called the police, but you know they won't do a thing about it. If it were up to me, I'd just send Charlie on down there with his gun."

She turns, rabbits marching, back toward her house, without saying good-bye. I've seen Charlie huffing around their lawn in summer, squirting weed killer on the dandelions and Queen Anne's lace, and I don't like to imagine him with a gun. Still, as I go back into the house, I understand some of my neighbor's anger. When I was a girl, my grandmother told me how it surprised her whenever she looked—really looked—into a mirror. *It's not how I feel,* she said, but I did not understand. Now I stand in front of the oval mirror hanging beside the French doors. My hair is brittle-looking; the skin beneath my eyes looks bruised. At five months, my pregnancy shows enough to make me look potbellied, though Adam says that isn't true. Dirty-looking freckles have erupted across the backs of my hands, my chest, the bridge of my nose. One long worry wrinkle runs parallel with my eyebrows. This is not the way I feel.

I often wonder what Sam would look like today, whether or not I would recognize him. At twenty-nine, he'd probably be getting our family's slumped shoulders and the beginnings of a receding hairline. Of course, if he was trying not to be recognized, he'd keep his blond hair dyed brown or black, though perhaps his hair would have changed naturally, turning reddish like my mother's. A few years ago, my mother and Auntie Thil were spending a day at the Wisconsin Dells when they saw a man with a long red beard who looked so familiar that my mother followed him from souvenir stand to souvenir stand, fingering T-shirts and postcards and mugs, until she heard his voice. "That fellow had a deep voice," she told Auntie Thil when she found her again. "Sam talked through his nose."

"Didn't Sam have a deep voice?" Auntie Thil said.

"No, he didn't," my mother said. And then she got very

upset. "I'm his mother! Don't you think I would remember a thing like that?"

Later, when Auntie Thil told me the story, I could hear my mother's voice rising above the sound of the falls, see the other tourists moving gently away, parents clutching their children's hands.

Laverne scratches on the door, and when I open it to let her in, I hear cars revving at the end of the street, bellowing male laughter, and a long, shrill wail that could be a teenage girl's giddy joy or else a cry for help. Which? The music swells again, and I can't hear anything else. Laverne hops up on the counter, butts her head against my hand. She knows that I don't have the heart to chase her off the way Adam would. But Adam isn't here, and I decide to walk down into the ravine, just to make sure I know the difference between the sounds of pleasure and pain. As I pull on my coat, all the warnings about walking alone at night play in my mind like a symphony, brief and discordant. What if there's someone hiding in the weeds? What if I were to take a wrong step, tumble into the open mouth of the ravine? But then, what if I am swallowing too many vitamins? What if, at this very moment, my cells are tingling with the radioactive kiss of a bomb detonated years ago? This is what Adam does not understand. No matter what we do, no matter how we plan, anything might happen at any given moment, and that moment will always be the one you least suspect—in the dark span of an eye blink, in the crick of a turned-away head, in the moment after you first awaken and realize that none of this is a dream.

The moon is so bright that I cast a shadow until I move beneath the sheltering arms of the trees that line the ravine. The music rumbles in my chest, in my throat, in the bones of my feet; bonfires flicker between the trees. When I stop to look back toward the house, all I can see are the windows. As children, Sam and I sneaked out into the cornfields at night, following parallel rows, zapping each other between cornstalks with the beams from our flashlights. Now and then we'd look back to see the porch light, a beacon reminding us where we belonged, calling us home. Once, I turned off my flashlight and waited, invisible and silent, as Sam's beam licked at the stalks around me, disappeared up into the sky. *Where are you?* he called. *Are you OK?* I heard him thrashing farther and farther away from me, his voice growing higher, shrill. *I'm not KIDDING! WHERE ARE YOU?*

Still I did not move, did not breathe, until his light winked out and left only the stars to watch over us. *Why are you so mean?* he sobbed, again and again. I crouched, hugging my knees, trying not to laugh and trying not to cry, every nerve in my body tingling, tingling. I mattered, I was needed. I was important to my brother.

At the foot of the ravine, the fires are giving off a cloud of thick, sweet smoke. Thirty or forty high school kids are standing around in groups, dancing close in the fallen leaves, their bodies weaving single silhouettes. A boom box is balanced in the low crook of a tree. Above it, girls sway in the branches, slapping at each other and laughing, and I realize I've discovered the source of the scream. If I called up to them and told them I had come out of concern, they would not understand. *Don't worry about us,* they might say, annoyance clouding their clear voices. *Nothing's going to happen to us.*

I walk around the outskirts of the bonfires, negotiating this odd sense of invisibility and remembering similar high school parties in Horton, on the bluff overlooking Lake Michigan. As soon as it was dark, cars began to line the winding dirt road, trunks packed with coolers of beer. Everyone drank and talked and wandered around the bonfires, the wood smoke clinging to our clothes and hair; I could smell it even after I got home and showered and slipped, still reeling, into bed. There was music in this too, a dizzying melody, and I wanted to get up and go downstairs to the piano and sound everything out: the craziness of the dancing, the brush of a boy's cold cheeks, his impossibly warm mouth. Now I watch the faces of the girls, their lips and cheeks done up in red and pink, the forced colors of cheer. I watch their darting eyes and the way they use their hands when they speak, painting the air around themselves, weaving invisible cocoons. I watch the boys, the way they walk with their hips tugging them in the direction they want to go, their heads and shoulders bobbing smoothly behind as if innocent, simply along for the ride, and I remember waking up in my bedroom after coming home from one of those parties, cotton-headed, confused. It was the ninth of August, four days after Sam's official disappearance on August fifth, four days before I'd be interviewed by detectives investigating *incidents* at Dr. Neidermier's and the drive-in and Becker's Foodmart, investigating an assault on Geena Baumbach of Oneisha. Boys were moving from the door to the window, led by the sleek pull of their hips. One of them—Sam—went through my jewelry box. One of them opened my purse, which was slung over the back of my rocking chair. One of them bent over me and began to stroke my hair. "What a nice ring you're wearing," he said, exaggerating his politeness. "Can I have it?" From a faraway place in my mind, I watched myself twist Elise's ring off my finger. There is no room for this in my mother's careful memories. There is no place for this in her longing for Sam's return. I never told; how could I? How could I be the one to finally break my mother's heart?

The music stops, and the yodel of a police siren billows unevenly through the air, bouncing off the sides of the ravine so it's hard to tell where it's coming from. Bodies scatter wildly into the brush, and I'm caught up in their panic and running too, clumsily climbing over fallen logs, branches whipping my face. *The cops!* we'd call to each other, and suddenly everyone would be scrambling down the side of the bluff, fighting for a foothold, the evening's dizzy drunkenness evaporating like mist. Then would come the long, aching silence, the crunch of footsteps on gravel overhead as we clung to the slender trees growing out from the side of the bluff, praying to Blessed Jesus that they wouldn't give way. Below, the lake sparkled diamonds in the distance, but all we could think of was the rocks directly below us and the murmur of gulls disturbed from their sleep and the cops' yellow beams stroking the leaves only inches from our faces.

I cannot imagine that the cops here tonight are much different from the cops I remember from Wisconsin. They all have their badges and billy clubs, their crisp uniforms and questions, a heavy walk that means *Do what I say*. Sam had disappeared before, sometimes for several days; and each time, they found him, or else didn't find him; but either way, he always ended up back home. Once, my mother found things missing—money, a tiny silver picture frame, her watch—but when Sam came in to breakfast his first morning back, it was as if she had forgotten these things had ever existed.

"Good morning," she sang as he sat down at the table. His eyes were like poison, and he kept them fixed on his cereal bowl. My father no longer addressed him directly; instead, he talked to the sugar dish, or the newspaper he was reading, or our ancient cat, Rose, who still loved Sam and struggled arthritically into his lap. "So he's finally come back from God knows where," he muttered to the ceiling, but Sam just blinked his poison eyes—he didn't speak to my father at all, directly or indirectly. Rose purred and purred, pushing the top of her head into his hand. I watched that hand, waiting for it to respond, and I knew something had been lost in Sam when it did not.

But how easily things might have been different! When the police asked their halting questions, my mother simply gave them the answers that should have been true. Sam had had his moments, like any teenage boy, she said, but he had no special difficulties, there were no fights at home. The friends and relatives who said otherwise were betraying Sam at the very time he needed them most; the truth was what you made it, and it was only by stating these things to strangers that they became terrible, unalterable fact. *If you can't say anything nice, don't say anything at all.* So I kept silent about the night that Sam came into my bedroom with his friends, looking for money, jewelry, anything they could sell. "So, Sam-boy, this is your sister," said the one who was stroking my hair. He looked older than Sam, and he had the knife Mrs. Baumbach would later describe: a leather grip, an odd tip curved like a question mark. "She isn't going to breathe a word of this, is she? Your sister can keep a secret," and he moved his hand over my shoulders and gown, lightly, as if he were soothing a child. Sam had my confirmation locket, the birthstone necklace my father had given me. "You got anything else?" was the last thing he said, but I was too scared to answer. Abruptly the one standing over me straightened, and then they were gone, filing out into the hallway, leaving only the smell of their cigarette smoke, and a bitter cologne I've never encountered since. For years, I worried I'd come home to find Sam waiting beside my door, or rummaging through my jewelry box, or pointing a gun to my head. I worried that someone would discover the part of me that hoped my brother would never be found.

I cross our lawn and sit on the steps that lead up to our deck, trying to catch my breath. Clouds have dimmed the moon to a quiet star, and the wind rises, shivering in the branches of the apple trees. I wonder why I was running in the first place—I wasn't doing anything wrong. *I heard the music,* I practice saying. *I was concerned. I came out to investigate.* Still, I am afraid as I listen to the cops thrashing through the trees below me, and when I see the glow of a flashlight moving in my direction, I stand up quickly and prepare my face, because this is what you do when the police ask you questions. You smile, a big, wide, friendly smile. You ask if you can be of any help. You assure them that, regardless of appearances, everything is really all right.

Seven

*H*alloween is Adam's favorite holiday, and this year he's offered to take Pat's girls around our neighborhood during official trick-or-treating hours at dusk. Pat lives above her antique store on a busy street in downtown Cobblestone; her neighbors are a hardware store, a liquor store, a gas station. But our streets are quiet, the houses set close together, the neighborhood windows plastered with cutouts of black cats and witches riding on brooms. Even our next-door neighbor Charlie hung a homemade ghost from the corner of the house, his wife calling shrill instructions as she held on to the stepladder. This morning, when I look out our bedroom window, I can see the white sheet flapping in the wind, its Magic Marker mouth stuck in a wide, pitiful howl. I want to walk over and pull it down, put the poor thing out of its misery. I don't like Halloween. There's something unnerving about skeletons in the grocery store, bats suspended from the ceiling at work, hay-stuffed corpses sprawled on people's lawns. I'm hoping we'll get by with a simple smiling jack-o'-lantern, but no such luck. Adam goes out to get one and, when he returns, the truck bed is filled with a dozen of the ugliest pumpkins I've ever seen. He carries them into the kitchen one by one, proudly, as if they're trophies.

"I'm going to carve them for tonight, surprise the girls," he says. "You want to help?"

Laverne eyes the pumpkins suspiciously. My expression is probably the same.

"How much did all this cost?"

"Next to nothing, can you believe it?" Adam says. "They're irregulars. Carl Jaeger let me have the lot for twenty bucks."

"Carl Jaeger should have paid you twenty bucks to take them," I say, staring at the odd shapes, the warty cheeks and splintered stumps.

"Wait and see," Adam says. "I have an idea. The girls are going to love it."

So I cover the linoleum with old newspapers, and we sit cross-legged on the floor, the history of the past months spread between us. Adam pulls the first of the pumpkins into his lap; he holds it steady against his knees, wiping its face with a warm wet cloth. He is gentle about this task, turning the pumpkin's face from side to side the way one might turn a child's face, alert for dirty ears, smudges, sleeping sand. My lap is already filled with my stomach, which is about the size of the next-to-smallest pumpkin—big enough to have made my descent to the kitchen floor unwieldy. Big enough so that strangers are starting to notice. Some make predictions: Most say it's a girl. Adam and I have told my doctor we don't want to know in advance.

My mother is predicting a healthy boy with my almond-shaped eyes and her own mother's smile. A boy just like my brother. She believes it's no coincidence that my revised due date—January fifth—is the day before Sam's birthday. "The doctor says that's just an estimate," I say. "It could be born in December, or as late as the middle of January."

"Or January sixth," my mother says. "Stranger things have happened."

She looks for signs in everything. She claims burning bushes are everywhere and that most of us just haven't learned how to

125

see them. Last Saturday night, when she and Auntie Thil joined
hands with the other members of their women's prayer group,
they saw a little boy, dressed in an infant's snow-white baptismal
gown, walking up the long gravel driveway toward our house in
Horton. This, she called to tell me, was the child I will have. Sam
coming home like the prodigal son.

She says, "Have you thought about naming the baby after
Sam?"

Adam outlines a pair of squinting eyes, a mouth that badly
needs a dentist. There's nothing he likes better than transforming
an idea into something concrete. Every day as I drive to work, I
pass things he has made, places where he's left his mark: this new
porch, that refurbished farmhouse, a delicate gazebo tucked between the trees. He's planning another sculpture for our side yard.
Inside the house, he rearranges our furniture. He paints and papers and plans. As my belly swells, he touches me—the small of
my back, the indentations behind my knees—as if he is evaluating
my structural integrity, longing to make improvements: a pillow,
supportive hose, sturdier shoes. He reminds me to take my cal-
cium supplements. He fusses over how much or how little I sleep.
Is there anything I can do? he asks. Is there anything you need?

He holds his pumpkin in front of his face."What do you
think?" he says from behind it.

"Scary," I say.

He lowers it, looks at it closely. "You think so?" he says.
"Scared, maybe."

"Aren't you going to make any happy ones?"

He chooses another knife. "You can make the happy ones,"
he says.

But my first jack-o'-lantern will turn out sad; I can already
tell by its flat, scarred cheeks, complete with tear-shaped blight
marks. I cut open its forehead, and there's that pumpkin smell—
rich, mildewy, dank, the odor of sealed, dark boxes, the odor of

secret things. I separate the seeds into the wooden bowl for baking; the orange goo goes into the compost bucket. My mother doesn't put her faith in things like supportive hose and vitamin tablets, what she calls *quick fixes*. The power of prayer will smooth the ache out of my tired back, reduce the swelling of my ankles better than elevation. The day she called me to say her group had prayed for my ankles, I got the giggles.

She sighed.

"I'm sorry," I said. "It's just a funny thing to imagine."

"Abby, when is it we remember to pray?" she said in her practiced businesswoman's voice. "When things are going OK? No, it's when we have problems that we remember God and turn to Him. That's why He sends us these little hardships."

"God's talking to me through my ankles?"

"Don't laugh," my mother said, but she laughed a little herself.

My jack-o'-lantern is an unhappy disaster. The mouth is lopsided, the left corner slicing too far down into its chin. One eye is smaller than the other. I turn it around for Adam to see.

"It's much scarier than mine," he says.

I'm surprised. "But it isn't scary."

"Yes it is."

"No it isn't."

We are looking at the same thing—how can we see it so differently? Adam squints one eye, widens the other, mimicking my pumpkin's expression. I nail him with a glob of pulp, and he whips back a handful of cold, wet seeds. When I yelp, the baby shivers sympathetically. Adam says it's bigger than the length of an outstretched hand. He reads all the brochures I bring home from the doctor; he even gets books at the library. There is nothing Adam loves better than a technical word, crisp in the mouth like a fresh stick of gum. Conduit, carburetor, compressor. Parturition, gestation, lactation. The baby, Adam reminds me, is developing according to the genetic blueprint we carry within our own cells. It is immune to my mother's prayers and premonitions. Visions of little boys dressed all in white.

"He's a goddamn encyclopedia," Pat complains, her big laugh like an engine that fires but won't catch. Pat suspects terminology of all kinds: She's at home with gizmos and doohickeys, whatchamacallits and thingamajiggers, sniggering references to ovens and buns and biscuits. She tells her own half-grown biscuits—three bone-slender white-haired girls—that the baby is in my stomach.

Uterus, Adam corrects her, and Pat snorts; I blush, the girls roll their pale blue eyes. Three plain little girls with elaborate frilly names: Alinda, Lorentina, Tamela. "My leeches," Pat calls them, running her hands through their strange white hair. They make me nervous—all children do—and I'm already dreading this evening, when they'll fill our small house with their shrieky voices, their pounding footsteps. Those spindly pumping arms and legs. Those gap-toothed mouths. "You won't feel that way about your own," Adam says, but I worry that I might drop it like a cup, overfeed it like a goldfish, leave it behind in the grocery store the way I'm always doing with my purse. I worry that I won't love it. I worry that I'll love it too much. I worry that I'll look into its eyes and see the figure of a boy, dressed all in white, walking up the driveway toward the house where my brother and I grew up.

Highway KL links the townships along Lake Michigan like so many rosary beads—Horton, Oneisha, Farbenplatz, Fall Creek, Holly's Field. Each summer, Sam and I played survival games in the fields along this road, stockpiling food in makeshift forts, estimating how long we could live off the land. We gathered the crisp young shoots of wild asparagus, sweet beans yellowing in the fields, sour gooseberries, tart wild raspberries. We invented a secret language. We carried clumsy stick weapons. At home, we explored my mother's pantry, dug our hands into the bins of corn-meal and oatmeal and rice, ran our fingers over the jars of pickles and tomatoes and beets in the root cellar; in the attic, we opened her cedar chest to inhale the bitter scent protecting our sweaters and scarves. It seemed that winter was always coming, a new virus constantly making its rounds, another bad influence seeping into the community—rock music, hip-hugger jeans, marijuana ciga-rettes. My mother looked in our ears and under our tongues, measured our height and weight against the chart in the bathroom closet. Once a week, we were forced to swallow a teaspoon of cod liver oil, *just in case.*

What were we preparing for even then? My mother still saves everything: string, rubber bands, slivers of leftover soap, bottles, rags, Christmas cards, our clumsy school projects, worn-out shoes. She collects discount dresses with crooked seams, bargain blouses, coupons. Her purse is heavy as an anvil, bulging with things she might need. Saint Christopher dangles upside down from the rear-view mirror of her car; each New Year's Day she blesses the house with holy water. And when these charms fail, there are always her intuitions, premonitions, dreams, which are true just often enough so that I can't dismiss them. Even now, she always knows when I'm thinking about her. If I say to Adam, "Maybe I'll call Mom today," she'll call me first. In Baltimore, at the beginning of my first and only semester of college at the Peabody Conservatory of Music, I tried to tell my roommate about my mother's gift.

"My mom's the same way," Phoebe said. She was from Con-necticut, wealthy and agnostic, and despite our differences we'd immediately become friends. I thought she was the most beautiful girl I'd ever seen. Her teeth were perfectly straight from years of braces; she saw a dermatologist and, she told me privately, a psy-chotherapist. It was the end of our first week of classes, and we were stripping our beds, getting ready to do our laundry.

"No, you don't understand," I said. "It's like she has ESP or something," and I told her how she'd sketched my father's face the day before she met him. I was showing off a bit. I'd never been to New York City or gone sailing off the coast of the Florida Keys like Phoebe, but I had a mother with a special gift. I'd impressed friends in Horton with this story, and no one had ever questioned it. But Phoebe said, "What does your dad look like?"

"He's tall, with brown hair, and he parts it on the side. He sometimes has a mustache."

"That could be half the men in the world," Phoebe said. "Did you ever see the sketch?"

The drawing hadn't been saved. The only ones who ever saw it were Auntie Thil and my mother.

"I don't think my mother would lie," I said, hurt.

"I didn't mean it that way. I'm just saying people believe what they want to, that's all."

"This is different," I said. "I'll prove it. I'll think about her right now and she'll call me."

"You want to put a dollar on that?" Phoebe said.

I hesitated; betting was a venial sin.

"No?"

"Sure, but you'll lose."

"Let's see if anybody else wants to bet," Phoebe said, and she headed for the door. But someone was already knocking. "Telephone, Abby," she said. "It's your mom."

Phoebe and I stared at each other. If someone had yelled "Boo!" we would have screamed.

"No way!" Phoebe finally said. "You arranged that in advance." She never would believe that I hadn't. But that morning, I'd caught a glimpse of my own beliefs through the eyes of someone else. *People believe what they want.* That night, as I struggled to undress for bed without exposing anything unnecessary, Phoebe said, "Can I ask you something? Why do you always have a penny pinned to your underwear?" A penny? Could she mean my Saint Benedict medal, which my cousin Monica and I had vowed, along with the rest of Girls' Catechism, to wear for life? I tried to explain: Saint Benedict medals prevented possession by the devil. "Do you think other people are possessed because we don't wear them?" Phoebe said.

"No," I said earnestly.

"So then it's just Catholics the devil wants? How come?"

It seemed as if everything I'd ever believed in was being exposed as wishful thinking, foolish superstition, or, at best, a matter of opinion.

"Can I ask you another question?" Phoebe asked, after we'd turned out the lights. "If your mother has this gift, why can't she find out what happened to your brother?"

The phone rings just as I'm finishing my third jack-o'-lantern, one with a growly expression and a frayed gray stump like a woman's hat. I pick up the receiver in the hallway, coating it with pumpkin slime; I already know who it has to be. "Happy Halloween," my mother says. "Are you having a nice weekend?"

"We're carving jack-o'-lanterns," I say, picking a pumpkin seed out of my hair. "Twelve of them."

"Twelve!" my mother says, and the pause that follows is her secret, silent laugh, the laugh that is now mine. I've always envied women like Pat, with their booming, sexy laughter.

"I won't keep you long," my mother says. "I was just thinking about that jack-o'-lantern you and Sam had, the one so big you both fit inside it. Remember that, Abby?"

"Not really," I lie. "I was pretty young."

"You were five," she says. "I've got the picture here in front of me. The two of you with just your heads sticking out. Like chicks in an egg. I'll send it on."

"Oh, that's OK," I say, but I know it will arrive by certified mail, just like all the other things she's sent over the past few weeks: Sam's baby clothes, preserved in cedar chips, his baby blanket, and, most recently, his handmade christening cap and gown wrapped up in acid-free paper. She has saved it all, every last bit, scented with sandalwood, preserved beneath plastic, and I don't need holy dreams to tell me she means to pass it along to my child in the same way that my grandmother passed Elise's belongings to me. It was hard for me to remember I'd never known Elise; my grandmother's memories became, at times, more real than any of my own. Even now, I remember the day of the cannery fire as if I'd actually been there. I remember the day of the funerals. I remember my grandmother's grief. I don't want my child to grow up that way, remembering things that belong to other people. It's too great a responsibility, living up to the perfection—or the imperfection—of the dead.

Now my mother is describing the day we brought Sam home from his christening. It's one of her favorite stories. My father lifts Sam out of his white blanket, plucks the lacy cap from his head. *There you go, sport!* he says in his booming voice, rocketing the baby around the room as my mother and grandmother cry in unison, *Support his neck!* But when they lay Sam across my lap, I support his neck without being told. I hold out my wrist when she checks the temperature of his milk. I soothe him when he cries in the crib beside my bed, singing little songs. And as I listen to my mother talk, I realize it's happening again—I *remember* this, and yet, of course, that's not possible; I wasn't even two years old. "You were always a natural mother," my mother says. "You took such good care of your brother."

"Adam's better with kids than I am," I say, but my mother doesn't want to change the subject.

"I mailed you Sam's christening gown. Did you get it?"

"We did."

"Your grandmother made that, you know. Now I'm glad I didn't give it to Monica."

"But you should have," I say. "It's so beautiful. Someone should use it."

"I keep hoping you'll use it," my mother says. "I keep hoping you'll change your mind."

"Mom," I say. "Why do we have to keep fighting about this? If the baby grows up and wants to get baptized, that's fine, but I'm not going to do it. You *know* I don't go to church, and even if I still believed in original sin, which I don't, I'd have to think long and hard about baptizing my child into a church that doesn't give women the same rights as men."

"I just hope you don't regret your decision," my mother says. "It's a comfort to me now, knowing Sam was baptized. Knowing that even if I won't get to see him again in this world, we can be reunited in the next."

It's the first time I've ever heard her mention the possibility that Sam won't be found. "I'm glad it's a comfort to you," I say, as gently as I can. "But it's not a comfort to me. I'm not even sure if I believe in an afterlife."

"Oh, Abby," my mother says, her voice full of anguish. "Then what's the point of anything? How can you live from day to day if you think we just end at death?"

"Look," I say, "I've got to go now. I'll call you later, OK?" I hang up, drained, miserable. In the kitchen, Adam is at work on a new jack-o'-lantern, one with a double stem like devil's horns. I remember sitting in the big pumpkin with Sam, back-to-back. The hard wriggling knobs of his spine. The cool walls of the pumpkin. That damp, secret smell.

"How's Mom?" Adam says. I can tell he is pleased with his jack-o'-lanterns; it's put him in a teasing sort of mood. "Any more holy visions of the baby?"

"No."

"Hallelujah." He uses a long-handled tweezers to pluck out a perfect oval eye. "Is she mailing us more stuff?" he says, but I've got my head in the fridge, so I can pretend I don't hear. Cheese. Eggs. Milk. I don't want to talk about anything. "It's lunchtime," I tell Adam. "You hungry?"

He shakes his head no. He is covered with pumpkin guts. He is consumed by his pumpkins, the idea of what his pumpkins will be. Absurdly, I think of Genesis, God bending over his new creation, dividing space, naming names. *And he saw that it was good.*

"I'm going to make an omelet," I say. If I were living in Wisconsin, if I were the person I used to be, I'd be having a baby shower, planned by my mother and Monica. I'd unwrap rubber nipples, disposable diapers, a breast pump, IOU notes for baby-sitting and housework. Monica would loan me clothes her babies had outgrown; she and my mother and Auntie Thil would make me special teas, accompany me to doctor's appointments, take me on trips to department stores to finger stuffed animals and jangly mobiles. We would make lists of ridiculous names—Garbanzig Rototiller, Chainsaw Elizabeth—before studying the worn *Christian Names for Babies* book that has been passed family to family for as long as I can remember. Of course, I would be planning the baptism—choosing godparents (my mother and Harv), making a reservation with the priest, preparing an announcement for the Baby News page of the weekly paper. Suddenly I am missing my mother terribly. I want to call her back and tell her I'm sorry, I'll baptize the baby, I'll start going to Mass, I'll do anything she says, just to feel like I'm part of that life again, blessed with that kind of certainty.

"What else is on the way?" Adam says.

"Just a photograph. You don't have to look at it."

My voice is as sharp as the sound of the egg cracked against the bowl. Adam gets up and comes over to the stove. "What's the matter?" he says. I open the shell, and there's the sudden surprise of a double yolk.

"Nothing." I puncture them each with a fork, add milk, beat them a bit too briskly. "My mother. You know."

"I *don't* know," Adam says. "What did you talk about?"

"She wants us to baptize the baby."

"So what else is new?" Then he sees my face. "I don't understand why she keeps after you about it," he says reasonably. "She knows we don't go to church."

I pour the egg into the hot pan. "That's not the point," I say.

"What *is* the point?"

"Salvation." How can I explain this to Adam, with his blue-prints, his careful reasoning, his twice-measured plans? Adam, who rearranges a room again and again, spinning each piece of furniture around himself as if it is a planet and he is the sun, the center, the confident source of gravity. I dump the omelet onto a plate. It falls apart, half cooked, ugly, nothing I want to put in my mouth. "Look," I say, "what would you think about having a baptism anyway? Just to keep everyone happy? I mean—"

Adam stares at me as if I've developed stigmata. "I would hate it," he says firmly. "You want to talk religion—fine. What kind of sin is hypocrisy?"

I scrape my omelet into the sink, turn off the burner, and go down the hallway to our room. The air smells of pumpkin, Adam's sleep, mine. The intimate odor of our lives. Beside the bed is the cradle he has made entirely by hand, the headboard carved with pineapples, those old pagan symbols of fertility, life. My grandmother's bed had four tall posts with a pineapple crowning each one. I remember being put down to nap on that bed beside my brother, the sour breath of the dog scorching our faces as we dreamed. Sundays after Mass, we'd burrow deep into the pile of guest coats, inhaling the dizzying clash of perfumes, scratching our cheeks on rhinestone brooches. Above the bed hung a large wooden crucifix. Once, my grandmother lifted it down to show us how the back could pop open to reveal blessed candles (half burned!), holy water, and oil, all that was necessary for an emergency baptism or last rites, the final cleansing of the soul.

I arrange my body in the center of the bed. The baby settles deeper into me, and I feel the click click of each fine bone in my spine separating. My hips pop too, first the right, then the left, my body coming loose in preparation for birth. "It'll be even worse than you imagine," my mother says, "so you might as well not think about it."

Just after I dropped out of the conservatory, she dreamed that I appeared in a cherry-colored nightgown and stood beside her bed, not quite close enough to touch. At the time of the dream, I was living in a room in an apartment filled with people I did not know. Downstairs there was a grocery store, where I worked part time, mostly nights and weekends; during the day I looked for a better job, a full-time job. It was the first time in my life I'd ever been hungry. I stole what I could from the grocery; I swallowed glass after glass of cold water to curb my appetite. My brother was still missing, I was a disappointment to my mother and grandmother, and worst of all, I'd confirmed my father's predictions: I couldn't make it in the world. One night, I decided that I'd cash my next paycheck and hitchhike to Mexico or Montreal or Alaska, somewhere far enough from where I was so that even God wouldn't be able to find me.

"What's wrong?" my mother asked my dream self, and I opened my chest and stomach to show her that emptiness there. The next night, I came home from work to find a delivery of fruit and chocolate. Attached was a note from my mother, saying a check for five hundred dollars was in the mail. "Abby, you can never disappear," she had written. "I will always know where you are, because you will come to tell me."

I awaken to the sense of someone moving through the room. It's late afternoon, already starting to get dark. My heart hammers in my chest even as I tell myself it's only Adam, it's all right. How much longer will I wake up at the slightest sound, thinking my brother and his friends have returned to stand beside my bed? It's guilt, I suppose, that brings them back. Maybe it would help if I told someone what I saw, what I didn't say, but whom? And after so many years, how could it make a difference? Mrs. Baumbach is dead; Dr. Neidermier has retired to Florida. The drive-in closed, and my mother has told me that even Becker's is in trouble, threatened by the new Piggly-Wiggly in Holly's Field. Adam's weary weight presses the bed beside my legs.

"You said your mom was sending a photograph," he says.

"Yes."

"What's in it?"

"Nothing. Just Sam and me as kids."

Laverne hops up on the bed, teetering between us. The sound of her purr is ridiculously loud.

"It's weird," Adam says, and his voice is soft, musing. "Your mother tells me all about your brother every time she calls. You won't talk about him even when I ask."

"I don't know what to talk about," I say, remembering the queasy feeling of having to answer questions, questions. Police with radios; reporters with cameras; detectives with notepads and busy scribbling pens. My mother hovering nearby, afraid I might say the wrong thing, afraid that our family would look as if there were something terribly wrong with us. Afraid of what happens when people begin their talk in a small town like Horton, people who would say it was all my mother's fault for being a career woman, a women's libber, a woman who'd lost sight of her duty to her husband. I would have said anything to protect her. I would have said anything to re-create my brother in the image she held up to us all.

"Then don't talk about anything," Adam says. "Just talk. Just tell me *something*."

And so I describe the pumpkin my father bought from the Luchterhands, so big Sam and I could both sit inside it. "After my mother took the picture," I say, "my father told me to get out of the pumpkin so she could take one of Sam alone. He asked if Sam could fit inside all the way, and when Sam scrunched down, my father fit the top back on and sat on it so Sam couldn't get out. We hadn't carved the face yet. At first, Sam was laughing, and my mother and I were laughing too, but my father put his finger to his lips. Then we heard Sam say something, and then he screamed, and the whole pumpkin began to shake. He was three or so, and my mother was pulling at my father and saying, *Gordon, please, you're scaring him,* and my father was laughing and saying she should lighten up. After a while, Sam stopped making noise and it got very still, so my father said, *All right,* and he lifted up the top. Sam had wet himself, and so my father spanked him."

The baby shifts inside me, a twinkling sense of motion. I try to imagine all the things to come: first steps, first words, wet kisses, lengthening limbs and complicated rages, slamming bedroom doors, car doors, front doors leading to the sidewalk, to the street, to the town and the whole wide world. I know my mother believes that by bringing Sam back, she can finally put things right. I want to believe that too. But here are the shapes of my brother and his friends moving through my room on careless tiptoe. Here is my brother's face, close to mine. Here I am looking into his cool stare and finding nothing that I recognize. How will I feel if, someday, I look into my own child's face and see that same flat stare? Adam puts his arm around me; I touch his sandpapery elbow.

"I finished the jack-o'-lanterns," he says. "You want to see?"

I get up and follow him out of the bedroom. The long hallway leading toward the living room seems like the tunnel we are told to expect when approaching death, the walls pulsing with a peculiar glow, the light at the end drawing us closer, close. The living room is alive with jack-o'-lanterns: flickering on the mantelpiece above the fireplace, leering from the log grate below, hunkered down in a row along the coffee table, balanced on the wide windowsill. Now I see that Adam had these places in mind when he chose the pumpkins this afternoon; no longer awkward or oddly shaped, each one seems perfect, tucked neatly into the bookshelf, snuggled in the cat's round wicker bed. I turn to let the shadows lap their way around my body. The pumpkin smell thickens the candles' scents: pine, vanilla, lavender, rich enough to eat. I'm dizzy with their odor, their color, Adam's arms spinning around me like a welcoming web, snug and warm.

"Sometimes I still believe in God," I say.

Adam shakes his head, his rough cheek scratching mine. He holds me tighter. "I can't even imagine what it's like to believe in something like that."

The jack-o'-lanterns keep their silence, eyes brimming with light, and I'm a small child sitting beside my mother as she drives along the web of rural highways leading home. Which way is north? I ask, and my mother points straight ahead of us.

How do you know?

I just do.

But how?

In the distance, in the wide spaces between smudged clumps of trees, shapes appear and fade like ghosts: here the peaked roof of a farmhouse, there a fat silo, the horizon seamless as the silent fields, sealed for the season beneath a bitter crust of ice. I notice places where deer have pawed away the snow, tearing at the dead winter grasses, the last of the maples and fruit trees stripped bare by hungry mouths. But I can't see *north*, and my mother never can explain to me how she feels it, how—like Adam—she was born with a perfect sense of direction. You can blindfold her and spin her around, and she'll still be able to tell you *north, southeast. West. West again.*

Back by Dark

(1984–1987)

Eight

*M*y favorite practice room at the Peabody Conservatory had windows that reached from the floor to the ceiling. I liked to open them all, though it was bad for the piano, and stand on the sill overlooking Charles Street and the George Washington Monument. Below, pedestrians walked along the cobblestone sidewalks: well-dressed people and homeless people pushing shopping carts, people holding the hands of children, people of different races and ages, people I would never see again and would not remember having seen. Even though we shared a city, a neighborhood, a street, we'd always be strangers. Sometimes one of them would look up, see me standing in the open window; once, a young man cupped his hand to his mouth and hollered, "Jump!" For a moment, I thought it was Sam; it *could* have been Sam. But by the time I ran down the three flights of stairs and out onto the street, he was gone. I saw Sam everywhere: in the grocery store, feeding seagulls at the harbor, waiting in line at the Morris Mechanic Theater, boarding a bus that wouldn't wait when I waved my arms. Nights, I'd stand in the practice room window, the skyline lit up with orange-tinted pollution, and I wondered if he was out there somewhere, watching me back. Perhaps he was waiting outside my practice room, and when I came out he'd grab my purse, my watch, my portable metronome. *You got anything else?* he'd say, just as he had that night in Horton. Sometimes I imagined receiving an envelope with Elise's ring inside. And a note, unsigned, of course: *I'm sorry. The other boys made me. I can explain.*

But no envelope came; no one was ever waiting outside my practice room door. In Horton, someone reported having seen Sam at the Laundromat in Fall Creek; someone else claimed he was in Milwaukee, hiding out from the law. There was a rumor that the police had enough evidence to charge him with Mrs. Baumbach's assault, but that wasn't true—there was no evidence at all, and Mrs. Baumbach could not remember enough about that night to make a coherent statement. In September, several weeks after I'd left for Baltimore, two of Sam's Milwaukee friends were picked up for questioning. Though there was nothing to connect them to Mrs. Baumbach, they were eventually charged and convicted of robbing both Becker's Foodmart and Dr. Neidermier's house. Under oath, they swore no one else had been with them. My mother, jubilant over this new evidence of Sam's innocence, sent me a clipping from our local weekly. When I saw the pictures of the two men, I recognized the two friends Sam had led into my room. I balled up the clipping and stuffed it in the trash. I tried to forget I'd seen it.

My parents had hired their own detective to look for Sam, someone recommended by a missing-children organization in Milwaukee. Saint John's Church took up a special collection to pay for an ad that ran in newspapers across the Midwest. But by now he'd been gone for over two months, and the police said there was little more they could do. He wasn't dead, but he wasn't alive either. He was in limbo, in a strange purgatory, and I was in my own. Had something awful really happened to him? Or was he merely hiding out somewhere? Should I grieve, should I be angry?

When people at school asked me, "Do you have any brothers and sisters?" I didn't know what to say.

I called Horton twice a week, waiting in line for the pay phone at the end of the dormitory hall. My mother acted as if Sam would be back at any moment. She changed the sheets on his bed once a week so that they wouldn't smell musty, and when athletic socks went on sale at Sears, she bought him a dozen pairs. "You know how he goes through socks," she said. My father developed ulcers, and one day, stooping down to pick up a newspaper, he slipped a disk in his back. At fifty-nine, he'd decided to retire from Fountain Ford at the end of the year. "Ready to come home yet?" he'd say. "Want your old dad to come get you?" Each time I talked with him, he sounded more wooden, resigned.

He hadn't wanted me to attend a school outside the state, but by the beginning of my junior year of high school, I had won several regional competitions, and my teacher, Mr. Robertson, believed I had a shot at attending one of the better conservatories: Eastman or Peabody, Curtis or even Juilliard. With my mother's permission, he took me to see a pianist named Peter Kozansky. We met in Kozansky's studio, on the east side of Milwaukee; it had two grand pianos, built-in bookshelves, and dozens of flowering African violets. I'd never been inside such a beautiful room. "Impress me," Kozansky said, and he paced the hardwood floors as I played the first movement of a Prokofiev sonata. I wasn't fully convinced I wanted to study music as a profession, even though everyone seemed to think it was my destiny. I was, according to Mr. Robertson, "big on emotion and short on intellect," and I knew that further study would involve the dry mathematics I hated. So when Kozansky said, "Enough," I was quietly relieved—until I saw that he was smiling. Would I do him the honor of becoming his youngest student? His lessons cost one hundred dollars an hour, far more than I could pay, but he brushed my concerns away with one expressive hand. He'd see me twice a week, and I would pay twenty dollars per lesson. If that was too much, I would pay less. I said I would have to ask my parents.

"Two lessons a week," my father said that night at supper. "Do you forget what they tell you the first time?"

Sam wasn't eating. He pushed the food around on his plate, breaking it up into little piles.

"Don't tease her, Gordon," my mother said. "This is a great opportunity."

"Who's going to pay for this great opportunity?" my father said. Once, that would have been enough to put an end to the discussion, but now that my mother had her own income, she could pay for my lessons if he wouldn't—and all of us knew it. "Goddamn it, Sam," he said suddenly. "Would you stop acting like a three-year-old and eat your food?"

"Can I have ten dollars?" Sam said. "It's for school."

"You can come to work for me, how's that?" my father said. He wanted Sam to detail cars at the lot on Saturdays and Sundays.

"You spend all this money on Abby because she's a girl," Sam said. "If I have to work, *she* should have to."

"We spend all this money on Abby because she's a hard worker," my father said, switching sides.

Now my mother jumped to Sam's defense. "Sam's a hard worker too."

"Then he can prove it to me at the lot. This Saturday, sport, eight to three."

"You can't make me," Sam said.

"Wanna bet on that, son?"

I excused myself from the table, cleared my dishes, and went into the living room to practice. Perhaps Sam and my father continued their fight; perhaps my father pulled Sam out of his chair, knocking his plate to the floor. Perhaps my mother was screaming, "Enough! Enough! Can't we just once have a quiet dinner like a normal family?" Or perhaps not. As soon as I touched the keys,

I wasn't aware of anything but the music I created. It was the same thing I felt when I prayed, a warm feeling of purpose, completeness, rightness. My grandmother said it was a *state of grace.*

But at Peabody, all of that changed. I spent eight hours every day in a practice room, in addition to ensemble rehearsals, ear-training classes, more classes in composition, conducting, foreign languages. I'd sit down to play the piano, and instead of losing myself in melody, I identified sequences, fumbled notes, forgot passages. For the first time in my life, I doubted my ear and relied on sheet music; at night, when I knelt down to pray, no words came. I slept in on Sunday mornings. I skipped classes, missed rehearsals, failed to complete my weekly piano assignment. One night in December, I climbed all the way out of the practice room window and lowered myself down to the ledge, where I sat with my feet dangling over Charles Street. My breath left my mouth in dreamy clouds. Christmas trees and menorahs shone in the windows of the apartments across Monument Square; streetlights glistened with wreaths. I listened to the sounds coming from the other practice rooms—a frenzied clarinet, a stubborn bassoon, dozens of violins—and then, with equal interest, I listened to the drawl of traffic, the occasional blaring car horn, the voices of pedestrians, who passed briefly into my life and then continued out of it. I'd been raised to believe that every least thing in our lives happened for a reason, and these reasons were born like seeds within the infinite mind of God. But what was the significance of the woman who walked below me now, wrapped in a long purple coat, carrying a black satchel? What was the meaning of my brother's disappearance, the long, bitter complaint my parents' marriage had become, my own musical talent, which, I knew now, was neither extraordinary nor miraculous? I'd met lots of people who could play the piano as well as I did, and they didn't have dead aunts to guide them. Some of them didn't even believe in God. And at that moment, I realized two things: I no longer believed in the Church, and I didn't want to study music anymore.

The knowledge hit me with the same unquestionable intensity Harv had described when he'd talked about his vocation. I shivered, my hands gripping the ledge. What was I going to do?

"How'd it go tonight?" Phoebe said when I came back to our room. It was only midnight; I'd reserved the piano until one. She was lying in her bed, reading Arthur Rubinstein's autobiography.

"All right," I lied. I felt changed, brittle, empty. Maybe I was just tired, and I'd feel different in the morning. Maybe I should call Harv, now a seminarian at Marquette, or even Kozansky—although his advice had always been: "The moment the piano fails to exhilarate you, go into real estate." I undressed, lay down on my bed, threw an arm across my eyes to block out the light.

"What's wrong?" Phoebe asked.

"I'm sick of everything."

"Me too," she said, and she turned out the light. "Hang in there. It's only two weeks till winter break."

Whenever Sam and I came in from playing in the fields, from wandering through the pines, from riding our bikes up and down the long gravel driveway, it was always my mother we looked for. We were her children, the way the dishes in the kitchen were her dishes. If my father was there, we'd ask him, "Where's Mom?" pushing past as if he didn't count, as if we barely noticed he was there. Perhaps he was only trying to get our attention, to force us to interact with him, when he'd answer, as he so often did, "She's hiding."

"No, where is she?"

"I'm serious. She got sick of you both and ran away."

"Da-ad."

"She's never coming back."

"I'm right here," my mother would call from the laundry

room in the basement, from the bathroom, from her bedroom. "Gordon, you shouldn't tease them like that."

One day, we came home from school to find my father sitting at the kitchen table. This was odd; he rarely got home before suppertime. "Where's Mom?" we asked. She'd recently started her job at the *Sell It Now!*, but we knew she wasn't at work because it wasn't one of her scheduled days. When my father, in an odd, wobbly voice, told us that she'd been taken to the hospital, we didn't believe him. "No, really, where is she?" we asked, waiting for him to tell us she was hiding, to hear my mother's footsteps coming from the back of the house, to listen to her scold, *Gordon, stop your teasing.*

"I told you," my father said, and then he said that her appendix had burst, that she'd had emergency surgery and was very, very sick. Sam giggled nervously, because my father simply didn't talk this way, with his face close to ours, with his voice nearly breaking. "C'mon, Dad, where's Mom?" he said, and my father jumped up and spanked him, first with his hand and then with the decorative wooden spoon my mother kept hanging on the wall. "Don't joke around with me," he shouted. "I'm warning you kids, this is no time for jokes."

In my room, we spoke in whispers. By now I believed my mother really was in the hospital, but Sam could not be convinced. "She's here," he said. "We just have to find her." His eyes were red from holding back tears. He searched under all the beds, in the hall linen closet, in the big cedar chest filled with keepsakes that we were forbidden to touch. There was no sign of my mother anywhere; in fact, her nightgown and bathrobe were missing from the hook behind the bathroom door. Sam would not give up. He slipped down the stairs and made a stumbling run for the barn. From the window, I watched as he squeezed between the warped double doors, reappeared, then disappeared briefly into the smokehouse. By the time my father called us downstairs for supper, Sam was back in our room.

I couldn't remember my father ever cooking before. He served us at the dining room table: toast, summer sausage, butter, milk, soft-cooked eggs, Cheerios, and two Flintstones vitamins apiece. Halfway through the meal, Sam excused himself and went into the kitchen. From the noises he was making, I knew he was still looking—in the tall cupboard that held the garbage pail, in the coat closet, in the mudroom. When he finally came back to the table, he was carrying the dull scissors my mother used for cutting garden flowers. His spanking had left him sore: I could tell by the way he moved, step by careful step. But something else was wrong: He looked different, older, deadly calm.

"What are you doing with that?" my father said. "Sit down and finish your supper."

"Where's Mom?" Sam demanded, and he raised the scissors over his head like a murderer in a cartoon. I felt everything I had eaten swim up into my throat and lodge there in a pulsing, sour knot.

My father blinked at Sam, then easily faked him out with his left hand while grabbing the scissors with his right. He tossed the scissors into the kitchen. "Jesus Christ!" he said, clamping Sam's hips between his knees and pinching his arms to his sides. They were eye-to-eye, mouths hanging open. Sometimes my father would challenge Sam to a wrestling match, and Sam—knowing he would not be allowed to refuse—charged violently. My father would let him twist and grunt for several minutes before offhandedly pinning him against the carpet. "Uncle," my father would say, until Sam repeated the word.

"Now say Uncle Sam."

"Uncle Sam."

"Uncle Sam please."

"Uncle Sam please."

"Gordon, you're hurting him," my mother would say.

"Uncle Sam please with a cherry."

"Uncle Sam—"

"Get off him, Gordon. I mean it."

My father would get up then and call Sam a sissy who needed his mommy to rescue him. And Sam would cry with rage, his cheek a bright red smear where my father had rubbed it back and forth against the carpet.

But this time Sam wasn't backing down. "What did you do to Mom?" he said, his face inches from my father's. "Tell me or *I'll kill you!*"

His voice was high, a kettle's desperate whistle, and something in my father seemed to give beneath that sound. "Look, sport," he said, releasing Sam's hips. "You just calm down, OK? I'll let your grandma explain it to you."

He got up, dialed my grandmother's number, and passed the phone to Sam. For a long time, Sam didn't say anything. Then he began to nod. Yes, he would pray for her. Yes, he would be a good boy while she was gone. He hung up and went upstairs to our room without looking at either of us. My father sat back down at the table, rubbing his temples with the tips of his fingers, an oddly delicate gesture.

"What gets into you kids?" he asked. It was clear he did not expect an answer.

My mother came home from the hospital with gifts for Sam and me: neat bars of hospital soap, paper shoes, a handful of tongue depressors. She let us look at her stitches and promised we could touch her scar as soon as it healed. When I tried to tell her about the scissors, the spanking, she didn't seem to hear what I was saying. Instead, she looked vaguely uncomfortable, the way she had the time my father sprained my shoulder, or the time he'd broken Sam's finger roughhousing, or the time Sam left his bicycle behind my father's car despite my father's warnings, and my father had backed over it deliberately. "I'm sure your father did the best he could," she said, and that was the end of it. Certainly my father never brought it up again. And so I doubted myself. Maybe I was exaggerating. Maybe I was making things up or misunderstanding what I'd seen.

In Baltimore, the night before I went home for Christmas, I packed everything I could carry: clothes, books, musical scores, stuffed animals, keepsakes, letters, folders of notes and completed assignments. "You're just going home for two weeks," Phoebe said. She was pacing wary circles around my matching faux-leather suitcases, garment bag, overnight bag, and carry-on case.

"Two and a half," I said.

The smallest of the suitcases was open; she knelt down to look inside. "Syllabi?" she said. "A campus map? Salt and pepper shakers—from the cafeteria? Nice touch. Oh, and six bars of soap. Of course." I was busy trying to cram my second swimming suit into a side pocket of the garment bag. A glove popped out like a drowning hand. "Abby, your parents will have soap, don't you think?"

How could I explain that I was afraid the past few months would disappear as soon as I opened my parents' front door?

My last final was on the morning of Christmas Eve; my parents picked me up at the airport that night. I was shocked by the gray in my father's hair. He hugged me briefly, awkwardly, before stepping back to let my mother throw her arms around me. Then none of us seemed to know what to say. As we went to get my luggage, I noticed how my parents didn't look directly at each other, how they kept their bodies separate, distant. "How are you?" they kept asking me. "How are *you?*" I'd ask back. But when my luggage came down the conveyor belt, item after item, that finally broke the ice. "Good God," my father said, restored to his own self. "I better go get a skycap. What did you do, bring the whole damn state of Maryland with you?"

"This isn't just an overnight stay," my mother defended me. "She probably had to bring a lot of schoolwork with her."

My father's back was clearly bothering him; still, he insisted on lifting each piece of luggage off the conveyor belt. I checked each one for my name. I hoped I had brought enough.

The next morning, I woke up at dawn, and for a moment I couldn't remember where I was. I listened for the traffic noise of Charles Street, but all I heard was silence. Then I remembered I was home. It was Christmas. I groped for the nightstand lamp; it was gone. Lots of things weren't where I'd remembered them to be: the owl-shaped wall clock in the kitchen; the collapsible TV trays in the living room; the portable TV in the kitchen. I assumed that my father had taken them to the shed, which was where, for all practical purposes, he was living. After coming home from the airport, he'd surprised me by saying good night at the kitchen door. Not knowing what else to do, I'd simply watched him cross the snowy yard to the shed. "I'll see you tomorrow, then," I called suddenly, and he waved before going inside.

"Do you eat separately too?" I'd asked my mother.

"Oh, goodness no," she said. "He just sleeps better there. Our bed irritates his back. By the way," she said, changing the subject, "I told Father Van Dan you'd sing the offertory at noon Mass."

"You did?"

"Just the Ave Maria. He only called yesterday to ask. Serina Oben was going to do it, but she's ill. I didn't think you'd mind."

Aside from chorus practice once a week, I hadn't sung all semester; this morning, I'd have some serious warming up to do. I got dressed by touch, my eyes gradually adjusting to the darkness, which was not darkness, I realized, but a vague, grainy dullness. There was light coming from somewhere. But who could be up this early? I opened my door and followed the light down the stairs and into the living room, where my father was standing by the mantel, clean-shaven, neatly dressed in corduroys and a button-down shirt and his leather bomber jacket.

"Good morning," he said, as if I still came down these steps every day. "I'm glad you're up."

"Hi," I said. "Merry Christmas."

"Yeah," my father said, and he made a wry face at the bare room. "Not much of a Christmas, huh?" There were no decorations; there was no Christmas tree. The house was the most orderly I'd ever seen it. The last of our cats, a battered gray tom, had died, and now there were no pets, no children, no family to clutter rooms that had seemed so much larger when I was young. "Say, look what I found," my father said. He held up a small orange ashtray made of coiled clay, an old school project of mine. I reached for it, but he put it on top of the mantel, carefully, as if it might crumble away.

"Sam was just five when he made that."

"I made it," I said.

He smiled at me the way adults smile at a child who is telling a lie.

"My initials are on the bottom."

"Those are Sam's initials," my father said. "Your mother can have it, if she wants."

"That's nice," I said. Perhaps Sam *had* made it. He'd had to make ashtrays in art class too.

"Tell her it's a Christmas present," my father said.

"You can tell her yourself," I said, and then I teased him, saying, "So where's *my* Christmas present?"

"I thought I saw a bag of coal outside," he teased back. "Have a cup of java with your old man," he said, and I followed him into the kitchen, where the coffee was already made.

"What time did *you* get up?" I said. He filled two mugs that had the Fountain Ford logo on one side and a slogan on the other. One said I'M THE BOSS; the other said DON'T BLAME ME. They were Christmas gifts from his staff. Each year, he got a new mug, a new slogan.

"Oh, fivish," my father said. "I want to be on the road by

six." The mugs steamed madly in the chilly air. "Choose," he said, and I took I'M THE BOSS. "Your mother's daughter, aren't you?" my father said.

"Where are you going?"

He seemed genuinely surprised that I would ask. "Didn't your mother tell you?" he said. He sat down at the kitchen table, pulled out a chair for me, and worked an oversize brochure from the inside pocket of his leather jacket. I looked at a series of glossy pictures: palm trees, boats, a fountain. Neat rows of trailers, identically landscaped, with tiny screened-in porches. " 'Pleasant Acres Adult Community,' " my father read aloud. " 'Pineland, Florida. Live the life of leisure in a mature environment.' "

"Are you going to live there?" I asked stupidly.

My father nodded. "Friday was my last day at Fountain. Got my gold watch, plus they gave me a pair of sunglasses. Ray Bans." He went through his pockets. "I guess they're already out in the car. They gave me a couple of those plastic flamingos too." He laughed.

"What about Mom?" I said.

My father drained his coffee cup and stood up. "Your mother isn't going anywhere," he said. "Your mother is going to stay right here and wait for your brother, for Sam . . ." His voice faltered. "You know, the goddamn cops aren't even looking anymore," he said, and he wiped his nose with the back of his hand. Then he handed me the brochure. "You can keep this, OK? And give your mother the ashtray. Don't forget."

He started to zip up his jacket. Then he stopped. "Hell," he said, looking down at it. "I sure won't be needing this where I'm going." It was an old bomber jacket I'd admired for years. "You want it?" he asked.

"Sure."

"Put it on," he said, and I did. The cuffs came to my fingertips; the shoulders were big and boxy. It was perfect, and I thanked him. "Merry Christmas!" he said. "There, something you like! I must be an OK father after all! One of you kids survived me anyway." He laughed bitterly.

"You were OK," I said. I didn't know what else to say.

He ran his hands through his hair. He looked at me, a quick, grateful glance, then looked away. "Well," he said, "you be careful. Take good care of yourself. Let me know if you need anything." He tugged affectionately at one of the jacket's lapels, turned, and left the house. It was starting to get light. I watched from the kitchen window as his Ford coasted down the snowy drive, the back seat packed to the roof. I wondered which pieces of his life with us he was taking along, which things he'd chosen to forget, to leave behind. It occurred to me that I might never see him again—too late, I wanted to run after him and tell him to stop. His wheels spun briefly at the bottom, where my mother was always getting stuck, but then the car lurched forward onto the highway, taillights glaring north.

I put the brochure in my new jacket pocket and wandered uneasily from room to room, sipping at my lukewarm coffee. I thought about the lamp that had disappeared from my bedside and imagined my father moving through the house, fingering this, deliberating over that, distilling the past into whatever fit best inside a four-door sedan. Already, the rooms were reshaping themselves, swallowing his absence the way they had swallowed my brother's. Soon there would be no clue, no sign, that either of them had ever lived here.

Except Sam's ashtray. I picked it up, enjoying the good firm weight of it in my hand, before flipping it over to read the underside. AES/1970. My own childish scrawl. I put it back on the mantel. I wanted to smash it. The stairway creaked, and I turned to see my mother coming down the stairs in her robe and a pair of glaringly new pink slippers.

"Where is your father going this early?" she said. She yawned, then covered her mouth after she'd finished. "You look good in his jacket."

"He gave it to me." I managed to keep my voice from shaking. "He's gone."

"Gone where?" she said. She came over to the mantel and picked up the ashtray. "My goodness, I haven't seen this in a while! Did Sam make it? I can't remember."

"I did," I said, my voice rising. "Dad left it for your Christmas present. Mom, did you know Dad was moving to Florida?"

My mother looked at me. "Is he leaving today?"

"*Mom,*" I shouted. "He just left!"

"Oh," she said. "Oh. I had asked him to wait until after Christmas."

"What's going on?" I said. "Why hasn't anybody told me anything? Are you getting a divorce?"

"I don't believe in that sort of thing," she said. "I've been telling him that for weeks."

I knew that if I didn't leave the room, I would grab her and shake her until her teeth rattled. "Can I get you a cup of coffee?" I said. I was amazed at how calm I sounded. "Dad made some before he left."

"That would be lovely," she said politely, and I knew that, at that moment, I could have offered her anything—a glass of cold water, a box of crayons, Sam's safe return—and she would have replied in the same way. "Look in the bread box too, if you would," she said, still gracious and lost. "There's a wonderful fruitcake from Thillie in there somewhere."

We wound up splitting the fruitcake, which was heavy with rum, and to help along my father's weak coffee, my mother brought out the bottle of Old Grouse he kept in the cupboard above the refrigerator. For a while, things started to look better. I turned on the radio, and we sang along with the Christmas carols. "Let's celebrate!" my mother said giddily. "I'm a bachelor now—I mean, a bachelorette!" And we made Christmas pancakes with walnuts and peach preserves; we ate strawberry ice cream and cold mashed potatoes and cherry Jell-O avalanched with Cool

Whip topping. It was such a disappointment to discover all the Old Grouse was gone. But there *was* an unopened bottle of Bailey's Irish Cream, a gift from one of my father's business associates.

"Wait!" my mother said, and she scampered up the stairs. I glanced uneasily at the bare space where the clock used to hang above the sink. I suspected that it was around ten o'clock; I was supposed to sing in two hours. But when my mother came back with two long-stemmed champagne glasses from the attic, I let her fill them up with Bailey's, and after a while she filled them up again.

"These glasses are great," I told her. "Where did you get them?"

"The Quick Stop. They were free with a ten-dollar gas purchase."

"You can't even tell," I said.

"I can tell," my mother said. "Everything I own came free with something else. Or it was on sale or it had a crack or stain somewhere. Or it was cheaper than the one I really wanted."

She licked her finger and rubbed it around the rim of her glass. It didn't hum; it squeaked. "What am I going to do?" she said. After Mass, she and my father and I were expected for Christmas dinner at my grandmother's. Thil and Olaf would be there, and Monica and her fiancé, Ray. Only Harv, who was on retreat, would be missing. And Sam, of course. And, it seemed, my father. And now my mother and I. We'd broken our fast with fruitcake, pancakes, whiskey, and Bailey's—how could we show up for Mass and not take Communion? Besides, my mother was still in her robe and slippers, and when we looked at the living room clock we discovered that, somehow, it had become eleven forty-five, and Oneisha was ten miles away.

My mother was crying, little sneaky tears, which she furiously wiped away. "What will your grandmother say when she hears about Gordon?"

"We don't have to tell her today," I said. "Half the time,

Dad makes some excuse and stays home anyway. She probably won't even notice."

"But the offertory. Oh my God, think of all those people sitting there, waiting to hear you sing. They'll think you were in an accident or something, they'll think you . . ." My mother was searching for the worst thing she could think of, and I winced as I saw the options march across her face. "I've made you commit a mortal sin," she said. "Missing Mass."

I took a deep breath. This seemed as good a time as any to tell her my life was falling to pieces too. "Mom," I said, not looking at her. "I haven't been going to Mass. And I haven't been practicing either. I don't think I want to stay at Peabody."

"Do I seem drunk to you?" she said. "I've never been drunk before. Well, maybe tipsy once or twice. But not like this."

She hadn't been listening. I didn't know whether to feel disappointed or relieved.

"You seem drunk," I assured her, and she beamed at me as if I'd told her she was beautiful.

"You get drunk too," she said.

"OK."

"But not too drunk. Because you'll have to call your grandmother later. I don't think I can do it. You'll have to tell her something. Tell her we overslept."

"OK."

"Why is everything falling apart?" my mother said.

"It isn't," I said, although it was.

"Maybe your grandmother is right," my mother said. "Maybe this is all my fault. Maybe I should have stayed home with you kids and kept house and agreed with everything your father said. Maybe that should have been enough." She stood up, weaving, and headed toward the stairway. "I'm going to take a little nap."

"You need help?" I said, but she didn't answer. I could hear her moving down the upstairs hall, the creak of the springs as she sank into bed. Then silence. *Where's Mom?* I heard Sam say, and I jumped up, shivering, and poured the rest of my drink back into the bottle, something my father had always done, saying, *Alcohol kills germs—even mine.* It was noon. In Oneisha, the Mass was beginning without us. My grandmother was sitting in her usual pew, with Auntie Thil and Uncle Olaf and Monica beside her. Father Van Dan was pacing up and down the hall, two nervous altar boys trailing him like woebegone angels. How long, he was wondering, should we wait for Abigail? Somewhere, my father was listening to the radio, steering with his knees the way he liked to do, muttering about gas mileage and shortcuts. Somewhere, my brother was thinking of us or not thinking of us, my brother was alive or he was dead, and it didn't really matter because there was no one to know which it was except maybe God, and God had His hands pressed over His mouth, sucking on the truth like a sour-apple candy, smug as any spoiled child refusing to share.

By the time he was in high school, my brother stopped asking for my mother; it was my father who asked after Sam. *Where is he?* my father would say, coming home from work, coming in from the shed. Perhaps Sam was kept after school? Or maybe he was in his room? Or studying at a friend's? In fact, nobody knew where Sam went on those nights he didn't come home until dawn, those days when he left for school and the principal called to say he had never arrived. Often, we'd sit down to eat without him, because Sam would come home late or not at all. "Where is he, goddamnit!" my father said one night, jabbing his fork into his peas so hard the plate seemed to chime the late hour. "Six-thirty sharp we eat. How many times do I have to tell him that?"

He pushed back his chair and stood up. "I've got work tonight at Fountain," he said. "I'll be home by nine, and Sam better be here." But minutes after he'd left the house, he came back inside. His hands were shaking; his arms and jaw were shaking. "That little fucker," he said. I had never heard him use that word before; I never heard him use it again.

"What happened?" my mother said, but my father did not answer. He opened the refrigerator and stared intently into that cold blue light.

I followed my mother outside. It was dusk, September, and each step shouted with leaves. My father's Ford was parked with its nose to the shed, and my mother stopped behind it. "Sam," she said. "Get up now, honey, get up," but I still didn't see him. Then the darkness behind my father's back tires took shape, and my brother crawled out. He was sixteen years old, drunk and laughing. Red and gold leaves were pressed like pleading hands to his face and hair and chest.

It was almost four in the afternoon by the time we finally left the house, my mother walking too carefully over the ice. When we reached the car, she handed me the keys, though I didn't feel very well either. "I am never going to make it through this," she said. She'd been chanting these words like a prayer ever since my grandmother phoned early in the afternoon, worrying about what had happened to us. "We overslept," I said, and this was partially true. I'd decided to lie down on the couch for a few minutes and had fallen asleep for two hours. When the phone rang, I'd been vaulted into the air by the sudden charged clarity of knowing exactly who was calling and why.

"Well, come for dinner at least," my grandmother said. "We're happy to wait till you get here."

I could hear my mother vomiting in the bathroom upstairs.

"Actually," I said, "Mom's kind of sick. I think she picked up the flu."

"It could be food poisoning," my grandmother said. Then, "Does she have a fever?"

"I don't know. I mean, I don't think so. I think she just needs to rest," I said. "You go ahead and eat. I'm sorry about all this, Grandma. I'll apologize to Father Van Dan. I—"

"Let me speak to your mother."

"She's getting sick," I said, truthfully.

"Your father, then."

"He isn't here."

My grandmother sighed, and when she spoke, her voice shook with terrible sadness. "Olaf heard a rumor that Gordon was moving out." My mother was coming down the stairs. Her eyes were red, wet-looking. *Grandma?* she mouthed, and when I nodded *Yes,* she held out her hand for the phone, but I turned away.

My grandmother said, "Is it true?"

I didn't say anything.

"It's all right," my grandmother said. "Your mother's standing right there, isn't she?"

"Yes."

"Do you think she'll feel better later this afternoon?"

"I think so," I said.

"Then come over when you're ready," my grandmother said. "Abigail, please, it's Christmas. I'll be expecting both of you."

I hung up, and when I told my mother I'd promised we would come later, her face took on the expression people use to face the inevitable: surgery, birth, death. "Do you think I'm still drunk?" she asked.

"Hungover."

"Drunk is the better part," she said, and she turned back toward the bathroom.

Now, as I drove down our long gravel driveway, my mother pressed her forehead against the cold window, gulped the damp winter air. It was that delicate time between daylight and dusk when the least brightness seems an exaggeration and the landscape loses its depth. Farmhouses twinkled with red and blue and green Christmas lights, intimate and warm, and they looked almost close enough to touch. We passed a manure spreader outlined in white lights; a mailbox transformed into an elf's toy shop; a stand of young pine trees, each with a gold star lashed to its tip, so that it seemed like a small constellation was hanging only inches above the snowy fields. Just before we crossed the railroad tracks into town, my mother finally lifted her head.

" 'Welcome to Oneisha,' " she said, reading the sign that Uncle Olaf had made years before. Now it was riddled with bullet holes, spackled with ice.

"Oh, God," I said, and I started to laugh because the Hornleins' rooftop was bustling with its usual arrangement of reindeer, and—look!—there was the faded grinning Santa at the Klopps', and, at the Pfiels', the electric-green swing set, quarreling with elves. Over the years, I had come to know each of these decorations by heart, and I loved them because they were familiar to me, because I had been taught to admire them. Now I saw them with the eyes of an outsider. The town looked like a carnival— garish, sparkly, a child playing fancy in rhinestones and glitter.

My mother was laughing too, a bit ruefully, as if it hurt her head. "Let's drive by the crèche," she said, and I turned into the Saint Ignatius parking lot. The crèche was life-size, made of wood, and it stood on a cordoned-off section of asphalt beside the front entrance to the church. There were real bales of hay, evergreen boughs for the floor and the roof, and metal poles for the stanchions. Every few years, all the figures were repainted: white sheep, brown mules, a dark-haired Joseph, a blond and blue-eyed Jesus. The animals wore exaggeratedly human expressions of piety, while the wise men looked at their feet like shy boys at a dance, wondering what to do next. As I pulled up close, my mother's face was bathed in the light of the floodlamps. Together we stared at the crèche. How deliciously warm and sleepy Baby Jesus looked!

"Where's Mary?" my mother said suddenly. "Look, they moved her all the way to the back!"

It was true; Baby Jesus was alone in the foreground, while

Mary knelt, open-armed, beside three candy-pink pigs, a brilliant red rooster. Even Joseph could have touched Jesus from where he stood, his arm resting on the back of a steer. "Can't let a mother get too close. Might sissify the boy," my mother said. She was imitating my father's voice. I had never heard her so bitter. "Let's go," she said, and I pulled away and continued up the street to my grandmother's house.

It was truly dark now, the gunmetal blackness of winter. As we pulled into the driveway, my grandmother opened the front door, waiting. Behind her, the light from the hallway blazed like flames, and yet there she stood, untouched. I thought of a story she'd told me once about a saint who had been thrown into a room of fire. There he'd lived for three days and three nights before emerging, healthy and whole. "Thank goodness," my grandmother said when we came up the walk. "I was afraid you wouldn't come."

"Merry Christmas!" my mother said, accepting my grandmother's kiss.

The remnants of the meal were still on the kitchen table: the half-eaten carcass of the turkey, a few slaughtered pies, green beans congealing in margarine. Why weren't the dishes already done? Where was Uncle Olaf? Where were Monica and her fiancé? Auntie Thil was there, but she was flushed, nervous. Her hands shook as she took our coats and carried them down the hall to my grandmother's bedroom. "Here, sit," my grandmother said, leading us into the living room. "I've sent the others home. I thought we could pray together, come up with a solution to all of this."

"To all of what?" my mother said.

"I know that Gordon's left you," my grandmother said, and my mother stepped back as if someone had struck her. "First your child, now your husband. What's next—I suppose a divorce?"

My mother glanced over at me, a brief terrible look that said, *Traitor.* Then she turned and walked out of the house, leaving the door open behind her. After a moment, Auntie Thil walked down the hall and closed it softly. I thought about my mother's coat, lying limp, dormant, across my grandmother's bed. I thought of the car keys, a cold lump in my pocket, and I wondered where my mother would go. My grandmother reached for my hand, and I pulled it away without thinking, staring at her as if she were someone I'd never seen before. *What right do you have to judge her or anyone?* I wanted to say, except that I was actually saying it, each word torn from my throat.

"Abigail?" my grandmother said. "What did you say?"

I ran down the hall, grabbed our coats, and I left my grandmother's house. Outside, the frozen darkness was pulsing with Christmas lights, bloody red, sickly green. The familiar street looked sinister, a fun house of mirrors and lights from which there was no escape. Where had my mother gone? I checked behind my auntie Thil's house, where the iced-over pond gleamed like an eye. I could see my uncle Olaf watching TV in the den, and I stared at him through the window the way once, at a county fair, I'd stared—fascinated, horrified—into a cow's stomach, which had been fitted with a transparent panel. I walked behind my grandmother's house and came up the side yard and onto the street, where I started toward the hazy glow of the floodlights surrounding the crèche at the church.

At first, I mistook my mother for one of the statues around the Baby Jesus, but then she moved, came closer to the cradle, closer than Joseph, the animals and wise men, until she stood right beside it. Her arms were wrapped around her shoulders, and when I saw her kneel down in that makeshift manger, I realized she meant to stay there for good, to curl herself up and rock herself, rock herself warm in that cold yellow light.

Nine

In the fall of my third year living in Baltimore, two and a half years after I'd left the conservatory, my mother called to say she'd received a letter from my father. He said that he was being watched. He said that he'd been awakened one night by someone trying the locks on his windows and doors. He said he had developed six of the Seven Deadly Warning Signs of cancer and was making out his will. Would she like the Ford?

"I suppose it's none of my business anymore," my mother said. Their divorce had been final for over a year. A priest at Saint John's had told her that as long as she didn't remarry, she was not in a state of mortal sin. "But he doesn't sound like himself."

"Maybe he's drinking."

"Or getting Alzheimer's or something."

"Or maybe it's just age."

"He's only sixty-two, Abby." She sighed. "And I certainly don't want his Ford. He knows what I really want." My father had gone through Sam's bedroom, through the house and the shed and the attic, collecting everything of Sam's that would fit into his car. Even now, my mother didn't know what, exactly, was missing, and this bothered her as much as the missing items themselves. My father, of course, denied he'd taken anything. "I'm entitled to half," my mother said. "I deserve more than that ashtray."

I'd heard all this before, but I was relieved to have a conversation with my mother that wasn't focused on what she referred to as my *lifestyle*. Adam and I were living together in a one-bedroom apartment near the basilica. We'd met in a Laundromat. He'd dropped out of the Baltimore School of Design the semester before I left Peabody, and now he worked as a carpenter. "All that abstraction," he said, "was starting to give me nightmares." I had a full-time job at a thrift shop and a vague idea about returning to school. But the longer I was away from it, the harder it was to make plans to go back. And I wasn't sure what I wanted to study.

"Well, what would you really like to do?" Adam said. "I mean, in your wildest dreams."

"I'd be like that woman who studies gorillas."

"Jane Goodall."

"That's her."

"Biology, then."

But that wasn't what I meant. I wanted a misty morning in the jungle, the cries of strange birds, the solitude of my tent. A place where my grandmother couldn't mail me prayer cards and religious medals and books on prayer; a place where my mother couldn't reach me with yet another far-fetched scheme to find Sam. As each month passed, and there was less and less chance that he'd be found alive—if at all—she became increasingly, unbearably optimistic. She'd enrolled in Christian counseling, encouraging me to do the same. She believed Sam's disappearance was a test of faith, one that she would endure and eventually pass with stained-glass colors.

Two nights later, she called again. This time, my father had phoned her, his voice so soft she barely recognized it. He wanted to know if she'd heard from Sam.

No, she said eagerly. Have you?

Wouldn't you like to know that! he said, and then he told her about senior citizens in Arizona being drugged and carried off to experimental labs against their will.

Is Sam there? my mother said. Have you seen him? Gordon, please! But my father hung up, and she had not been able to reach him since.

"Did you call the police?" I asked.

She had. They'd contacted the police department in Cape Coral, the nearest city of any size, and Homicide sent a detective to visit my father. She judged him a lonely eccentric who knew nothing more than anyone else did. She advised my mother, through the Horton police, to forget about the incident.

"I think it might be better if we handled this ourselves," my mother said. "The police down there don't know your father. They don't realize how he can be."

"What are you going to do?" I said.

"Well," she said, "what if you were to visit him? You could post flyers. I looked at a map, and there are lots of little towns around there. I'd pay your bus ticket, if you'd go."

"I don't know if I can get the time off," I said. But I couldn't help imagining myself as the hero, the one who—against all odds—rescued her brother, returned him safely home, redeemed herself in the eyes of a mother who, for months, had been telling her she'd *thrown away her future*, who gave her gift subscriptions to *The Catholic Digest, Leaves, Guideposts*, who warned her that God has ways of making stubborn people listen to His voice.

"For all we know, Sam could be there right now," my mother said. "Maybe Sam's the one who's been watching him. Maybe he saw himself on TV."

"Maybe," I said.

A few weeks earlier, my mother had been interviewed on a talk show, along with other parents whose lost children—if alive—would be adults by now. There, on national television, Sam's face was displayed, first as a seventeen-year-old, then aged three years by forensic experts. They showed him clean-shaven, mustached, bearded. They showed him wearing different styles of hair.

"You can ask the neighbors if they've noticed any visitors. You can post a flyer, in case he shows up nearby."

"What if Dad doesn't want me to visit?" I said. "I mean, we haven't exactly kept in touch." In fact, I'd sent him cards on his birthday, but he'd never acknowledged them, or sent me anything on mine.

My mother paused. I could hear her clicking her tongue against the roof of her mouth, a habit that meant she was formulating a careful reply. "I just wouldn't tell him you're coming," she said. "And while you're there, if you wouldn't mind, you could ask him what he's done with Sam's things."

The next day, the owner of the thrift shop gave me a week off without complaint. "You've been with us over a year," she said, and I felt the long, gray winter of my failure. If I wasn't careful, I might end up spending the rest of my life in that same dark shop, collecting my minimum-wage check twice a month, worrying because I had no health insurance. That night, desperate for any kind of change, I cut my long thick hair in front of the bathroom mirror and, afterward, buzzed it with my Lady Bic. "Good God," Adam said when I came back into the living room, but I liked how it made me look: knowing but indifferent. The sort of look my father would despise on any woman. The sort of look that Sam would recognize.

Now I was tired, catching a cold, cramped by the duffel bag I'd wedged into the tight space between my feet and the seat ahead of me. It was October, one week before Halloween, and the bus—the last in a series of complicated transfers—was hot and sour-smelling. The cutout paper jack-o'-lanterns in the windows we passed seemed too vivid, frightening in a way I'd never noticed up north. Gaping mouths. Glowing orange teeth. Faces as round as the souls we used to draw in Sunday school, rising from their unsuspecting bodies. All Souls' Day—we weren't supposed to say Halloween—was followed by All Saints'. Still sick from trick-or-treat candy, we dressed as saints and marched into the church holding candles, singing "When the Saints Come Marching In." My mother would be sitting on the outside edge of the pew so that she could wave to me and Sam as we walked past, hot wax nipping our fingers. I always chose to be Saint Cecilia, the patron saint of music, who was beheaded after she refused to marry a wealthy man. For three days and nights she lay dying in her cell, while beautiful music filled the air. As a teenager, I'd sit at Elise's piano with my hands spread over the keys, praying to hear what Cecilia heard as she was drawn up into heaven by the force of God's desire.

I believed these stories in a way my brother never did. I hoped that I too might be chosen, God's capricious wishes revealed, my life irrevocably changed. When Sam first disappeared, I was strangely envious that he'd been singled out, the prodigal son who'd come back to a grand celebration. But now, ironically, I was the one returning to my father.

The bus finally arrived in Pineland, which was no more than a dozen houses, a gas station, and a fruit stand. We stopped at a crossroads, where several people got off, before continuing on toward the Pleasant Acres Adult Community, two miles down the road. I carried my duffel up the long crushed-shell driveway, past the trailers with their birdbaths and plaster rabbits and windmill ducks, until I reached number 26, solemn and plain, its curtains pinched like wary eyes. I saw the Ford in the carport, and I knew my father was home. Slick with sweat, I climbed up the porch steps, dropped my duffel and rang the buzzer. Immediately I heard footsteps moving away from the door. The light behind the front curtains dimmed. The rooms seemed to hold their breath.

I leaned on the buzzer again, imagining the sound like a needle, stinging the tender back of my father's neck. I pictured him flattened in his La-Z-Boy, the volume on the TV turned down to a hum as he waited for me to go away. Or perhaps he was crouching below the kitchen counter, the way Sam and I once did, warned not to let anyone into the house while our parents were at work. We'd take turns peeking out the window over the sink, popping up like startled jack-in-the-boxes, knees cracking. Eventually, the stranger—a girl selling cookies, a woman with a Mary Kay smile—would go away, though we always worried someone might think to lift the welcome mat and discover the spare key.

That was an idea. I lifted the braided plastic mat that grinned the same Welcome, and there it was. I picked it out of the diamond pattern of dirt and rang the doorbell one last time. "Dad," I called, and the front curtains moved slightly. He'd seen me. He wasn't going to let me in.

The sun was starting to set, sending orange streamers across the crushed-shell driveways, and I noticed that faces had begun to appear in the windows of the neighboring trailers. A man came out onto his porch to give me a hard stare. I unlocked the door, but it would not open. Furious, I threw my weight against it. I pounded it with my fists. More people appeared on their porches, and I was yelling at them to mind their own goddamn business when the sirens, no longer in the distance, distracted me. Two police cars fishtailed up the driveway, skidding to a halt in a spray of shells. I picked up my duffel bag as doors popped open, uniformed men launching into the air like springs. "Drop it, man!" one of them yelled. "Hands in the air, move, move!" *Man?* They weren't kidding. They had guns. I leaned against the door, arms and legs apart, the way I'd seen people do in movies.

I'd forgotten about my haircut. In Georgia, two little boys had run over as I opened the door to the women's room. "That's for *girls*," they said, and even when I spoke, they were not sure what to make of me. "My name is Abigail Elise Schiller," I called over my shoulder. "This is my father's house."

When the officers heard my voice, they seemed to relax a little, but they cuffed me anyway. The cuffs were hot, like everything else. They led me to one of the squad cars, which, mercifully, was air-conditioned. In the front seat, an officer was punching my name into a computer. On the porch, two more officers were opening my duffel bag, rifling through the manila folder of flyers my mother had sent me. They opened the map she'd marked with red circles—one around each town where she hoped I'd post the flyers. The officer rattled the cage that separated us from each other, and I squinted at him pleadingly, remembering the long interviews after Sam disappeared, the scribbling pens that meant no one believed what you were saying.

But all he asked was, "Do you know that man?"

My father was standing on the porch, gesturing grimly. The officers followed the movements of his hands, as if he were hard to understand. He'd lost most of his hair and at least twenty pounds; his blunt chin was hidden in his collar. *Only dogs look at the ground*, he used to say, his chin pointing at you, a challenge. "Gordon Schiller," I said, trying not to sniffle. "That's my father."

"He doesn't seem real glad to see you," the officer said reflectively.

"We don't get along."

By the time I was allowed to step out of the car, most of the neighbors had accumulated on their porches, smoking, sipping cool drinks, exchanging comments. The men wore polyester pants held up with broad leather belts; the women reclined in floral-print dresses, nylon hose, cracked white sandals, floppy hats. They looked past me without curiosity, as if they'd seen my type before and knew exactly what to make of it. It was my father they were all staring at. He ignored them, watching closely as the officers removed my handcuffs, wearing the expression he always wore when observing anything vaguely mechanical.

"You called the police," I yelled. "I don't believe this."

"I didn't know it was you." He scratched at the seat of his pants unselfconsciously, the habit of someone accustomed to being alone. A few thin, greasy strands of hair had fallen across his forehead.

"You looked out the window!"

"With that hair, you look like a goddamn boy."

Furious, I rubbed my wrists, more for show than because they hurt. "What if I'd been Sam?"

I recognized the haughty look he always got when someone said something stupid. "You and Sam look nothing like each other."

I picked up my duffel and started to walk down the driveway, back toward the road. A woman followed me, carefully lifting her feet as if she were walking through several inches of water. The sandals she wore had three-inch heels, and her face creased with makeup when she spoke. "He's missing a few pieces to the jigsaw," she called to me.

"What?" I stopped. Back on the porch, my father was going through all his gestures again, the officers nodding, shifting their feet. I wiped my nose with the back of my hand. My eyes watered, and for a moment the woman's face blurred into a clown's colorful leer.

"He's cuckoo." She twirled her finger near one ear. "We've been worried over him. You family?"

"Daughter," I said, and, for the second time that day, "We don't get along."

"Well, somebody's got to do something about him." The rings she wore were attached to one another by a delicate web of gold chains. "My name's Lily," she said, and she encircled my wrist with her fingers. "You come by and visit me tomorrow. Number thirty."

I waited for her to release me. A flock of iridescent grackles landed on the single grassy plot, where there were park benches and a fountain spouting colored water. They argued in their wheezy voices, gobbling up things I couldn't see. It occurred to me that I didn't know where I'd go and how I'd get there once I reached the foot of the driveway. And what would I say to my mother? Lily, as if sensing my change of heart, let me go with a little wave in the direction of my father, as if to say *Shoo*! I turned around and walked back up the driveway to his trailer.

Inside, the living room walls were bare except for the owl-shaped clock that had once hung in our kitchen. There was a short couch, covered with a plastic sheet, a glass coffee table, a squat porcelain lamp. In the kitchenette, there was a table with one chair. The countertops were empty. Spotless. My father's black lace-up shoes were cuddled head to toe by the door; beneath the window was a stationary bicycle, its split seat held together with duct tape. There was no sign that anyone else was here, had been here, or would be coming. I didn't see anything of Sam's. I watched as my father wedged an iron bar between the doorknob and the floor, twisting and double-checking the door locks as if they were delicate controls on an unstable aircraft.

"Is the neighborhood that dangerous?" I said sarcastically.

"You never can be too careful."

My nose was running again, and I searched my pockets for a tissue. He turned and stared at me suspiciously.

"You got a cold?" he said.

"Me and everybody else in Baltimore," I said, and I waited for his favorite lecture, the one on Mind Over Matter that he always gave whenever Sam and I threw up or coughed or asked to stay home from school. Sickness, he claimed, was all in the head—after all, he hadn't been sick a day in his life. But now, instead of lecturing, he seemed to shrink a little. "You keep away from me," he said. "Come all this way to give me a cold."

"I'm sorry," I said, bewildered.

"I go to bed early," he said. "You can sleep here on the couch. Wash your hands and don't touch anything. That's how a cold spreads, hand to hand." He didn't ask me why I'd come, how long I wanted to stay. He took a deep breath and walked down the hall to his room, and it was then that I realized he'd been holding his breath—afraid of my germs. My father, who had never been afraid of anything or anybody, was nearly paralyzed with fear.

I remembered him instructing Sam about bravery. Without warning, he'd strike out at my brother's face with the back of his hand, stopping a bare whisker away from contact. "Made you flinch," he'd say, and Sam's thin shoulders hunched with the weight of his shame. He was eight, or nine, or ten, and always small for his age. "Try *me*," I'd say, but my father never would. "You're ready now," my father would tell me. "It doesn't count once you're ready." Our relationship wasn't a physical one; my body was something delicate and, by implication, slightly inferior, something to be protected.

At fourteen, Sam was still small for his age. One morning, when my father came downstairs for breakfast, Sam whipped his fist into the cushion of air around my father's chin. My father slapped him hard, a reflex. "Made you flinch," Sam said. His cheek was already swelling like a yellow pear; my father knew how to hit a man so it would count. My mother started yelling at them both. "This has just got to stop," she said. But it never stopped, it went on and on, my father and Sam like precarious lovers, testing each other until the time came when neither of them flinched, ever.

At the end of the hall, across from my father's room, there was a single door, which was locked. Beside it was a bathroom, cramped with a toilet, a sink, and a shower stall. There were no towels, no soap—just a roll of white toilet paper. I stripped off my clothes and showered in the empty chamber, letting the water beat my chest like pointing fingers, you-you-you. In Wisconsin, my father's clothes dominated the closet he shared with my mother; their bathroom was tangled with cords from his shaver, his electric toothbrush, his nose-hair clippers, toenail clippers, soaps, aftershaves, tweezers, foot powders, tiny scissors and combs for his on-again/off-again mustache. And his smell—Old Spice cologne and something else, not unpleasant, but heavy, pungent, spilling out ahead of him, claiming space.

When I stepped out of the shower into the steam, I felt as if I were still underwater. My cold made me shiver, feverish. Dripping, I pulled my clothes back on and walked around the house, searching for . . . what? In the kitchen, I looked in each of the cupboards: empty, empty. I opened the refrigerator, and there I found a few plates and cups, pieces of silverware, pots and pans. The door was crowded with bottles of vitamins, white-capped rows like cadets. The only food was on the top shelf: bottled water, stone-ground bread, organic peanut butter, a paper bag of apples. Health food. I selected an apple and bit into it, the cold electrifying my teeth. The Florida detective had been right. There was nobody here but an eccentric old man, and I had arranged to visit him for a week. I lay down on the couch, put my head on my hand to keep my face from sticking to the plastic cover, and slept.

In the morning, I got up and ate another apple, waiting for my father until it became apparent that he wasn't going to come out of his room. "I'll be back for lunch," I hollered through the door. I could hear a TV, the chatter of morning talk shows. Outside, the fine morning mist was already burning away. The heat felt good. I walked past the tiny grassy park toward the canal, eager to see the water. The trailers were like dolls' houses, squatting exactly in the middle of their lots as if placed there by a child's careful hand. Each was equipped with an air-conditioning unit, and the humming was like the sound of distant traffic, constant, dull, distracting.

It was quieter by the canal, except for the boats and, occasionally, an airplane passing overhead. I saw an anhinga—a bird I'd read about in books—spread itself over a clump of mangroves like a shiny black scrap of cloth. Woodpeckers rattled the palm trees, and tiny lizards scuffled in the dry fronds beneath them. There were only two trailers at this end of the park, and one, I realized suddenly, was Lily's—number 30. The mailbox was shaped like a bullfrog with a wide-open hungry mouth. LILY ANN SWEET was painted in pink block letters down the side of the post.

I knocked at the door, and after a moment Lily appeared, in a satin nightgown. "Yes?" she said pleasantly. A matching sheer robe hung from her shoulders like a bridal train, and her slippers were covered with peach-colored feathers. "Oh!" she said then, recognizing me, and she pulled me over the threshold. Within minutes I was sitting in the sunny kitchenette, with an antique teacup balanced on my knee and my mouth full of English muffin. "Thanks," I said gratefully. "My father doesn't have much in his refrigerator." Lily's trailer was identical to my father's, only here the windows were an explosion of greenery. Furniture turned the rooms into a flowery obstacle course.

"I'm not surprised," Lily said. "It doesn't seem like he's taking good care of himself."

I asked her if she had ever seen my father's place.

"Oh, we all used to visit him, the way we do each other," Lily said. "But now he won't let anybody in. The death of a child, it's hard on anyone, but he only makes it worse by shutting himself away."

I must have looked at her strangely.

She said quickly, "He told us about the accident when he first got here. He showed me the room where he keeps your brother's things."

I put down my teacup. "What accident?"

"The car accident?" Lily's earrings and bracelets were jangling like alarms.

"Oh," I said, trying to sound casual.

"It sounds like your brother was a wonderful young man. Makes it all the harder, I suppose, when you think of all the things he might have gone on to accomplish."

I thought about that for a moment. "What did he tell you about my mother and me?"

She seemed to relax. "Why, nothing," she said. "He never mentioned his wife. Or you. I didn't even know you existed."

It was worse than any lie he could have told. The sun had found its way through the plants and was warm on the back of my neck. "I'd better get back," I said. "I don't want my dad to worry."

"Well, I'm sure you're doing him a world of good," Lily said. I thanked her, trying to gauge how quickly I could pack up my things and get on the next bus. But my father was waiting for me at the door. He was wearing the same clothes he'd had on yesterday: pants too big around the waist, a soiled white shirt buttoned all the way up to his chin. "You left the goddamn place unlocked!" he shouted. Sweat rolled down his face like tears; his hands clutched each other, slipped free, then fluttered at his sides. "Just waltzed right out, leaving everything wide open!"

"How else was I going to get back in?" I said, trying to step past him, but he blocked my way with his body; I realized he was offering me a key pinched between his thumb and index finger.

"The one under the mat is for the first lock," he said. "This is for the second. For Christ's sake, keep the house locked up or we'll end up with our throats slit." He dropped the key into my hand. "You can't trust anybody," he said. "You can't let down your guard for a goddamn minute."

"Why can't you trust anybody?" I said. "Is that why you lied to Lily?"

He backed down the hall and pounded his fist on the door across the hall from his room as if he expected somebody would open it from within. "This is all I have left of him. All I have left!" It had to be the room Lily had seen, filled with Sam's things, the things my father had taken. And I realized each of them was a clue that would help me to know the difference between what I remembered and what I'd been told, between the answers I'd given to neighbors and friends and detectives and the unspoken ones I'd learned to hide even from myself. *You're exaggerating,* my mother said whenever I tried to talk about Sam. *I don't remember anything like that.* But my father had the evidence, facts I could pick up and hold in my hand. I knew I wouldn't leave until I'd been inside that room.

Over the next few days, my father and I settled into a wary routine, avoiding each other politely unless I happened to violate a rule, in which case he would come to me, shaking, sometimes too terrified to speak. The pots and pans and plates and silverware had to be washed in special detergent. The curtains could not be opened because someone, a stranger, might look in; also, the sunlight raised the temperature of the air, which made it more hospitable to bacteria. He kept his toothpaste in an army trunk beneath his bed, in case, he explained earnestly, someone spiked it with acid like what happened to that retired man in Punta Gorda.

"Maybe you should see a doctor," I told him.

"I never felt better in my life. Remember how my back used to hurt me?"

I nodded, recalling his slipped disk.

"Cured it myself," he said proudly. "High-protein diet. Low sugar, low fat."

Mornings, he vacuumed, exercised on the stationary bike, and then scrubbed the kitchen and bathroom with ammonia. I offered to help with the cleaning, but it was clear I was not reliable—look at me, sick with a cold! I might miss a spot in my youth, in my carelessness, in my eagerness to get outside and into the carcinogenic sunlight. My father avoided sunlight, drafts, hot drinks, cold drinks, synthetic fibers, furry animals, and all situations where there might be spiders, mosquitoes, or flies. He rarely left the trailer more than once a day when, late in the afternoon, he walked to the Pleasant Acres Community Service Center to buy whatever food we needed for our evening meal. I trudged behind him like an uneasy pickpocket, hovering a bit too close. Once, we ran into Lily, but he scurried past her, leaving me to exchange pleasantries for us both. Lily didn't take offense. "Poor man," she said, shaking her head.

I spent most of my time sitting by the canal in the shade of the gumbo-limbo trees, dangling my feet over the concrete seawall. My hair was growing out quickly; the stubble had turned soft. A coral snake came to sunbathe every day on the same, sizzling rock. Pelicans glided past in groups, splashing down so close I could smell their fishy breath, and beneath the surface of the water their pouches ballooned, hideous as sausage casings. My cold had left me bleary-eyed, tired, and I convinced myself I wasn't well enough to think about the flyers in my duffel bag, the map with its neat circles. My mother had printed thousands of flyers in the weeks after Sam disappeared, and now, whenever I tried to imagine my brother, I inevitably saw the picture on the flyer. The original had been taken on his seventeenth birthday. He'd been gone for two days, coming home just as my grandmother and Auntie Thil showed up for a Sunday afternoon visit.

"There's the birthday boy!" Auntie Thil said nervously. "Good thing we brought a present." Sam looked like hell. His T-shirt was torn, and blood caked the corner of one nostril. My grandmother held out a brightly decorated gift box; the wrapping paper boasted tiny boy angels blowing horns. Congratulations! the paper read, over and over. I watched the careful horror in Sam's face as he reached across the table, gingerly taking the gift. Each movement released waves of cigarette smoke and the cloying sweet smell of marijuana.

"I'll get the camera," my mother said, and when she came back into the room she snapped the picture. The gift was a hand-painted china statue of Saint Francis. "It's an antique," I could hear my grandmother saying, her voice a broken whisper. My mother said, "Oh, it's lovely," and Sam turned the statue over and over in his hands, his fingernails black with dirt, a broken blood vessel blooming in the soft skin inside his elbow. But out of context, printed on a flyer, Sam merely looked serious, somber, reflective. My mother had chosen the picture for that reason. Sitting by the canal, I tried to remember my brother's face when he smiled or scowled or laughed. I couldn't—there was only the picture on the flyer, the pop of the flash, Sam's red-rimmed eyes.

One night, just as my father and I were finishing our supper, the phone rang, a sudden, violent trill. My father leapt up. "Stay right where you are!" he said, pacing circles around the table as the answering machine kicked on, his own disembodied voice stating that no one could come to the phone. After the tone, there was a pause before the click of the receiver. "Who the hell was that?"

"How should I know?" I said, but I thought I'd recognized my mother's sigh. I could see her sitting at the kitchen table, her decaffeinated coffee chilling in its cup, her work pushed to one side. She was looking out the window toward the highway, the old pear trees lost in the fiery lace of autumn, the sunset a crimson line. She was wondering how to find out if I was OK, without my father discovering she had been involved in my visit. And as my father checked the locks on the doors, mumbling about thieves, I realized that even though the material things in his life had grown spare, he was still as large as he'd ever been. My week in Florida was almost up. Tomorrow would be my last full day, and I promised myself it would not go to waste.

In the morning, I got up early and went out to the carport. The Fords' keys were under the driver's-side floor mat, which was where my father had always kept them. I was surprised to see a quarter-size starburst on the windshield, a scratch that ran the length of one fender. In Horton, he'd babied his cars, purring to them in cold weather, oiling their dark, mysterious coils. He'd spent one summer working on an old Mustang, going from junkyard to junkyard like a crow, scavenging for that perfect piece of shining metal. He enlisted Sam's help, but Sam's aptitudes, much to my father's disappointment, were not mechanical ones. His scold—"Goddamnit, son!"—rang through the apple trees on hot summer nights when Sam misunderstood an instruction or dropped one of my father's pristine heirloom tools. By the time Sam started high school, the Mustang had become the hub of an argument that had circled for so long its track was worn permanent, private, deep. They never did get it running.

"What were you up to out there?" my father said when I came in for our breakfast of peanut-butter toast, which, according to my father, would boost our energy.

"I was thinking about spending a day at the beach," I lied. "Would it be OK if I borrowed the car? I could stop at a grocery store, get you some things they don't have at the center. I'll be going home tomorrow," I said. "So if there's any other errand you want me to—"

"The beach!" my father exploded, his shock catapulting us over the issue of the car, my departure, his possible grocery store needs, and into new, dangerous territory. "No, definitely no." His chin shook faintly; a diamond of saliva was caught near the corner of his mouth. Didn't I know there were dirty needles in the ocean off the coast of Virginia, Massachusetts, New Jersey? "You could get hurt. Something could happen."

After we'd finished eating, he scraped the crumbs from our plates, scrubbed the table and countertops vigorously with ammonia. I waited until he had gone into the bathroom for his shower, which I knew by now would last precisely ten minutes, and then I got the flyers from my duffel bag. *Back by dark*, I scrawled on a paper towel, and I left it on the table for my father to see. I eased myself out the front door and locked up the way he had shown me.

The Ford was like my father, suspicious, unwilling to move beyond its daily routine. When the engine caught, a thick black cloud drifted over the other driveways and lawns. I backed out and eased along the narrow lane toward the highway, expecting to see my father burst from the trailer, partially clothed, foaming cinnamon Crest. But he had three more minutes left to shower as I spread the map across the seat. The first town on my mother's list was Matlache; it was on the way to Pine Island, where there were two more circled cities. Away from my father and the close, chilled air of the trailer, I became aware that my cold was finally gone.

Matlache was unincorporated, the small green sign like a chewed leaf, rough with bullet holes. The town was a parallel chain of stilt houses caught between Highway 78 on one side and the bay on the other. The bay bisected the east and west sides of the town briefly; they were tenuously connected by a long, narrow bridge, where people gathered to fish and smoke, staying close to Styrofoam coolers of beer. There was an ice cream shop, a turquoise store, a marina and fish market, surrounded by pickup trucks. There was also a small, tired-looking bar and grill, called The Mullet. The sign in the window said it opened at eleven.

I parked at the marina and walked down to the waterfront, where shrimp boats were docked. A group of fishermen had gathered around a giant stingray that hung from a winch, suffocating under the weight of its own body. Gulls squawked on the pilings, hissing at one another along the rotting docks. A great blue heron stood in their midst, evil-eyed, its long bill an eager spear. The birds, like the men, kept their eyes on the ray. Its beautiful body bucked once and was still. I shivered and crossed the street to the gas station, where I bought gas and then a Coke, craving caffeine. "You mind if I post a flyer?" I asked the teenage girl working the cash register.

"I don't care what you do."

"Have you seen this person?" I said. My voice didn't sound like my own; it was pleading, the voice of someone who needs a favor. I struggled to lower it. "He's my brother." Now it sounded like a lie.

"I seen nobody," the girl said, not looking, staring into her hands. Her nails were long and polished red, with a clear decal of a sunflower pressed to each tip. I posted the flyer and went back outside. The Mullet seemed like a more visible place, but it wouldn't open for another hour. To pass time, I walked up the street to the group of little shops, each tended by a middle-aged woman in a similar floral smock. I explained that my missing brother might be in the area, and the women nodded, their lips narrowing sympathetically. One refused to let me post the sign; the owner might not approve: They catered to tourists who came to Florida to look at beautiful things, not the faces of missing people. But she took a flyer for herself, promising to post it at her church in Saint James City. Looking at it closely, she said, "I haven't seen this man before, but I think I've seen this picture."

"On TV?" I asked.

"At The Mullet!" she said suddenly. "You know the bar by the water? It's up on the wall there as you walk in. They should be opening pretty soon."

I thanked her and left, figuring she'd mistaken Sam for another missing person on another flyer. I often read the bulletin boards in laundromats, at bus stops, in grocery stores and libraries, scanning the litany of lost names, deliberate facts. Four feet tall. Brown hair; red hair. Green eyes; black eyes. Can't speak. Answers to Sweetheart. The faces on the flyers were fuzzy, smudged, the eyes staring like the eyes of the dead.

The neon sign in the front window of The Mullet still glowed

CLOSED, but the door was open, propped back by a straggly potted palm. There was a faint fishy odor of fry-grease lingering in the parking lot; two trucks and a rusted Chevy Nova were parked in the half-shade of the awning. I went inside, conscious of my shorts and bare arms. The air was cool and dark, stale with cigarette smoke, and it took a minute for my eyes to adjust.

"We're not ready for ya, hon," a woman called to me from the grill behind the bar. "Coffee's making, but that's all we got right now."

"Coffee's fine," I said. There was no bulletin board, no place to pin a flyer. I sat down at the far end of the bar, wrapping my feet around the legs of the stool.

"Bottomless cup," the woman said, giving me my coffee and a quick smile before hooking the phone off the wall and dialing briskly. "It's me," she said into the receiver. "You better get your ass in here. I got customers." She rolled her eyes at me. "I don't want to hear about it." When she hung up, she was laughing.

"My son's got himself a little girlfriend. Makes it hard to get him up in the morning."

I could see how it would be when her son finally arrived, the good-natured back-and-forth between them. "Could you tell me if you've seen this person?" I said, taking a flyer out of my bag. "He's my brother."

"Just a minute," she said, turning down the grill. When she came back to the counter, she sighed, pushing her hair behind her ears, revealing tiny sparkling earrings, the brightest things in that room. "Haven't found him yet?" she said. "So sorry, hon. I still got his picture posted at the waterside entrance."

"This same person?" I asked, astonished. "How did you get his picture?"

"Some old guy brought it in a while ago. Maybe a year . . . was it that long?" She put one finger to her cheek, thinking. "He asked for a glass of water, and he drank it like this"—she pantomimed, mouth open, head back—"so his lips wouldn't touch the glass. You could tell he had some sort of nervous problems. He thought your brother might be working one of the boats, but these are all our local boys. I'll tell you what I told him—if this boy shows up, I'll sure call."

I wanted to touch my own face to see what expression I was wearing.

"Hon," she said. I must have looked sad. "I am sorry about your brother."

"Thanks," I said, and after I finished my coffee, I ordered a beer. The woman's son arrived and served it to me, rumple-headed, his face still faintly creased from the bedsheets. "Hustle up there, Romeo," the woman said.

"Aw, Ma."

She winked at me, bumped his hip with her own.

"Aw, Ma."

"My Romeo," she said. "My lady-killer."

When I left, they were working at the grill, side by side, the son smiling back at her beneath the tangled curtain of his hair. I spent the day doing what my mother had asked, posting flyers in Saint James City, Bokeelia, swinging back inland to Cape Coral. Nearly everywhere I went, I found my father's faded flyers. Eventually, I ended up in Fort Myers, where I walked along a crowded beach, stepping over sand castles, broken shells, the tanned feet of lovers. It was getting dark by the time I returned to Pleasant Acres, sunburned and thirsty, eager to put the week behind me. My father was waiting for me at the kitchen table. "Where'd you go?"

"Beach."

"I remember telling you no."

I felt as if I'd been sucked back into childhood: I saw myself standing before him, small, frightened, trying to keep my face impassive as I waited to be punished for whatever rule I'd broken. But then I came back into myself, into the present: I was not a child anymore. "It's good to know you remember something right," I said. "All that crap you told Lily Sweet about Sam."

My father looked away from me, stared into the cup of his own clasped hands. "Sam was a good boy," he finally said, so gently he could have been my mother. "Isn't it something, how he could just disappear like that? How anyone of us"—he snapped his fingers—"and that's it. That's all." He touched the tips of his index fingers together, over and over. "I worried about you all day."

"I'm sorry."

"All day long."

"I'm sorry," I said again.

He got up and went to the kitchen. I sat down on the couch as if nothing had happened. But the interaction had shattered the balance of caution and silence we'd woven between us. During supper, we made polite conversation. We watched each other, caught each other watching. Before he went to his room for the night, my father dug into his pocket and handed me another key. "You can look in Sam's room if you want," he said, in a voice I didn't recognize. "Just don't change anything, OK? I got it all laid out the way I like it." And then, without warning, he started to cry, his arms at his sides, not hiding his face. I put my arms around him, and for a moment, he did not pull away.

The room smelled of cedar and the underlying odor of Florida tap water, mildewed, swampy, strange. The only light aside from the dull overhead fixture was the lamp that had once been beside my bed. It belonged to both Sam and me when we'd shared a room as children, arguing whether to leave the door open or closed, the night-light on or off. There was the tricycle that had first been mine, pink, with pink tassels streaming from the handlebars. I remembered how my legs had stretched to reach the pedals. When Sam was old enough to inherit it, my father had repainted it red, white, and blue. Now, in old age, its true color showed through. There were Sam's old skateboards leaning up against the wall and, beside them, the baseball and bat and glove that he never used much, despite my father's earnest lectures on How a Sport Builds Character. There were boxes of schoolwork my mother had saved, Sam's and mine jumbled together; the childish drawings hanging on the walls were the ones I had given her because she said she liked them. The Horton Wildcats banner on the wall had been my father's gift to Sam, but I'd never seen the football trophies before. I picked one up; it belonged to my father's brother, my uncle who had died in the war. The plaques behind them were mine; I'd assumed they were still boxed up in my bedroom closet. *Chopin Competition, Third Prize, Milwaukee. Contemporary Musical Festival, First Prize, Minneapolis. Milwaukee Conservatory Medal of Achievement.* I touched them, remembering a time when I thought myself capable of great things. I touched the drawings, the schoolbooks, the fishing pole Sam hadn't wanted for Christmas. I touched the padded varsity jacket hanging in the closet, the kind football players wore.

This was not Sam's jacket. These were not Sam's old-fashioned athletic shoes. Sam wore black leather jackets and combat boots, the tongues hanging out, obscene. Sometimes, at night, he wore eye makeup and bracelets studded with metal, his hair spiked tall and fierce. A car would be waiting, there was always a car waiting, with the radio thumping and the windows rolled up and tinted dark so you couldn't see who was inside, and then Sam would be passing through the kitchen and out the door as if he were already invisible, safe, gone. Outside, a door would swing open like a welcoming arm, and for a moment the music would be crisp and sharp, and maybe we'd hear voices and the sort of laughter men use only among themselves. And then the car would squeal down the long gravel drive and roar toward Milwaukee, most nights not returning until dawn.

It seems to me now that the past belongs to those who have the self-possession, or the arrogance, or enough sheer determined longing, to stamp their own particular imagination *history*. It was no use wondering what I would have put in this room were it mine to fill, because it was not mine, it never would be. I remembered Phoebe telling me, People believe what they want. But there was also this: People want to believe. And somewhere in between wanting to believe and believing what we want, there is the story we call the truth.

I walked outside into the humid air and followed the path toward the canal and the sleepy sound of the gulls. My sneakers crunched the shells and stones that made up the path, and it was a brittle sound, a bitter sound, the sound of many small things breaking.

Grace

(1995–1996)

Ten

My job at Turkey Hill consists of many jobs: running the information kiosk, preparing the displays, mowing the small front lawn in summer, helping to clear the nature trails of debris each spring. Today has been a quiet day, but as I'm getting ready to close the kiosk for the night, the bells on the front door jingle merrily and two women come inside. They're wearing identical neat black coats, boots trimmed with stiff fake fur, and they stand beside the winter mammal display as if they are posing for a photograph already labeled and pasted in an imaginary scrapbook. Gloves bulge from their pockets, and the mouths of the purses they carry are sealed with scalloped clasps. One of the women is holding something; the other tugs off her kerchief, and the ripple of fabric, the blue and green and gold diamond pattern, reminds me of the sheer scarves my grandmother used to wear.

"We close in five minutes," I say, and I continue sweeping the floor around the pellet dispensers, where, for a quarter, you can purchase a handful of food for the Canada geese outside. "Our winter hours started this week." But I know I'll let them poke around for a while. It's my favorite time of day, no longer afternoon, not yet twilight, the feeling like the moment between wakefulness and sleep. Overhead, beyond the skylights, the dull shapes of clouds pass like coils of smoke, making the bird skeletons suspended from the high ceiling beams appear to be moving through the air. Only the golden eagle, posed on the ledge above the winter mammal display, keeps perfectly still. Its glass eyes shine the color of cracked corn, watching the small dry mice and slender quail, watching my progress with the broom, watching the women, who, I realize, haven't moved since they first came inside. "Lottie thinks it's her fault," the woman with the kerchief calls to me, and as I cross the room, I see that her companion is cradling a great horned owl. Blood drools from its nares. "I told her maybe someone here could fix it."

I reach for the owl, but a slight shift in Lottie's weight lets me know she will not release it. One magnificent wing stretches away from its limp body, pulled long by its own weight, longer still, until the tip brushes the floor. There is no response when I press my index finger to the cornea. "I'm afraid it's already gone," I say. I can smell the women's coats, that stale church smell of hair spray and liniment and sweet, sweet perfume. "Sometimes we work with a vet in Binghamton, but there'd be no point calling her now."

"Fool thing flew up off the road, straight at us. Cracked the windshield," the woman says. "Could have killed us both." Her kerchief flutters beside her. "Oh, Lottie!" she says. "You got bugs all over you!"

Lice are streaming over Lottie's hands and wrists, disappearing underneath the sleeves of her coat. "Bird lice," I explain, my own skin itching in sympathy. "You can shower them off with regular soap. This kind of lice doesn't like people."

Again, I try to take the owl, but Lottie is staring into its crushed face, those liquid yellow eyes. I remember the time Auntie Thil hit a doe, driving us home from an ice-skating lesson—me and Sam, Monica and Harv. The doe was winter thin, ribs heaving, the tendons in her legs taut as string. She lay on the side of the highway and kicked, her body spinning around and around. We were in the back seat, looking and not looking as Auntie Thil got out of the car, hands outstretched in front of her the way you do when you've just said something unforgivable, when you just want to take it all back.

"Let me find something to put it in," I say, and by the time I return with a plastic trash bag, Lottie is ready to let go. In a low, rough voice, she asks if she can wash her hands, and I point her toward the rest rooms. As she walks, the bottoms of her boots skim the floor as if the weight of them is almost too much to carry. The owl is a large specimen, probably a female. I turn to carry her over to the gift shop counter, and my ankle pops. I wince, catch my balance. "Are you all right?" Lottie's companion says, and then, without waiting for my answer, "When's your baby due? Christmas?"

"January," I say, bracing myself; lately, I've found myself trapped in gruesome conversations about induced labor, cesarean sections, crib death. But this woman does not say anything more about it. She picks up one of our promotional mugs, on sale at $5.95. "Wild turkeys," she says, examining the Turkey Hill logo. "They certainly are foolish-looking things."

Lottie comes out of the bathroom, her mouth bright with fresh lipstick. She wanders over to the winter mammal display and stares out the big glass windows at the sun setting over the heated pond. Canada geese form a tight raft at the center; others walk in slow, proud pairs across the frozen lawn. There is snow in the clouds, in the softness of the light that deepens the sadness in Lottie's thin face. She's been crying, and I can see that this owl is just one more thing to be added to a long list of small, private sadnesses. On her way out the door, she stops at the donation box and slips something into it with the furtive look of the perennial almsgiver, one who knows she can never give enough. A person like Harv, who has taken vows of chastity, humility, poverty, believing that somehow he can suffer for us all.

I carry the owl down the narrow wooden steps to the base-ment. The walls are lined with snowshoes and cross-country skis, flashlights, NO TRESPASSING signs, an assortment of aging tools. On the back table, pinned to a piece of Styrofoam, is the Cooper's hawk—found electrocuted on a fence—I finished preparing ear-lier today. People often bring us birds: a blue jay, a grosbeak, a waxwing. They open the shoe box, the paper bag, their own cupped hands, and it seems so wrong that even in death, the plumage is that same vivid blue or rust or ocher, soft to the touch, lifelike. Over the past few years, I've taught myself the fundamen-tals of taxidermy, keeping records of stomach contents and par-asites, healed-over bones and half-formed eggs, reconstructing whatever moments I can from these small lost lives.

"How can you handle dead things like that?" my mother asks. But I'm fascinated by the way we live beyond ourselves, how our very bones can tell our stories. I lug the owl to the freezer, stacking and restacking the other, smaller birds like so many bun-dles of kindling, making room. Already, death is filling its body with a heaviness that doesn't register on any scale. Poor Lottie, I think. How awful to drive home peering through that cracked windshield, wondering, What if I'd swerved, what if I'd gone a different route? What if. I unsnag my coat from its hook, dig a pocket's worth of pellets from the storage barrel, and begin the long climb back up the stairs. My mother believes, the way my grandmother believed, that each tragic thing we suffer is a spiritual lesson, something we bring upon ourselves, something we deserve. My refusal to baptize the baby terrifies her, and it's this last, blas-phemous straw that has broken her determination to see the past decade of my life as simply a temporary lapse of faith. Our most recent fight was a week ago; we have not spoken since.

I lock the front doors, and the geese, hearing the chime of my keys, begin their slow migration out of the water. Their white cheeks shine like double moons. I spill the pellets from my pockets and they eat—snapping, hissing. The clouds descend, snuffing a

sunset that looks like fire running wild along the horizon, and I
remember the cannery fire, the same dark, cold November day
that my grandmother remembered whenever she saw a rosy winter sky. "That's just what it looked like in the distance," she'd say,
"like the sun going down at noon, like the end of the world had
come." She'd told me over and over how she'd known all along
that the cannery was no place for girls. The dusty air gave them
coughs that lasted through the summer; the noise left them cock-
ing their heads—*What did you say?*; there were rumors that the
foremen used bad language. But my grandmother wanted money
to buy sugar and seed, cloth and fertilizer, all the things that had
run low since my grandfather's death, and so, each day, she sent
Mary and Elise to meet the cannery truck that lurched from farm
to farm at dawn, collecting workers.

The morning of the fire, the wind froze the air in people's
noses and sealed the eyes of the cattle, grinding its way through
scarves and cloaks and wool stockings, speaking in the white voice
of static, making it hard to hear. There was half a foot of hard-
crusted snow on the ground. *Zero degrees in November!* the mothers
cried, hurrying their daughters off to work. *Zero degrees in November!*
the fathers cursed, out in the barns already, hands so cold they'd
become weak. *Zero degrees!* the girls crowed as they greeted one
another at the cannery, hurrying toward the hum of the machines.

The first oily belch of smoke was torn into loose ribbons,
wavering on the horizon like the shadows of large birds. Children
pressed up against windows to stare; mothers and fathers finishing
chores, crossing at a run from barn to shed, from shed to house,
from house to henhouse, now paused and danced in place, refusing to understand. Then they dropped the eggs, the bales of straw,
the tins of milk, hollering against the wind, running for trucks and
cars. The smoke was thickening, funneling into the clouds, a
slanted black arrow with a blazing root. People came from
Oneisha and Farbenplatz, Ooston, Horton, Holly's Field, and by
the time the fire truck arrived from Fall Creek, a line had formed

to pass buckets of snow, which liquefied in midair. Men and women flung off their coats, rolled up their sleeves as if preparing to fight, danced forward with their buckets until their faces browned like pork and the hair on their arms turned to ash and blew away. But the heat forced them back, the water splashed short. The wind roared, feeding the fire, snatching the words out of people's throats, though behind the sound of the wind were the other cries, fierce at first, then fading like smoke. My grandmother never stopped believing my young aunts' deaths had been her fault, the result of her lack of faith that God Himself would provide.

"Watch out what you want or you'll get it," she'd say whenever I began a sentence with *I wish* or *I want* or *Wouldn't it be nice.* To want was to take the reins from God's hand. To want was to suggest that you yourself presumed to know what was best. When she started to work outside the home, my mother began to want, to wish and dream. *A career woman,* people said, and when Sam disappeared and never came back, they consoled her with the cruel, fevered look of the righteous. When I went away to college and then stayed away for good, it was clear my mother had gotten what she had been foolish enough to ask for. *Watch out what you want.* I toss the last handful of pellets to the geese, and the wind unwinds the scarf from my neck. The air smells faintly of wood smoke; the trees are scorched black and bare. How much longer will I find myself remembering pain that is not my own, raw and undigested hurts belonging to the communities of Oneisha, Ooston, Farbenplatz, Horton, Holly's Field? Stories told again and again until they belong to us all. My grandmother's grief becomes my mother's. My mother's fear becomes my own.

———

"Harv called," Adam says as he lets me into the house. It's good to find him here, warm cooking smells wafting in from the kitchen. "He said he'd call back later."

"What did he want?"

"He wouldn't say, but I can guess." Adam's voice holds the same weariness I feel. "What will your mother try next? A call from the Pope? Crusades?"

"Harv wouldn't get involved in this," I say, but Harv doesn't call without a reason. Our relationship has been cautious ever since I left the Church. The last time we talked, I was still in Baltimore, *living in sin* with Adam; he'd been nervous, awkward, reluctant to speak. "Your mother," he finally said, "wants me to let you know that I'm here in case you ever want to talk about your faith."

I didn't know what to say.

"Well," Harv said, "I told her I'd say that, even though I knew you'd just tell me to mind my own business."

"Mind your own business," I said, but I had started laughing because he sounded so foolish and shy.

"And it's another success for the good father," he said in his dry, self-deprecating way. "Another lost sheep returned safely to the fold. My God, they should have me canonized."

I was still laughing. "I don't want to talk about it."

"Promise you'll tell your mother I argued with you for hours. Tell her I quoted Scripture. Tell her I threatened to have God strike you dead."

"I'll tell her," I said, and then we both relaxed and talked about other things. But before we hung up, he said, "I can't imagine what it would be like to lose my faith."

I didn't say anything. Was he going to make some sort of religious pitch after all?

"Well?" he said.

"Well what?"

"What's it like? I mean, as a kid you were just as devout as I was. You were even praying for a vocation for a while."

I told him the truth. "It's lonely."

There was a pause as he thought this over; I could almost see him shaking his head. "I can't imagine," he said again.

As I wash my hands for supper, I tell Adam about the ranch house where Harv and Monica grew up, the pond in the back, which Olaf decorated with floating plastic ducks. How, in winter, he set the temperature to sixty before locking the thermostat controls back inside their plexiglass box. How even the toilet paper was rationed: one square for number 1, two squares for number 2. Adam listens to me with the expression of someone who's waiting for the punch line. "I've told you all this before," I insist, but he shakes his head.

"You never talk about your family."

"Well, now you see why."

We are laughing as we sit down to the supper he has made: meat loaf and green beans, potatoes with gravy. "Watch him call again right now," Adam says, and with that the phone starts to ring.

"Let me get it," he says. "I'll tell him you'll call back when we're done eating."

He goes down the hall and picks up the phone. I play connect the dots with his responses, and the picture I come up with isn't a friendly one. Steam rises from the meat loaf, and I hear Adam say, "Look, you can just tell me. Did Therese ask you to call?"

"Adam, don't! Let me talk to him," I yell, but before I can get up, Adam's standing in the doorway.

"Great," I say. "All I need is a fight with Harv too."

I push past him to the phone. "Harv?" I say. "Hi, Harvard. Look—"

"When have I ever pushed my beliefs on you?" It takes me a moment to recognize Harv's voice; I can't remember ever hearing him angry. Adam is standing beside me, too close. "Your mother asked me to call you," Harv says, "because they found the remains of your brother in a dry well on the Luchterhand's old property. The ID came back positive this morning."

For over ten years, I have imagined this phone call, expected it, dreaded it, wished for it. But what Harv has just said cannot be true. I shrug Adam's hand off my shoulder; I'm so relieved I start to laugh. "That's crazy," I say, almost smugly.

"The developers found him. They were digging a foundation for those condos going in. There must have been an old homestead along the bluff. Even the Luchterhands didn't know about it."

"Mom told me about that subdivision," I say. "She says the Luchterhands made out like bandits when they sold that land. She's thinking she could sell our place for some serious bucks."

"Did you hear what I just told you?"

A strange thought is occurring to me: *This is real.*

"Abby," Harv says. "Listen. They also found the knife Geena Baumbach described, which means Sam was one of those boys who . . ." I pass the phone to Adam and go back into the kitchen. Everything looks delicious. Should I wait for Adam, or should I eat now? I can hear him asking questions about Sam, and it annoys me to hear him speak my brother's name. *You never even met him,* I want to say. I help myself to a slice of the meat loaf. He's mixed the meat with chopped sweet onions, the way I like it best, then baked it with bread and egg and dried tomatoes from our garden. I spread my slice with mashed potatoes, thick as sour cream, and drizzle gravy on top. It's hot, but I'm greedy, I swallow it down. Next I ladle green beans onto my plate; I pop them into my mouth with my fingers.

"Did he fall down there by accident or did someone . . ." I can't hear the rest. Then, "How can they know what really happened?"

I cut another slice of meat loaf, cover it with ketchup. Adam hates it when I do this; ketchup, he says, is an insult to meat. I fill my glass with milk and drink it down in long, aching gulps. I've drifted through this pregnancy on a shallow wave of nausea that leaves everything around me dull, unappealing. But tonight the food has color again; I taste salt, sweet, the richness of beef. Adam comes back into the kitchen, stops, stares at the collage of food on my plate.

"I'm sorry," I say. "I should have waited. I was just so hungry."

"It's OK," Adam says. "Harv says you should call him back when you can. Your mother is staying with his mother, and she doesn't want to talk to anybody."

"I think I'd like dessert," I say. "Do we have anything sweet in the house?"

"We'll come up with something," Adam says. He himself doesn't seem to have much of an appetite, but he sits with me as I finish my meal, and afterward he makes baked apples for dessert. When I start to get up to clear the dishes, he puts his hand on mine, holding me in place. Then he tells me everything he's learned about my brother—tells me over and over until I hear him, until I understand.

Sam wouldn't do a thing like that. My mother's voice, a fragment of a dream I can't remember, awakens me in the gray hour before true dawn. I get up to go to the bathroom, marveling at the way familiar things look unfamiliar at this time of day: the toothbrush, the soap, the long, limp slope of the bath towels. The sound of my mother's voice winds around me like the refrain of a simpleminded song. *A thing like that*—her euphemism. I put on my bathrobe and creep to the kitchen, the cold floorboards biting the balls of my feet, and I sit in the rocking chair beside the French doors as light spills over the tops of the trees like a slow, persistent leak. The baby awakens, and for the first time I feel its conscious presence. It *knows* me, I think with amazement. And I don't know whether to feel comforted or afraid.

A thing like that. My mother and I heard Geena Baumbach's story from my grandmother, and it's not hard to imagine how it was. What woman hasn't awakened in the night to a noise that shapes itself into a man's heavy footstep? What woman cannot hear of a break-in and see that same shadow fall across her own bed? Mrs. Baumbach remembered it had been a long day of tornado warnings, the sky above the swollen lake purple as the underside of a tongue. Twice, a peculiar twisting finger bled through the cloud cover to touch the fields the way a child might slip a sly finger into a bowl of cake batter—just to taste. Late in the afternoon, Father Van Dan came over at a run. The wind flapped his black skirts into a frenzy, and when he leapt up onto her porch, his hair was standing on end. "Don't go taking chances, Geena," he said. Lightning shattered the sky like an omen. "Come on over with the rest of us." But Mrs. Baumbach was unwilling to spend a day in the basement of the church, making small talk, playing cards, drinking lukewarm coffee with the group of nervous parishioners who lived in the trailer park west of Oneisha. She had work to do: a sinkful of dishes humming with flies, that tacky kitchen floor she'd been meaning to wash for days, the set of matching pot holders she wanted to finish on time for her niece's wedding shower. She showed Father the pattern—two pale yellow geese, their long lovers' necks entwined, a sprinkle of daisies beneath them.

"I still got some git left in me," she told him. "I can run over quick as a rabbit if I must."

"You think a rabbit won't get blown away?"

"Not this rabbit."

Father Van Dan studied her face to see how firmly she'd made up her mind. "Suit yourself," he finally said, and she watched him dash back to the church, a wayward crow fighting the wind. For a while, she thought she might go on over to the church basement after all. There'd be plenty to do helping Sister Mary Andrew and Sister Mary Gabriel with the clutter of coffee and Kool-Aid and Styrofoam cups, the tangle of children forced to share toys, the anxious parents worrying over fallen trees and flying glass. But now the worst of the storm seemed to be blowing out over Lake Michigan, and her kitchen was finally clean. She was happy she'd stayed at home. She hung a fresh strip of flypaper from the light fixture and made herself a cold supper: sardines and soda crackers, a can of diet cola, and—a treat—two butter cookies from the Christmas tin in the closet. She relished those cookies, allowing each one to melt into velvety slush between her teeth. The heat didn't bother her much. The lightning was far away, delicate as thread. Harmless.

A thick fish smell from the lake drifted in through the open windows, ruffling the homemade curtains with their embroidered heart borders, shivering through the leaves of the plants suspended by macraméd hangers, shuffling through the pile of letters and bills and advertisements on the coffee table. The storm was spinning itself into the lake; tomorrow night after work, she might drive to Herringbone Beach to look for the interesting pieces of driftwood and polished glass she used to make Christmas tree ornaments. She settled down on the sofa to finish her niece's pot holders. The portable radio beside her crackled with bursts of static like laughter. Ninety-two degrees. Humidity ninety percent. Tornado warnings in effect throughout Wisconsin until midnight. She pictured the families in the basement of the church, unfolding the cots, passing out pillows and sheets, snacking on peanut butter and jelly. There was no need for all that; this was clear. You just had to smell the air. She hummed to herself as she worked. The twilight passed into evening.

What woman hasn't had the uneasy feeling that she's being watched, stripped bare of potential and promise, broken down into muscle and sinew, bone and flesh? Mrs. Baumbach was seventy-six years old, a widow, an innovative cook, Father Van Dan's closest friend outside the clergy. She made toys for the parish children out of toilet paper rolls and egg cartons and glitter; she was admired for her watercolor paintings of lakefront scenes. She kept the books at the rectory, something she'd taught herself to do. Oneisha was a town of less than seven hundred people, a place where people proudly announced that no one ever locked doors. Of course, there were incidents now and then: teenage boys speeding up the Fox Ranch Road; drunkenness; rabid animals; family disagreements; the occasional suicide.

Now Mrs. Baumbach was finding it difficult to concentrate. She got up to pull the shades, the fish smell oiling the back of her throat, and then—an odd impulse—she walked around the tiny house, latching screens. Perhaps the weather had unnerved her. Perhaps the butter cookies had been too rich. The wind whispered in the bushes as she sat back down to her work. It was after nine by the time the last puckered daisy was sewn into place. She thought about all the years she'd lived alone, how feelings like these had come and gone, leaving nothing in their wake but a vague sense of foolishness. She peeked between the curtains. The town was dark. There were no stars. She got into bed, tugged her white cotton nightgown over her knees, and pulled the sheet up to her lips.

She would never be able to remember their faces. She would never be able to say, exactly, how many boys there were. Five or six, she thought. Maybe two. She was certain the time was after midnight—or was it? No, she had just gone to bed. It took several days before she could weave a ragged story from the scraps, the false cuts, the oddly shaped pieces: faces like white moons hanging too close; the rough talk; the forced walk to the kitchen as they took turns stepping on the back of her nightgown. Certainly local boys wouldn't do such a thing. Certainly they must be boys nobody knew. She sat at the table with her head in her hands as one of them opened the refrigerator, pulled the pickle relish and mustard and cherry Jell-O onto the clean linoleum floor. The

juice pitcher shattered, and the boys kicked at the pieces, grinding
them under the heels of their combat boots. *Bitch. We're hungry.*
Cook us something. Cook us some eggs. And there was the knife, its
question-mark tip: *Won't you do as I ask?* She got up and walked
on her bare feet through the glass. She collected, eggs, margarine,
milk. She turned on a burner, reached for a pan.

The smell of the margarine melting too fast. The smell of
the boys, their sweet cologne, and the cigarettes they smoked as
they waited for her to feed them. Sweat. The smell of her lilac
talc rising from the folds of her nightgown. The pop and hiss of
the eggs in the fat. The scold of the bacon, its irritable writhing.
The angry burn of toast left too long in the broiler. The boys'
mouths opening and closing over their laughter. Her own mother's voice like a faraway dream: *The way to a man's heart is through*
his stomach. They found her Christmas tin of butter cookies and
swallowed them, one by one.

What woman cannot recognize hunger? What woman can
live for long in this world without being seen as merely a body,
nourishment, egg and margarine, breast and belly, mouth and
hip? Sam loved eggs—scrambled, poached, fried, hard-boiled,
slathered with ketchup or mayonnaise. His favorite meal was a
fried egg sandwich, which my mother often made on weekends,
and as children we'd compete to see who could avoid rupturing
the yolk, as my father intoned, *Don't play with your food.* I was
allowed to make soft-boiled eggs for our after-school snacks; I
served them in metal egg cups, so we could knock off their heads
with a spoon, scoop up the salty yolk with the buttered tip of a
piece of toast. Mrs. Baumbach could not remember how many
eggs she prepared. She could not remember the boys' hungry
faces. She could not remember how many boys there were. Maybe
there were five boys. Maybe there were three. The only thing she
was certain of was the knife—its unusual tip, its dark leather grip.

It was the parishioners coming up out of the church basement, heading home after the all clear had sounded on the radio,

who saw the light in Mrs. Baumbach's kitchen window. Someone noticed a torn window screen flapping like an injured wing. Someone called, "Hello-oh! Geena, are you still up?" while someone else, stepping through the wet lawn toward the back of the house, caught the last rush of a man's shape disappearing into the tall field of corn. The parishioners gave chase, but corn swallows everything: raccoons, skunks, foxes, dogs, unmindful children. Don't go into the corn, we were warned every year, but there was always another story of a child who disobeyed, wandering miles into the corn before he or she was found, dehydrated, exhausted, even dead. While the men searched the fields, the women cleaned up the mess in the kitchen and did the dishes and wiped the counters and straightened the house and swept the porch clear of last year's leaves—whatever they could do to help out, to put things right. The police, arriving from Horton, would find no footprints, fingerprints, no physical evidence of any kind. And the next day, a medical exam revealed that Mrs. Baumbach had *not been hurt,* though she required twenty stitches in her feet. Surely there had been at least four boys. Surely they were boys nobody knew.

The sun is coming up now; the tips of the bare trees quiver like the warning hairs along a dog's curved back. It should not take long for the police to reconstruct the ghost of my brother's last hours. I called Harv back for the facts, and here, at last, is the evidence I've needed. The ruptured well cover. The broken bones: left tibia, right femur, a shattered ankle, three cracked ribs. The knife, by now encased in plastic, labeled along with the other samples: teeth, hair, bits of rotted denim. For the rest of my life, I'll see Sam walking through the fields, through narrow strips of woods, following the lakefront toward the house where we are sleeping. Coming home. And I'll wonder, What if he'd made it back?

Adam comes into the kitchen, stands behind me, presses his lips to my hair, and I cry harder because this feels so insincere, these tears that he thinks he understands. Last night, after talking to Harv, I called my mother at Auntie Thil's, wincing at the cheery message on her answering machine: *Hi, it's Mathilde! So sorry to have missed you!*

"Mom?" I said. "Are you there? Pick up. Please, pick up."

But no one did.

"Mom, please," I said. "I'll try again later. Call me as soon as you can." How I want to tell her that Sam was lost long before he disappeared. How I want to tell her what I could not tell my grandmother: *It was not your fault.*

How badly my mother wanted to work at the cannery with her sisters, but she was young, always too young. *Watch out what you want or you'll get it,* my grandmother said, but my mother stared after them longingly when they left the house, laughing and swinging their lunch pails. Summers they spent sorting vegetables, picking bad beans and stray leaves and dead field mice from a conveyor belt; in winter, they bottled the company's sweet fruit pop: cherry, orange, grape, lime. Mary, seventeen and known for her capable nature, supervised Elise and the other girls, warning them whenever the man they called The Company was coming by tugging her kerchief low on her forehead. It was noisy work, hot in the summer, cold in the winter, sticky with sugar and dust. The day of the fire, they went to work with scarves wrapped around their noses and hot potatoes tucked in their pockets to warm their hands. It had snowed six inches the day before, and another six inches stretched the faces of the clouds. *Keep warm,* the mothers murmured as they sent their daughters out to board the company pickup, which went from farm to farm, and because it was a Saturday, the bed of the truck was filled with teenage girls and women, huddled into the straw.

Keep warm, mothers told their husbands and sons and younger daughters as they split up at the barns to do chores. The mothers milked, pressing their foreheads into the cows' warm sides, wondering about their daughters who must be standing on those awful wet concrete floors by now, shivering under those high fans, which blew chill air across their shoulders. The mothers calculated again how much the family needed that little bit of money. The mothers worried over frostbitten toes and misshapen ears, poor circulation, wool. The mothers planned what they would fix that night for supper—thick meat stew over mashed potatoes, pepper-and-flour gravy, buttered beans, steaming tea laced with honey and a splash of lemon extract. *Lord God*, the mothers prayed, *keep them warm.*

Eleven

Sam's burial must be delayed until after the ground thaws, and so it's May by the time I fly back to Wisconsin, my first trip home in more than ten years. Adam cannot come with me; spring is his busy time. For the past three weeks he's been working on an apartment complex going up south of Cobblestone. When the sun sets, the crew works by artificial light, and there are nights when he doesn't get home until midnight. Sometimes I'm up feeding the baby, and Adam stretches out on the floor beside the rocking chair, still wearing his dirty clothes. "I feel like we're the subjects of a sleep deprivation experiment," he says. By seven-thirty, he'll be on his way back to the site; I'll have fed Joe at least once more before he goes. For me, the days and nights have blurred: the baby cries and I feed him; I sleep and the baby cries. He has colick, and there are times when nothing will comfort him. Then, I leave him wailing in his crib and walk out onto the deck, and I'll stand there for a long minute, breathing in the piney scent of the woods, before going back inside. And yet, when I drop him off at the sitter's to go to Turkey Hill, it's everything I can do to leave him behind.

He screams all the way from Albany to Chicago, but by the

time we board the plane to Milwaukee, he gives up and sleeps until our descent. In the airport lobby, I see my mother first and though, of course, I'm expecting to see she has aged, I'm not prepared for how much she is starting to resemble my grandmother. Her hair is permed tight to her head and rinsed a uniform steely gray. She's eating an ice cream cone with the same unselfconscious enjoyment that used to annoy my father, embarrass Sam and me. "Mm!" she'd say, biting a piece of fruit, chewing a slice of meat, her eyes rolling blissfully, reverently. When she sees me, she extends the ice cream like a bouquet. "Try this," she says—her first words to me, in person, since her visit to New York—and what can I do but take a big sloppy bite? Before I can object, she's given Joe some on the tip of her pinkie finger. "He won't know why," she tells me, "but years from now, when he thinks of his grandma, he'll always remember something sweet."

Driving home from the airport, she tells me she's putting the house on the market, she's found an apartment near her office in Sheboygan. "I guess I should be more nostalgic," she says, "but now that I've made up my mind, I'm eager to get rid of it." As we pull into the driveway, I see the exterior has been freshly painted, and all the old car parts and broken appliances are gone, leaving bald patches in the grass. Inside, I admire the new linoleum in the kitchen, the bright fixtures, the wood banister polished to a rich, glowing warmth. But the water still runs yellow in the bathrooms. The fruit trees have grown too old to bear; the barn finally collapsed last year. Sam's bedroom in the basement smells of mildew, and though my mother has replaced the carpet, it's already dark along the edges, slick with wet.

I feed Joe in the living room, sitting in the white wicker rocking chair that used to be in my bedroom. Half-packed boxes are scattered everywhere, and the walls are bare of photographs. Elise's piano occupies the space where the couch once was; the couch itself is gone. "The new place will be much smaller than this," my mother says when I ask, and she shows me a picture of the complex she'll be living in, her unit circled with red pen. "If you want any furniture, let me know."

She glances at the piano. At various times, she's suggested moving it to New York, but I always say she should keep it. My grandmother gave it to me as an instrument, not an ornament, and I don't want to see it sitting in my house, day after day, a silent reproach. "Why not offer it to Monica?" I say.

"I promised your grandmother I'd keep it until you were ready to have it."

"You did? When was this?"

"Oh, way back. Before you got married."

"It's been longer than that since I've played. I've probably forgotten everything."

I shift Joe to my other breast, and my mother watches, suddenly shy.

"You were the only one I breast-fed," she says. "By the time Sam was born, the doctors had decided formula was better. Now they've changed their minds again. You can't imagine." She shakes her head. "There I was, taking pills to dry up my milk, and Sam would be screaming his head off because he had to wait while I warmed the formula. It didn't make sense, that mother's milk wasn't good for babies. But I went along with it anyway."

"Why?"

My mother sighs. "That's just how it was back then. When Doctor told you something, you did it. It was a different generation. We didn't question things the way you do today."

I tense, waiting; it's the closest she's come to bringing up the baptism since Sam was found. But she says nothing more. Later, after supper, we play cards at the kitchen table, discussing everyone and everything but ourselves. It occurs to me that tomorrow is Sam's burial, and yet neither one of us is mentioning it. It's like something that happened years ago, distant as my father's leaving or my grandmother's death. We talk about the rising price of real estate, people moving in from as far away as Chicago, eager for a country setting. "The broker says I can get one seventy-five for this place," my mother says. "Can you believe it?"

"You're rich," I say. "What are you going to do with all that money?"

"Some of it's your father's," she says. "The rest—I don't know. I guess you'll inherit it at some point."

"You should take a vacation. Go on a cruise."

My mother makes a face.

"Or buy a sports car. Something red and sexy."

She laughs. "Maybe I'll ship you that piano," she says. "Whether you want it or not."

"Not."

"You might use it if you had it. Especially now, with Joe. It's nice for a child to grow up with music in the house." We've drifted away from our card game, and now my mother turns her hand faceup on the table. "Well," she says, and she stands, yawning. "Think about it. I'm going to turn in; how about you?"

I'll be sleeping in my old bedroom; my mother has set up the same bassinet that Sam and I once slept in. She brings me extra blankets, a glass of water for the nightstand. "Sleep well," she says, but I don't. I'm restless with half-dreams, unable to get comfortable. The wind picks up. A tree branch thumps the side of the house like an irregular heartbeat. When Joe starts crying around midnight, I'm almost grateful. I change him, prop myself uncomfortably against the headboard to feed him. He's fussy; he won't take much. He cries off and on for an hour or so before, at last, he closes his eyes. I ease him back into the bassinet, lie down, and will myself to fall asleep. I'm almost there when I hear the floor creak beside my bed. Old houses, I tell myself. Wind. The floor creaks again. I think of Sam's friend sitting beside me on this very bed. The gleam of the knife. I open my eyes, and a low sound escapes from my mouth before I can stop it.

"Shh, it's all right," my mother says.

I sit up. I'm shaking so hard the bed shakes too.

"I'm sorry," she says. "I couldn't sleep. I just wanted to look in on the baby."

"It's OK," I manage to say. The tree branch thumps the side of the house.

She sits on the bed. "Listen to the wind. I hope the weather's good for tomorrow."

"Could you pass me that water?" I say, and I take the glass, drink, water dribbling down my chin.

"I must have really frightened you," she says. "I'm so sorry."

"I'm all right."

"He's such a beautiful baby," she says. "He looks a lot like Adam, don't you think?"

"Sometimes."

She pats my hand. "Go back to sleep. I'll see you in the morning."

But in the morning, I find a note in the kitchen; my mother has gone in to her office for a couple of hours. I fix myself toast and eat it, wandering from room to room with Joe balanced on my hip. It's an overcast, windy day, and the house seems smaller, darker than I remember it. In the living room, I notice my mother has pulled the blanket off the piano, opened the cover to reveal the keys. Sly move, I think, but I finish my toast and sit down at the bench. My left hand is occupied with Joe; I attempt a C-major arpeggio with my right. I miss. Joe stiffens at the dissonant sound. I get his blanket from the kitchen, spread it out for him on the floor. He kicks happily and I go back to the piano, try the arpeggio again. I execute a chromatic scale. I feel my way through the beginning of a Chopin Prelude. Suddenly it's almost noon, and my mother is standing in the doorway, listening.

"That's how you always were," she says. "The world could have fallen down around you, and you wouldn't even have noticed."

"How was work?" I say, trying to change the subject.

"Busy," she says. "Cindy Pace will be at the service."

"That's nice."

"Look how the baby's listening," my mother says. And it's true: Joe is wide-eyed, jerking the way he does when he's excited. "Maybe he's got your good ear."

"Or Sam's," I say, surprising myself.

My mother sighs. "It doesn't make any difference now to think of everything I'd do differently. But I wish I'd stood up to your father more when it came to Sam's interest in things like this." She lifts Joe into her arms, brushes her lips against the top of his head. "You could always escape if you had to. But Sam had nowhere to go."

"Neither did you."

"I had my work," she says. Then, correcting herself, "Have it. And my faith, of course. That's a comfort." She hands Joe to me before I can say anything. "We better get ready for the service."

"Mom," I say. "I've been thinking. Maybe I'd like the piano after all."

She looks at me curiously. "Really?"

"Don't give me a chance to change my mind."

"You know, I almost broke down and gave it away last year."

"Why didn't you?"

"I told you," she says. "I promised your grandmother I'd keep it for you."

Sam will be buried at Saint Ignatius Cemetery; the service is set for two o'clock. Harv is driving down from his parish in Peshtigo to perform the ceremony. My mother and I arrive hopelessly early, but Auntie Thil is already there. She hugs me long and hard, exclaims over Joe, helps me negotiate him into his harness. The sky promises rain, and I button my jacket around us both. "It must feel strange to be back," Auntie Thil says, but what's strange is that it doesn't. Looking past the stubble of the graves, I see the flat fields stretching mile after mile, and it occurs to me that this is the landscape of dreams, of nightmares in which you run as fast and as far as you can, only to discover you haven't left the place you started from.

"I sure hope the rain holds off," my mother says as we start down the dirt service road that bisects the cemetery.

"They had hail to the north," Auntie Thil says.

"That's unusual for spring."

"Doesn't it seem like the weather gets crazier every year?"

"Along with the rest of the world."

They continue talking about the weather, seemingly oblivious to the gravestones all around us, and I remind myself that they come here all the time to tend the family plot. But when they stop to admire the wildflowers growing in the ditch, I walk on ahead. Already, I can see the new rectangular stone that belongs to Uncle Olaf. Auntie Thil's name is etched beneath his, a blank space left for the date of her own death. And beside it is Sam's wide-open grave, shadowed by a pile of rust-colored dirt. Coming closer, I see his coffin has already been lowered inside, white with gold trim, an otherworldly star in that odd dirt sky. My eyes burn with sudden tears; I blink, look away. To the left are the spring flower beds around my aunts' graves, and here is my grandfather's plot, the only decoration a tiny American flag. My grandmother shares his headstone, of course, and I touch her name: Gretchen Anna Grussen, 1910–1994. I want to believe that she sees me, that she's with Sam in the heaven she always described with absolute certainty. I wish her angels blowing trumpets, streets paved in gold. I wish her the faces of Mary and Elise, forever young and whole.

Thunderheads hang on the horizon, and the light has that peculiar glassy quality that intensifies color, making the sky seem close enough to touch. When I look back down the service road, I see that my mother and Auntie Thil have started picking wildflower bouquets. The irregular peaks of their conversation come to me on the damp gusts of wind. I wave, and they wave back, but they don't make any move to join me. Other people are arriving now—mostly members of my mother's prayer group, I suspect, plus a few people from A-1 Advertising. They carry umbrellas, glance nervously at the clouds. I recognize Cindy Pace; she smiles and nods to me, and I nod back. When I overhear one woman ask another, "So is Gordon going to be here?" I deliberately focus all my attention on Joe, making sure he's warm enough, adjusting his harness. I'm not sure what my mother has told people; I don't want to be the one they ask. My father wanted to come to the funeral, but he just isn't able to travel anymore. Each year he grows more locked into routine, more terrified of crowds, sickness, disease. Yet, in a strange way, he's grown closer to my mother and me. When we call, he picks up the phone, keeps us talking for hours. After Joe was born, I sent him a whole roll of pictures, and he actually wrote back, a letter filled with advice about electrical outlets and swallowed coins.

When I look up again, Harv is walking briskly down the service road. He sees me and breaks into a clumsy run, his long robe tangling around his legs. "Careful," I say as he bends down to hug me, and then I feel his body freeze, as he realizes the baby is between us.

"Can I see?" he asks, and I unbutton my coat, trying to reveal as much of Joe's face as I can. The bags beneath Harv's eyes are the color of strong tea. I've heard from my mother how busy he has been, serving a combined parish of six hundred people, driving hundreds of miles each week throughout the rural townships north of Peshtigo.

"My goodness, he's a tiny thing," Harv says, using the baby voice people adopt without even realizing it, and I love him for it. "How old is he?"

"Three months, three weeks," I say. "Mom was hoping he'd be born on Sam's birthday, but he held out till the middle of January."

"Good for him," Harv says. "It's rotten to share a birthday." He stares at me fondly, and I stare back. "So what's it like?" he asks. "Having a baby, I mean. Being a parent and all that," and

I remember him asking me, long ago, *So what is it like to lose your faith?* His voice had been incredulous, almost reverent, eager for my answer. The way it is now.

"It's hard," I say. "You never really know if you're doing things right."

"Like serving God," Harv says.

"Not that bad," I say. "Babies give you more concrete feedback."

But Harv doesn't smile. "I envy you," he says. "I think I would have been good with kids. I sure would have been better at it than my dad was."

"Or mine," I say.

It's almost two o'clock. Monica and Ray are walking toward us across the grass, towing children and assorted stuffed animals. "I guess I better let you mingle," Harv says, and he kisses my cheek. "See you after the service, OK?" While he greets people, I intercept Monica, who introduces me to her boys, David and Donovan. Ray is carrying their third child, four-year-old Daisy, in his arms; she struggles to be put down. By now there are about two dozen people waiting by Sam's grave, and when Harv takes his place beside it, everybody steps into a loose half-circle. Donovan asks me if he can hold Joe.

"Later," I tell him. "He's sleeping now, OK?" The rush of disappointment sharpening his face makes me want to cry.

"Don't worry about it," Monica tells me as Donovan hides against her hips. "He's at that age when they take everything personally."

"And some never outgrow it, believe me," says a woman standing with a teenage girl who has to be her daughter. The girl blushes, and I remember the exquisite embarrassment I felt at that age, pinned in the spotlight of this cruel, kindly laughter. My mother and Auntie Thil are finally coming to join us, and I desperately want them to hurry, I want this to be over, I can't imagine waiting one moment longer. My mother has a handful of wild irises. She passes them to me; the stems are wet and pungent. I lift the flowers to my face, but the blossoms themselves have no scent.

"Are you sure that baby's warm enough?" Auntie Thil asks.

"He's fine."

"It's a long day for such a small baby," my mother says.

"For kids too," Auntie Thil says. David is hanging on Monica's purse in the deliberate, dead-weight pose of a very bored child. Donovan has started to cry. Daisy has managed to slip off one shoe, and she stands, sock-footed, in the wet grass. "This isn't going to work," Ray says to Monica. "I'm taking them inside. We'll meet you afterwards, OK?" She nods, wiping her hand across her forehead in an exaggerated gesture of relief, and he leads the children across the street toward the entrance to the church basement, where, already, volunteers from Ladies of the Altar have set up chairs, spread tables with paper tablecloths, counted scoops of Folgers into tall metal percolators.

"It's a long day for us all," my mother says to no one in particular, and for the first time she looks down at Sam's grave, at the bright white coffin, which I realize she must have chosen by herself. She removes her glasses, puts them back on. She frowns at the grass, frowns at the sky, fighting tears. Harv has been trying to catch her eye; now, at last, she looks at him, and he clears his throat, hushing us, begins. And still it doesn't seem real, it doesn't seem possible that Sam is really inside this clean white casket. Perhaps there's been a mistake. Perhaps it's somebody else inside, and the real Sam will reappear someday, as happy to see us as my mother always promised, eager to explain. Even now I want more answers than the concrete facts can offer. I want each door of my life to close behind me with a perfect, resonant click.

I drop the irises into Sam's grave and walk away from Harv's words, passing between the rows of gravestones until I reach the edge of the fields. The long furrows are straight as an index finger, pointing at me, urgent, accusing. I lower myself down onto the damp grass and rock Joe to and fro. Gulls flutter like moths in the distance, fighting the wind, settling down to hunker close against the land. A white cat follows a fence line toward a secret distant point.

After the service, we all walk over to the church and descend the echoing stairwell to the basement. The painted concrete floors have cracked from years of changing seasons. My mother and I stand at the base of the stairs, and a line of mourners forms around us. Suddenly I'm shaking hands with them all. They tell me that I'm looking like my mother. They ask if I still play the piano, and what's my young one's name? Joe wakes up, so I turn him around in his harness. People examine his hands, proclaim that he's inherited my own long fingers.

Eventually, everybody forms a new line in front of the percolators. They sweep my mother along with them, patting her shoulder, pressing her arm. Two long tables are laden with cakes and kuchens and tortes, as if these small, sweet things can somehow erase the bitter aftertaste of grief. Someone hands me a Hello Dolly, still warm from the pan, and when I bite into it obediently, I find that I am strangely comforted, a child slipped a lollipop after a fall. Licking my fingers, I take Joe over to the community playpen that's been set up in the same corner since I was a little girl. Beside it there's a new wicker stand for changing diapers, a sealed bucket marked WASTE, and a few battered toys in a cardboard box. I change him into one of the diapers I stuffed into my coat pocket before we left the house and powder him with cornstarch from a Ziploc Bag. There's already one baby in the playpen, a little girl older than Joe. She chews on a pacifier, widens her eyes in a worried way when I lower him onto his back beside her. "Who's your mother?" I say to her, wanting Joe to hear my voice and relax.

"Jessica Blaunt," Monica says, sitting down on the floor beside me. She balances a plate filled with brightly colored things:

angel food cake with blue frosting, green finger Jell-O, fudge with rainbow sprinkles.

"Jessica Blaunt?"

"She used to be Jessica Hardy."

"Oh," I say, but I don't remember anyone by that name either.

"So." Monica tugs on one of Joe's feet, then looks at me expectantly.

"What?"

"Inquiring minds want to know."

"Know what?"

Monica rolls her eyes, then makes an exaggerated sign of the cross over Joe. "Are you going to baptize the little heathen or what?"

"His parents are heathens," I say, rubbing his firm, round stomach. "He comes from good heathen stock. Besides, Mom doesn't care anymore. She hasn't brought it up since they found Sam."

"She's probably planning to baptize him herself. Or whisk him away to Father Van Dan on the sly, like my mom did with David. Didn't you hear about that?"

"No," I say, scanning the room for my mother, but she's out of earshot, helping Ray and Auntie Thil with the kids.

"Well," Monica says, lowering her voice, "Ray and me, we started going to this Bible church for a while, and when David was born, we decided we'd have him baptized at this big summer ceremony they have at the Waubedon River. My mom kept trying to talk us out of it, but then all of a sudden she seemed to accept it, and I thought it was great that she was respecting my beliefs. But things at the church started getting real intense—people speaking tongues, that kind of stuff—and we thought, no way, and came back to Saint Ignatius. It's *dull*," Monica says, "but at least you can understand what people are *saying*." I laugh, and she laughs too. "Anyway, we called up Father Van Dan and asked if he would baptize David. *What?* he says. *Once wasn't good enough for you?* And that's when we find out that Mom took him to the church the first time she baby-sat."

"Well, my mom won't be baby-sitting Joe," I say.

"You always did take this stuff too seriously," Monica says. "You and Harv. Me, I'd just go ahead and do it. What's the harm? Make your mother happy."

"It's the principle of the thing."

"You and Harv," she says again. "His principles get him in trouble, too. Did you know he got reprimanded by the arch-bishop? They say he's too liberal, he should straighten out. He's like you, he thinks women should be priests. He thinks gay people should get married"—she whispers the rest of her sentence—"and women should have a choice on abortion."

"What are you girls so hush-hush about?" my mother says, sitting down beside us. She has a plateful of food to share: more Hello Dollys, fruit cocktail torte, cookies, finger Jell-O. Her plaintive face says, *Take this,* and though I'm not hungry, I eat because I have to, because it would be wrong to say no. The afternoon is passing, and now people are starting to leave. Harv touches Joe's hair, hugs me goodbye; we both promise to be better about keeping in touch. Auntie Thil accepts a ride up the street from Monica and Ray. My mother and I wave them off before going back downstairs to help the volunteers clean up. We fold the paper tablecloths, wipe down the tables, sweep the vast expanse of floor, empty the percolators into the unisex toilet off the hall. When I return the trays and utensils to the kitchen, I see that nothing has changed here since I helped prepare and serve church suppers fifteen years ago. The trays are still kept on the shelving unit behind the door; the utensils go in the row of drawers along the sink. I feel as if I've become my own ghost, moving through the kitchen—bending, opening, stacking, straightening—trapped within this particular memory, destined to repeat myself forever.

And then comes the awkward moment when every last thing has been cleaned and put away. The volunteers are tucked into their jackets. Joe senses the emptiness in the air and begins to fuss, a rasping, breathless sound. Still, my mother isn't ready to go home. I walk him from one side of the basement to the other, while she chats too eagerly with the last volunteer, a woman in her early forties who listens and nods even as her feet take her backward, step by step, toward the stairwell. I offer Joe his pacifier; he spits it out so suddenly that it falls to the floor. "Shit," I say beneath my breath, trying to pick it up without losing my balance, wishing I'd put him back in his harness so I wouldn't have to worry about dropping him. Suddenly I'm missing Adam, who is strong enough to swing Joe high above his head, who will say, "Give me the baby," at moments like these, when I'm not sure what to try next. I take Joe with me into the kitchen to wash off the pacifier, and the abrupt, familiar sound of running water temporarily calms him. This time, when I give him the pacifier, he takes it, keeps it, works his mouth over it. I am overwhelmed by an unreasonable sense of accomplishment. I do not want to leave this kitchen. I do not want to face my mother, to watch her return home yet again without my brother, this time without even a miracle to hope for. But when I come back out of the kitchen, she is standing in the middle of the concrete floor. Waiting. "Let's go," she says, briskly collecting her purse, her sweater. She wears her most private face.

Her car is the last one parked in front of the church. Joe sucks his pacifier; he's overtired, and I'm eager to get him home. The sun has been lost to a glaze of clouds, and there's a strange heavy feeling in the air. My mother drives out of town at her usual quick pace and crosses the railroad tracks into the countryside, heading for Horton, passing feral farmland, rickety corncribs, old clapboard houses. Laundry trembles on drooping wash lines—corsets, undershirts, yellowing slips—the undergarments of widows who are the last living members of farm families that could once sit down to a noon dinner of fried chicken, potatoes, squash, bread and butter, sauerkraut, and rhubarb pie. Now a single light shines in each window, and it is easy to imagine the meager supper laid out on the table before it gets dark, to save the few cents on electric. Hot cereal, overripe bananas. Day-old bakery from Becker's Foodmart. I see an old dog moving arthritically up the steps of a porch. I see a swaybacked horse grazing a slow circle around two derelict trucks in a pasture gone wild. As we approach the site of the cannery fire, I turn my face away just like my mother always did, thinking about getting Joe fed and bathed and put down to sleep for the night. Thinking about Adam and how good it will be to get back to New York. Thinking about how sorrow is like a vaguely familiar scent, dissipating if you try too hard to identify it, reappearing to return you to places and people you thought you'd left for good. The car slows, and the unexpected motion tugs me forward in my seat.

"What are we doing?" I ask.

My mother has turned down the service road leading to the cannery. She parks behind the burned-out foundation. In the distance, the dark line of the freight tracks follows the highway, playfully, dipping close, curving away. "I used to come here sometimes," she says. "When you and Sam were kids. I'd stop on my way home from work and sit for a while, think about things. I always worried that someone would drive by and see me." She opens her door. "Do you want to walk around? There's something I want to tell you." The wind comes in gusts that rock the car like a cradle.

She waits while I lift Joe out of the car seat, and then we follow her into the scorched foundation of the cannery, stepping over crumbling cinder blocks, charred pieces of wood, broken glass. It's hard not to imagine the snap and snuffle of flames in our footsteps. It's hard not to imagine we are walking on the remnants of bones. Perhaps what we hear are not the close cries of gulls blown in off the lake but the ghost voices of the cannery girls, high and shrill, filled with pain. The air tastes of ash. My mother stops beside a pile of blackened metal doors, stacked like outdated magazines.

"This is from the investigation still," she says. "These doors were supposed to be the exits, but the company kept them locked. There used to be one door where you could see, here"—she touches the bald, scarred face of the top door—"where they'd scratched and beat at it, trying to get out, but that one disappeared years ago. Everything else is here, though, the way that it was. People come," she says, gesturing at the scatterings of crushed beer cans, fast-food wrappers, bottle caps, "but they don't seem to take anything with them. I guess by now there's nothing left to take."

The rolling clouds absorb the daylight. I imagine dropping to my knees, crawling blindly beneath the dusky layer of smoke. The press of bodies in front of me. The push of bodies behind.

"All these years, I was certain we'd find Sam back some-how," my mother says. "But I thought that when he was found, there'd be a way to make sense of everything, maybe even put things right. All day I've been waiting for a revelation, a sign, I don't know—" The wind whisks her words into the fields, scatters them as easily as cinders. "I have this strange feeling that none of this is really happening. Like I'm standing far away from myself. Like nothing's quite real. Have you ever had a feeling like that?"

She doesn't wait for me to answer.

"They say that's how a person feels during a violent attack. I keep thinking that maybe I'm feeling what Geena Baumbach felt. Like all of this is happening outside myself. I wonder if I'll feel this way for the rest of my life. Like nothing matters. Like it doesn't not matter either. Like it just . . . *is*."

What did my aunts and the other girls do when they first realized they would not be rescued? Did they continue to beat and pound and scratch and sob against the doors? Did they fall into each other's arms, wait in silence for their lives to flicker out?

There's a low groan of thunder, then another, and I see the high walls of the cannery collapse, hear the explosions of the machinery, the roof buckling, slapping everything beneath it to the ground.

"Mom," I say. "I lied to the detectives. I knew Sam had that knife."

"I knew it too," my mother says. "It was your father's. It came from the war. He gave it to Sam when he was eleven or so, and it looked like such a dangerous thing that I hid it in my dresser drawer. I figured I'd give it back when Sam was older, but he must have found it, snooping—or maybe Gordon did. Anyway, one day it was gone.

"For years, I've prayed for forgiveness. Each night, I asked God, What else can I do? How can I atone? And then, last night, after we went to bed, I understood what I had to do. It came to me as clearly as if it had been spoken. *Baptize the baby.* I got out of bed and I heard it again. *Baptize the baby.* It began to make sense: This was the test I'd been waiting for, and if I did what God asked, He'd forgive me everything. He'd give me the reasons I needed so that all of this would finally make sense. I got the holy water from my nightstand and went into your room. I could see everything as clearly as if it was day. It was like God was helping me see."

"You baptized Joe?" I say. I'm so angry I can barely speak. "You sneaked in and baptized my baby?"

"You don't understand," my mother says. "There were times when faith was the one thing I could give you, the only thing your father couldn't control. Nobody could, not even the priests, not even the Pope or any of those men—and God knows they do try. But I gave it to you, and it's there if you need it, and don't get mad at me for saying that, sweetheart, because I don't mean the Catholic Church, or even God, I mean"—she pauses, searching for the right words—"*faith.* The ability to believe. The ability to see beyond the place where you are. Do you understand how important that is? Because Sam couldn't do that. And neither could your father. You could, and now you're the only one I have left."

My mother flinches as if something has struck her, and now I feel a rap on my head, my shoulder, the back of my hand. Hail is falling, the size of buttons, pennies, the sterling-silver charms the girls in my high school wore for luck. Shielding Joe with my body, I run back toward the car; my mother gets there first, opens my door so I can get him safely inside. Hailstones bounce off the roof, the windshield, and the world around us disappears beneath a flurry of pounding white fists. Will the glass break? I glance at my mother; she's wide-eyed, pressed back in her seat. I cup Joe's head with my hand, twisting to shield him, and it occurs to me how fragile all our lives are, how at any moment the sky can open and drown us, the earth can open and swallow us. I think of all the intricate ways our bodies can betray us, the accidents and atrocities, the missteps and misunderstandings. Joe hiccups, a sure sign he's ready to cry, and I feel him tensing up, the slow burn of rage balling his fists. What will happen the first time he looks beyond the concrete hungers of the body? What if he sees nothing but this frail shelter, bones and breath and skin, without the comfort of imagination, transcendence, hope? The hailstorm passes over us as suddenly as it came, and in the silence, I hear my mother take a deep, ragged breath. She turns on the engine, starts the windshield wipers. We watch the cloud move across the fields, the long shadow fluid beneath it, and a part of myself I realize I will never leave behind—the teenage girl singing for the congregation, the child still praying to be chosen—wants to see more than what's actually there: a message, a confirmation. Perhaps I'm only seeing a reflection of myself when I search for possibility in everyday things. But it's a better self, a bigger self. I turn to face my mother. I'm not angry anymore.

"I just want so much for Joe to grow up with faith in something," she says. "To have what you had when you went to the church, or sat down at the piano. All the things Sam didn't."

"You want him to grow up with—grace," I say. "So do I. But you have to trust I can find my own way to give him that. And I will. I promise." I reach for her arm, but she shrugs my hand away.

"No, don't," she says quietly. "People have been touching me all day, and it doesn't help a bit. In fact, I think it makes it worse."

"I won't touch you, then."

"We'll never know anything more about Sam than we do right now, will we?"

"I don't think so."

"I feel like God has let me go. It's like I'm falling from His hand. It's like one of those dreams where you just fall and fall, and there's nothing you can do to stop it."

Joe begins to cry, and my mother turns the car around, pulls back onto the highway. All the way home and long into the evening, he cries and cries, sleeps fitfully, wakes up and cries again, as if he's crying for us all. My mother and I take turns walking him. I offer him my breast, the pacifier, my finger. We sing to him, rock him. None of it is enough. When he finally abandons himself to sleep, it's more a result of his own exhaustion than anything we have done. We make hot chocolate and sit at the table, sipping that sweetness, too tired to speak. I can't stop hearing the sound of his crying; I'm raw with it. When my mother finally stands up, the scrape of her chair makes me jump. Hot chocolate sloshes across the tablecloth.

"Sorry," I say automatically, but my mother nods, understanding.

"Such a terrible sound," she says, and I know she's seeing my brother's face, "when you hear your child crying and you don't know what to do."

6/2001- stains